continued . . .

Praise for the M. J. Holliday, Ghost Hunter Mysteries

"Laurie's new paranormal series lights up the night."
—Elaine Viets, Anthony and Agatha award–winning author of *Half-Price Homicide*

Ghouls Just Haunt to Have Fun

"[A] fun, suspenseful, fast-paced paranormal mystery. All the elements combine to make this entry in the Ghost Hunter series a winner."
—The Romance Readers Connection

"A hair-raising tale that will keep readers engrossed in the ghost-driven action. *Ghouls Just Haunt to Have Fun* has as much dark and danger-filled action as ever, and introduces a wonderful new character that readers will be hoping to see more of in the future. This is a must read in the series!"
—Darque Reviews

"A lighthearted, humorous haunted hotel horror thriller kept focused by 'graveyard'-serious M.J."
—Genre Go Round Reviews

Demons Are a Ghoul's Best Friend

"Ms. Laurie has penned a fabulous read and packed it with ghost-hunting action at its best. With a chilling mystery, a danger-filled investigation, a bit of romance, and a wonderful dose of humor, there's little chance that readers will be able to set this book down."
—Darque Reviews

"M.J.'s first-person worldview is both unique and enticing. With truly likable characters, plenty of chills, and even a hint of romance, real-life psychic Laurie guarantees that readers are in for a spooktacularly thrilling ride."
—*Romantic Times* (4½ stars)

What's a Ghoul to Do?

"A bewitching book blessed with many blithe spirits. Will leave you breathless."

—Nancy Martin, author of the Blackbird Sisters mysteries

The Psychic Eye Mystery Series

Abby Cooper, Psychic Eye
Better Read Than Dead
A Vision of Murder
Killer Insight
Crime Seen
Death Perception
Doom with a View

The Ghost Hunter Mystery Series

What's a Ghoul to Do?
Demons Are a Ghoul's Best Friend
Ghouls Just Haunt to Have Fun
Ghouls Gone Wild

A GLIMPSE OF EVIL

A Psychic Eye Mystery

Victoria Laurie

AN OBSIDIAN MYSTERY

OBSIDIAN
Published by New American Library, a division of
Penguin Group (USA) Inc., 375 Hudson Street,
New York, New York 10014, USA
Penguin Group (Canada), 90 Eglinton Avenue East, Suite 700, Toronto,
Ontario M4P 2Y3, Canada (a division of Pearson Penguin Canada Inc.)
Penguin Books Ltd., 80 Strand, London WC2R 0RL, England
Penguin Ireland, 25 St. Stephen's Green, Dublin 2,
Ireland (a division of Penguin Books Ltd.)
Penguin Group (Australia), 250 Camberwell Road, Camberwell, Victoria 3124,
Australia (a division of Pearson Australia Group Pty. Ltd.)
Penguin Books India Pvt. Ltd., 11 Community Centre, Panchsheel Park,
New Delhi - 110 017, India
Penguin Group (NZ), 67 Apollo Drive, Rosedale, North Shore 0632,
New Zealand (a division of Pearson New Zealand Ltd.)
Penguin Books (South Africa) (Pty.) Ltd., 24 Sturdee Avenue,
Rosebank, Johannesburg 2196, South Africa

Penguin Books Ltd., Registered Offices:
80 Strand, London WC2R 0RL, England

First published by Obsidian, an imprint of New American Library,
a division of Penguin Group (USA) Inc.

First Printing, July 2010
10   9   8   7   6   5   4   3   2   1

For my dear, dear friend, Dr. Jennifer Casey.

Acknowledgments

My humble and most profuse thanks goes to the following people:

My editor, Sandra Harding, whose attention to detail and marvelous enthusiasm make my job sooooo much easier! Thank you, Sandy, for all that you bring to the table and for being delightfully fabulous to work with!

My agent and dear friend, Jim McCarthy. What is there left to say after fourteen published books together except, lovie, you *da bomb* and I heart you so! Thank you for being SO great both personally and professionally and here's to the next fourteen! (er . . . assuming the workload doesn't kill me, of course . . .) Mmmmwah!

My publisher, Claire Zion—thank you for the faith you've placed in both Abby and M.J. Your support has meant everything to me.

My gratitude also to the marvelous Michele Alpern for another awesome copyedit!

A special thanks to Dr. Jennifer Casey, who has been the Candice to my Abby and who has blessed me with one of the greatest friendships of my life. Thank you, sweetie, for all your help on this book, and for being such a great sidekick!

Extended thanks to my family and friends with a few honorable mentions to those of you who have given extra-special support to me and the books, and you are: Elizabeth Laurie, Mary Jane Humphreys, Hilary Laurie, Chris Humphreys, and Jessica Najdowski, Nora and Bob Brosseau, Karen Ditmars, Katie Coppedge, Leanne Tierney, Suzanne Parsons, Silas Hudson, Shannon Dorn, Pippa and Betty Stocking and my marvelous webmaster, Jaa Nawtaisong. I am eternally grateful for the difference each and every one of you have made in my life.

Hugs and love,
Victoria

Chapter One

Let me just state for the record that being the FBI's "civilian intuitive profiler" (aka resident psychic) was not the cake job I thought it'd be. I'm not sure what I actually expected when I took the position: perhaps my name printed on the door to a nice candlelit room with soft cozy furniture, where I'd jot down my impressions as they came to me and hand them off to an attentive agent for follow-up. I learned quickly that the FBI doesn't do cozy and candles. Nope. They're all business. "Just the facts, ma'am." Oh, and paperwork. The FBI is *all* about its documentation . . . in triplicate.

But back on April first, I had no idea that I was about to be strapped to a desk in a crowded room, lit by the unflattering light of fluorescents, while piles of files stacked up around me, threatening to crush me in a tsunami of recycled paper. No, on this day I was actually feeling pretty upbeat as the bureau's newest civilian profiler. I was super-excited about my prospects, in fact, and all I thought to contribute to solving crime and bringing in the bad guys.

I should have known then that nothing good ever happens on April Fools'.

Still, as my sweetheart, Dutch, and I cruised through Waco on our way to Austin on that last day of March, I will admit, I could have been overly optimistic due to all the exciting changes taking place in our lives.

Now, Dutch has been my steady for the past three years. Until the end of March, we'd been doing the "living in sin" thing at Dutch's bungalow back in Royal Oak, Michigan—a quaint suburban town just outside Detroit. Then the offer had come in to relocate to Austin, and we'd said yes.

The move was driven a little more by Dutch—it meant accepting a promotion for him and helping to pioneer a brand-new division: two challenges that my S.O. really wanted to tackle. And because I genuinely love him, I'd gone along with the idea. Okay, so maybe there'd been a job offer for me in there too, but it hadn't come without strings attached, believe me.

Anyway, as far as our relationship goes, I will freely admit that, of the two of us, I'm the lucky one. Dutch is a manly sort of man; heck, even his five-o'clock shadow arrives by four, and his voice is this wonderfully rich baritone that reminds me of chocolate and espresso: rich, smooth, and earthy. And did I mention that he's also really easy on the eyes? No? Well, let me just state for the record, then—the man is fan-yourself-when-he-passes beautiful and then some.

More specifically, he's thirty-six, with square chiseled features, light blond hair, a body I like to climb like a rock wall, and the most gorgeous pair of midnight blues you've ever lost yourself in.

He's also a great cook, doesn't leave his laundry on the floor, and patiently puts up with *me*. Which, given my lack of homemaking skills, inability to distinguish the floor from the hamper, and penchant for getting into serious trouble on a regular basis, definitely qualifies him for sainthood.

Dutch's day job is at the FBI. He's the assistant special agent in charge of . . . something. What, exactly, I'm still not clear—but he's one of the good guys, assisting in the managing of a group of other good guys at a brand-new bureau office in Austin, Texas.

Dutch's boss is a guy named Brice Harrison, a man I'd come to know and like, even though he and I had gotten off on the wrong foot when we'd first met.

More specifically, he thought I was a nut. I thought he was an ass.

We were both a little right.

Since then, I'd managed to win Brice and his superiors over by helping to solve a big multijurisdictional case involving some missing teenagers. After proving myself on that case, Brice had been so impressed that he'd specifically recruited me as a civilian profiler for the new branch in the Texas state capital.

I'd gratefully accepted, as I realized that Dutch really wanted the promotion that Harrison was offering him, and that my income as a professional psychic had been significantly dampened by the downward-spiraling economy in Michigan.

So, after the holidays, Dutch and I had packed up his house, scouted out a rental home in Austin, and were ready to move. And that's when my test results came back.

See, for all positions within the bureau—even those considered "civilian"—you must pass a lengthy and difficult interview process along with one incredibly intense psychological profile. By asking you a series of questions, which I assume are largely devoted to determining if you're a nutcase, the bureau can decide if they should hire you, or lock you up and throw away the key.

Don't believe me?

Sample one of the actual questions from the test: "Was there ever a time when you wished your parents were dead?"

Ummmm . . . no?

Maybe?

Okay, yes, when I was about sixteen and on the heels of being unfairly grounded for something my sister did, I will admit that I *did* fantasize about it but only for a second. I . . . um . . . pinkie swear.

The actual test, however, didn't allow for any elaboration or explanation; it was just "yes" or "no," and from my perspective, that all added up to a whole lotta bad news for me.

So, I was very surprised when the results came in a week later and showed that I was actually quite sane . . .

Score!

. . . but angry.

Say *what,* now?!!!

According to some FBI behavioral "genius" at HQ, my psychological profile suggested that I was likely given to frequent and unpredictable outbursts—particularly those expressing a sense of rage and frustration. Based on that analysis, the bureau was requiring me to attend "anger management" classes prior to being offered the position with the Austin bureau.

This disclosure was followed by a rather comedic outburst of said rage and frustration, and for a long while, my response to the idea that I attend the AM class was to tersely spout off a list of the vast and varied ways the FBI could go stuff themselves . . . and, yes, in hindsight I *do* see the irony!

Whatever.

In the end, it was the only choice I had; otherwise, bureau policy dictated that I couldn't be hired. After considerable study of my shrinking bank balance, my dwindling client list, and the sad face that Dutch displayed every time I looked like I might refuse to go to the classes, I gave in. Which is why our move was delayed two months from February first to the end of March right after I received my certificate. (The FBI will have to excuse me if I don't rush to frame it and mount it on the wall for everyone to see.)

After meeting the terms, I was officially hired, and

we were on our way. The trip itself had been long and uncomfortable—I'm not a fan of extended road trips—but I'd seen some beautiful scenery all the way from southern Michigan to Oklahoma. But right around the time we entered north Texas, things got . . . well . . . dull.

"Yo, Abs," Dutch said as I stared with concern out the window of his SUV, which had my MINI Cooper hitched behind it. "Penny for your thoughts?"

"It's so stark," I said, pulling my eyes away from the window. "I mean, I had no idea Texas was so flat."

Dutch smiled wisely. He'd been flying down to Austin every week since the end of January to help Brice set up the new office and interview candidates for the squad. "The topography changes just outside Austin. Don't you worry. Central Texas is almost as gorgeous as you are."

I blushed. Dutch was laying on the charm extra thick these days, mostly, I assumed, because he was so happy I'd agreed to the FBI terms for hiring me. "Yeah, yeah," I said with a wave of my hand. We rode again in silence for a while and I stroked the top of Eggy's head. Both of our pet dachshunds were in the cab and I had to admit they had been incredibly well behaved on the long journey.

"How're they doing?" Dutch asked as I moved Eggy over into my lap and Tuttle nudged her way closer to my thigh.

"Really well. But I think we're close to the edge here. At some point they've got to be as sick of riding in this car as we are."

"There'll be plenty of room for them to run around at the house," Dutch assured me.

"You swear you loved it?" I asked. The bureau had purchased Dutch's old house in Michigan, which allowed us to rent something temporary in Austin until we found our own home to buy.

"It's perfect for the time being," he assured me.

I sighed heavily and tried to think happy thoughts. I'd lived in Michigan almost my whole life, and no matter how many times Dutch tried to tell me that Austin was the shizzel, for me, seeing was believing.

"You nervous about tomorrow?" Dutch asked into another stretch of silence.

I glanced sideways at him. "That's the seventh time you've asked me that, cowboy. I'm starting to think I should tell you something other than 'no.'"

He laughed. "I'm just trying to let you know that it's okay if you are. I mean, these guys can be a little rough at first."

Dutch was referring to my new job with the bureau, which began the next morning at eight a.m. As far as I knew, my new job description entailed giving the Cold Case Squad, or CCS, my impressions on various cases, and teaching the other agents in the office how to open up their own intuition.

"Harrison has my back, though, right? I mean, he keeps telling me he won't allow anyone to disrespect me, which is incredibly ironic coming from him of all people." Harrison had been one of the most skeptical, hardheaded nuts my intuition had ever had to crack.

"Oh, he'll have your back, all right. Candice would kill him if he didn't."

"I can't wait to see her," I said wistfully. My business partner and closest friend, Candice Fusco, was a private investigator by trade, and she had followed Harrison down to Texas two months ago. I knew from the few e-mails that I got from her that she was ridiculously head over heels for him, and the two were even talking about moving in together.

"They've invited us over for dinner," Dutch added. "I heard that Candice laid down a big chunk of change last week for some swanky condo in downtown and she moved in a few days ago."

"How is it you know more about Candice than I do?"

"Harrison keeps me in the loop," Dutch said with a bounce to his eyebrows.

I smiled. "You're pretty proud of yourself, aren't you?"

"Little bit."

I shook my head and stared out the window again, but Dutch's cautionary words about my first day on the job were settling in and making me nervous. "Do you really think they'll give me a hard time?" I asked him after a bit.

"Who?"

"The other agents on the squad."

"Yes."

My mouth fell open. "Gee, cowboy, thanks for cushioning it a little."

Dutch reached out and squeezed my hand. "Sorry, doll, but you're better off knowing what you're about to walk into."

"Do you think it'll be as bad as the first time I met Harrison?"

Dutch considered that for a minute, which made me even more nervous, because the first time Harrison and I had met had been *baaaad*. "Maybe just a little less awkward than that," Dutch said.

"Shit," I said, and that won me a sideways glance from him. My anger management instructor had forbidden us to swear. "Zu," I amended quickly. "Shih tzu!"

Dutch laughed and shook his head. "That's a new one."

Since I'd been conditioned the last two months not to swear because my instructor was convinced it led immediately to an anger impulse, I'd been coming up with some rather "colorful" alternatives. "I'm never going to be able to stop," I admitted. Of all the alternate behaviors we'd learned in the class, the single greatest challenge for me was the no swearing. I'd yet to go a full day without letting at least one expletive fly.

"Anything's an improvement," Dutch muttered. And although I leveled my eyes at him, I knew he was right. My mouth could put most sailors to shame.

"Yeah, yeah," I said, then got back on topic. "So, what's your advice for making my first introduction to these agents less awkward?"

"Don't be yourself," Dutch said, and it took me a minute to realize he was kidding.

"I'm *serious*!"

Dutch laughed heartily but then sobered a little when he noticed I wasn't laughing. "I think it can't hurt to be as professional and down-to-earth as possible. You don't want to go in there and talk about your crew like they're real or anything."

That shocked me. "My crew" was the term I used for my spirit guides, and they were such a part of my intuitive process that I was aghast at his suggestion. "Why the hello-dolly not?"

That won me another smile. "Because the minute you start talking about the voices in your head is the moment these guys will earmark you for a nut and discount everything you tell them after that. Then they'll discount both me and Harrison because we believe in you, and pretty soon we'll have another political mess on our hands."

Now I understood why Dutch had continued to pester me about whether I was nervous and what I planned to say to the agents when I met with them. "So what should I talk about?"

"Well," Dutch said, scratching his chin thoughtfully. "I think you should stick to basics. Dumb it down as much as possible and maybe give them a demonstration. But don't read them. Read a case."

"Why can't I read them?" I asked. That was my forte after all.

"Because you'll intimidate them."

It was my turn to laugh. "Come on," I scoffed.

But Dutch wasn't smiling. "You don't think that going

in there and publicly revealing all their secrets will turn them immediately against you?"

My eyebrows shot up. I hadn't considered that. "Okay," I conceded. "I see your point. So, I tune in on a case, then what? Have them go out and solve it?"

Dutch shook his head. "Nope," he said. "What you should do is tune in on a case that has already been solved. Something where we've already nabbed the bad guys, but something that took a while to solve, which will be totally relevant because that's this group's specialty after all."

I sat with that for a bit and realized he was right. "Okay," I said. "I get it. So I'll go in there tomorrow and do my thing, but not overdo my thing, and impress the heck out of these guys and we'll all be singing 'Kum Ba Yah' around the campfire by dinnertime."

Dutch grinned. "That's the spirit," he said, adding, "And up ahead is the city limits. We'll be at our new house in about twenty minutes."

I looked ahead, and saw that Dutch had been absolutely right before when he talked about the change in topography. As I-35 coasted into North Austin, the road began to undulate over more hilly terrain. I tried to take in as much of my new home as possible.

Dutch took an exit, and not long afterward, my breath caught; as far as my eye could see, there were great sandstone cliffs, the color of champagne with amber and brown undertones, sometimes jutting up alongside us, other times dropping away and giving us breathtaking views. Interspersed in the cliffs were willowy trees with pink, purple, fuchsia, and white blooms, lush green grass and bluebonnets covering the highway median as far as the eye could see. Dutch glanced over at me as we cruised closer and closer to our destination and asked, "What do you think?"

"It's so beautiful," I said softly. And then I turned to him and smiled. "I think we're home, cowboy."

Later that evening after we'd supervised the movers unloading our things into the new house (and Dutch was right: the rental was large and spacious with a lovely fenced-in backyard for the pups), we cruised into the city, heading to Candice's, which was right in the heart of bustling downtown.

After pulling into the underground parking for a huge modern-looking building, we took the elevator up to the thirty-eighth floor and stepped out into a narrow hallway lit by artsy sconces and painted an earthy brown. We walked only a few steps when Dutch stopped in front of number A12 and knocked. The door was opened almost immediately. "You made it!" Candice exclaimed, and threw herself at me, crushing me in a giant bear hug.

"Hey, Candice!" I squeaked.

Candice let go but held my arms as she eyed me with interest. "You look amazing!"

I smiled. It was Candice who looked amazing. Love had done wonders for her complexion, and there was a little extra glint in her eye and an extra wattage to her smile. "Thanks, honey. You look pretty good yourself. This place agrees with you."

Candice's smile broadened even more, and she gave Dutch a big hug too before grabbing my hand and pulling me inside. "It does, sugar," she said. "And just look at the view!"

We entered Candice's condo and I will admit, the view was pretty spectacular. Only, I'm not talking about what was just beyond her window; I'm talking about Special Agent in Charge Brice Harrison, who was leaning relaxed and gorgeous against the bar.

Brice was dressed to kill; he wore black dress slacks and a cashmere V-neck sweater that hugged his trim, fit body like a second skin. His face had always been ruggedly handsome, but the last time I'd seen him, that frown that he seemed to never go without had vanished, and now he wore something closer to a smirk.

It changed him dramatically. He was still the cool-as-a-cucumber, humming-with-testosterone man I remembered, but there was a softer element now. And it looked gorgeous on him. "Hey, Brice," I said, surprised that I was actually happy to see him.

Harrison's smirk turned into a full smile and he walked smoothly over to us, shaking Dutch's hand and even giving me an unexpected hug. "Great to see you two," he said warmly.

I was so stunned I couldn't think what to say next. Most of my encounters with this man had been—at best—hostile. At worst they'd been downright murderous, so this change in our relationship would take some getting used to.

Candice seemed to pick up on the effect Brice was having on me, and she giggled, then took my hand again and pulled me to the balcony. "Come on, girl," she sang. "You have got to get a load of this!"

We walked out onto the terrace and I gasped. "Holy cow!"

"It's pretty fabulous, isn't it?"

"Honey, it's amazing!" I said, thinking she was one lucky duck to live with this kind of view. You could see the entire city and well beyond into the surrounding countryside from here.

I stared down, observing all the people who looked like ants. "The place really rocks with pedestrian traffic, doesn't it?"

Candice leaned back against the railing, tilting her face up to the last rays of sunshine. "Downtown is always bustling," she told me. "And the food here, Abby!" she said. "I don't think Brice and I have had a mediocre meal since we arrived. It's been one fabulous dish after another. And the night scene! Abs, wait until we take you guys clubbing!"

I smiled tiredly. "Can't wait, but maybe not tonight. It was a long drive down."

Candice moved over to wrap an arm around my shoulders. "Right, right," she said. "I'm just so excited that you're finally here. I've missed you, Sundance."

"Who'd like some wine?" Brice asked from behind us, and we turned to see him holding two glasses of red.

Candice and I took the wine and he and Dutch joined us on the blacony. Brice sat close to Candice and held her hand. The two were obviously taken with each other, and my heart filled with happiness for my dear friend.

Still, I will admit that I was a bit surprised at how serious the pair had gotten so quickly. I'd seen the moving boxes stacked neatly in one corner, and all of them had labels like "Brice's dishes," or "Brice's books."

It seemed that the talking about moving in together had turned into the real deal. And it was about then, as I was watching them and seeing my new boss hold my friend's hand, that my radar *ping*ed and a sudden thought went through my head. I let out a tiny gasp as I stared in earnest at Candice's left hand, and my expression must have changed, because all of a sudden Brice abruptly said, "Hey, Abby, can I see you in the kitchen?"

I pulled my eyes away from Candice's hand and stared at him. "You . . . ," I said, more words failing me.

Brice stood up quickly. "Kitchen?" he repeated urgently. "Now?"

"What's wrong, honey?" Candice asked.

"Nothing's wrong," Brice replied smoothly. "I just want to go over a few things with Abby before her first day at work tomorrow."

Dutch gave me and Brice a funny look. "Should I come?"

But Harrison shook his head and motioned for me to go ahead of him. "No. You two sit out here and enjoy this great weather and the view. We'll be right back."

Once I was through the door, Brice reached for my

elbow and guided me into the galley-style kitchen. "Don't say a word until we're out of hearing range," he cautioned softly.

I pressed my lips together and attempted to hold in the giggle that was burbling around inside me. When we got into the kitchen, Brice stood in front of me and asked, "How much do you know?"

"I know her ring size," I said with a big fat grin. "Did you need it for anything *special*, Agent Harrison?"

Brice looked truly uncomfortable, which was an unusual expression for him. He was always confident. And cool. And collected. And I'd just made him toss all of that right off the balcony.

He ran a hand through his hair and glanced nervously over my shoulder to the terrace. "It's crazy, right? I mean, we barely know each other."

I laughed and he flinched. I attempted to rein in my humor and talk to him seriously. "It's not crazy," I assured him, but he still looked torn. "Listen, Brice, I know Candice, and I can tell you that she is as crazy about you as you are about her."

Harrison chewed his lower lip, and a small line of perspiration appeared on his brow.

"Do you want me to tell you what I see?" I asked him coyly. I will admit, I was delighting at the opportunity to flaunt my intuitive abilities in front of him. I'd earned that right after all he'd put me through in the beginning of our work relationship.

Brice sighed and stared at his shoes. "Would you?"

"Of course!" I said. I waited until he raised his eyes

again to say, "She's not going to want a big, fancy wedding, so I hope you're okay with something small."

Brice's face flushed with relief and he let go of the small breath he'd been holding. But then he seemed to think of something that gave him pause. "Will I make her happy?"

"Not always," I told him honestly, and when he looked taken aback, I added, "But that's normal, Brice. No couple always gets along. Overall, however, I think that you two will have one of those relationships that last. All the elements are there for a terrific future together. You're good for each other. You push each other—you're both driven, loyal, and ridiculously honest. You're also both stubborn as mules. It's almost like you're the same person. And that kind of understanding for someone else is a rare thing, and mostly why I think you two could really work. It'd be an unbreakable bond, and a deep, deep love, Brice. One most people spend their whole lives looking for."

Brice's smile returned. "Thanks," he said, and I was surprised again when he leaned in and hugged me for a second time. As he let go, he whispered, "Just don't tell her before I get the chance to pop the question, okay?"

I stuck out my hand to shake his. "Deal."

Later that evening after we left Candice's place, Dutch suggested we take a drive along the cliffs near our home. "There's a spot I want to show you."

I smiled and stroked the side of his face. He could be wonderfully romantic sometimes. As we drove, he asked me, "So, what'd Harrison tell you about tomorrow?"

"Hmm?"

"The meeting in the kitchen you two had," he said, reminding me. "Did he tell you much about the squad?"

My brain raced to make up details and failed. "Um . . . ," I said, pressing my temples with my fingers.

"Hey," he said, knowing me too well. "What gives?"

"We didn't talk about tomorrow."

Dutch eyed me. "So why'd he pull you aside?"

"Can you keep a secret?"

Dutch's eyebrows arched.

"Okay, I know, stupid question. Of course you can. Brice is going to ask Candice to marry him."

The car swerved and veered to the left, pushing us perilously close to oncoming traffic. I grabbed the door handle and squealed.

"Sorry," Dutch apologized, quickly righting the SUV.

I put a hand on my chest. "What happened there?"

"Just tired," Dutch said, and offered me what looked like a forced smile. "Maybe we should just head home and save the view for another time."

I laid my head on his shoulder and sighed. "That sounds awesome," I told him. "We'll do romantic view next time."

When we finally got home, I climbed into bed and had only a moment's worry over what I might encounter at my new job the next day. I was honestly just too exhausted to give it much thought. In hindsight, maybe I should have braced myself for one heck of a turbulent ride.

Chapter Two

I rode in to the office with Dutch and spent much of my time sweating about how I looked and what I should say when I was introduced to the other agents. Mostly my introductory speech read like a corporate conference nametag, "Hello! My name is Abigail Cooper!" Beyond that, I figured I'd wing it and hope for the best.

The bureau office was on Nueces Street between Eighth and Ninth, a block away from the Austin Public Library. It was located inside a gorgeous plantation-styled home that had been converted into an office building but still held the original charm with beautiful trim and plenty of character.

When Dutch and I got out of the car, I stood for a minute just admiring it. "Doesn't look much like I expected," I admitted.

"Why? Because it's not square, steel, and tinted glass?"

I glanced at Dutch, who was smiling back at me. "Yeah," I said. "This place has way too much personality for the FBI."

Dutch laughed. "Maybe," he said, reaching for my hand. "But it's probably only temporary."

"Temporary?"

"Remember, this division is strictly experimental. The bureau doesn't officially have an Austin location yet. The Central Texas office is still in San Antonio."

"So why aren't we in San Antonio?" I asked as Dutch held the door open for me.

"Too much opportunity for us to get sucked into other bureau business," Dutch explained. "Harrison pushed hard to get us our own setup away from all the usual bureaucratic noise and distraction. He wanted this division to be focused only on cold cases, and he knew that if we were located in one of the other offices, our investigators could be temporarily reassigned whenever the other division chiefs wanted to borrow one of our guys on a case they thought might be more important."

"Sounds like a bunch of politics."

Dutch winked. "Exactly."

I sighed. I'd never been good at office politics. To be well skilled in that area, you had to occasionally ignore it when someone fed you a line of buffalo chips. I wasn't so good at that. I was much better at calling people out on their shih tzu.

Which was why I was particularly anxious about going

back to a corporate office setting. Still, the idea of solving some old cases and bringing closure to a family or two appealed to me. And, I'll also admit, I was a wee bit excited about teaching some old FBI dogs a few new tricks.

Dutch and I climbed the stairs to the third floor and pushed our way through a door marked only with the suite number into a brightly lit office with several desks arranged in pairs of twos, split by an aisle and flanked at the end by two glassed-in offices.

To one side was a brand-new gleaming whiteboard with "WELCOME, AGENTS" written in large black letters. New filing cabinets lined the side walls, and boxes and boxes of files were stacked along the floor in front of them.

Crouched down next to one of the boxes was a pretty woman with curly auburn hair who was busy arranging the boxes by date and grouping them next to the coordinating cabinet.

Gathered around one of the desks were several men dressed in shirts and ties. I guessed they ranged in age from midthirties to early sixties. Everyone looked up when we entered and the place got quiet real fast.

Gulp.

"Good morning," Dutch said to the men. He sounded confident, which helped stem my anxiety a little. "It's good to see you all again."

The men nodded and a few muttered, "Good morning, sir."

Dutch turned slightly and introduced me to the group. "This is our new civilian profiler, Abigail Cooper."

Immediately there were exchanged glances and the faint buzz of mumbled commentary, none of it loud enough to reach my ears, but it was clear—these guys had heard about me and what I was supposedly bringing to the table, and if I'd hoped they'd be open-minded, it was obvious from their expressions that I'd hoped wrong.

Feeling the heat rise to my cheeks, I was saved by the woman on the floor, who got up quickly and came directly over to us. "Good morning!" she said happily, sticking out her hand to shake mine. "I'm Mrs. Katherine Copperidge, the office manager here. It's great to finally meet you, Ms. Cooper."

I shook her hand and attempted a smile. "Nice to meet you, Mrs. Copperidge," I said.

Her smile widened. I could tell she saw my discomfort and was working hard to put me at ease. "Please, call me Katie."

"Abby," I said, feeling a little better.

"Hello, Katie," Dutch said when she turned to him. "It's great to see you again."

"Agent Rivers," she said, taking his extended hand. "Special Agent Harrison is in his office, and he'd like to meet with you briefly before addressing the squad."

Dutch left me for Harrison's office, and Katie took my elbow and led me to one of the desks closest to the whiteboard against the window. All I had to do was turn around to see the beautiful trees just outside. "This is your desk," she said, pulling out the new chair for me to try. I sat down and swiveled from side to side. The chair was one of those ergonomic numbers meant to give optimum support to the back. It was actually pretty comfortable.

"This is great," I told her. "Thanks."

Katie placed a paper in front of me. It was a list of office supplies. "Just circle any items you'll need from that list and I'll have it on your desk by the end of the day." Next she gave me a lanyard and pulled a small camera from her blazer pocket. "We'll also need to take your photo for your civilian badge and key card. The security system for the doors is being installed today, so you'll need to swipe in and out after tonight."

I plastered a smile on my face as she took the picture, and then, with a pat on my shoulder, she hurried off to make my ID.

I looked again at the group of agents on the other side of the room, who were speaking softly but sneaking an occasional glance my way. Uncomfortable, I averted my own eyes and stared around at the big room. I'll admit I had a moment of buyer's remorse and seriously considered bolting for the door.

My old office back in Michigan had been so comfortable and cozy. And most importantly—save for Candice in the next suite—it had been all mine. This sterile, stiff, and fluorescent-lit atmosphere was really going to take some getting used to.

Brice and Dutch came out of the office at that point and Brice's eyes caught mine. I swore I saw something like indecision there, and I wondered if he was now regretting offering me the post as much as I was regretting taking it.

With nothing more than a nod to the other investigators and to me, he approached the whiteboard and began to erase the "WELCOME, AGENTS." Dutch stood with his arms folded across his chest on the other side of the whiteboard, and a few of the other agents came forward to take their seats.

The desk next to mine was taken up by one of the younger-looking investigators, a Hispanic man with jet-black hair and large brown eyes. I watched him covertly out of the corner of my eye. There was something in the way he moved, with the grace and stealth of a panther. I figured bad guys didn't really stand a chance when he faced off with them.

I avoided making eye contact with him and kept my expression neutral; I thought it best to wait until I figured out where I stood with these guys before I tried to make nice.

Brice began writing a list on the whiteboard. The first item was labeled "CCS Introductions," the next "Departmental Procedures," then "Audits," and finally "Stats."

Brice then turned to face us. He waited until he was sure he had everyone's attention before he began speaking in a low, even tone, which was his trademark.

"Good morning, agents and staff," he said. "I would like to officially welcome you to the FBI's newest office here in Austin. As you know, we're a special group with our own budget and our own agenda. We've been located away from any other bureau office for the specific reason that when we begin investigating these cold cases, we don't want any animosity reaching our squad from other departments. We're not trying to show up other investigators, merely taking a second look at their dead files to make sure they meet the FBI's investigative protocols.

"Being located in Austin also allows us to operate from a central location in relation to all the other main cities in Texas. We're within a three-hour drive to both Dallas and Houston, and only an hour and a half away from San Antonio.

"Which brings me to my next point," Harrison said, and he paused here to look around the room as if measuring us up. "This job will come with a lot of downtime and paperwork. Far more than you're used to, in fact. You'll be required to thoroughly audit these old files, looking for missed clues or leads that were not thoroughly vetted. Once we have determined that a case may be viable, it will be assigned to one or more of you for follow-up, which will require you to travel to wherever the case originated.

"Airfare will only be approved for areas further than six hours away by car. I know you were briefed on these requirements before you committed to joining this squad, but I wanted to emphasize it again."

I let my eyes swivel around the room. No one seemed fazed by anything that Harrison had said, and he continued. "We've been given the official division name of the Cold Case Squad, or CCS, and if you haven't already noticed, we're a diverse group of some of the best investigators Texas has to offer.

"Because we're the first division of its kind, and something of a test case to my superiors, we've been allowed some leeway when it comes to our investigative techniques. As a department we will be relying heavily on gut instinct, and those of us already bearing a successful track record in that area will help mentor the rest of the group."

Harrison's steely gaze settled on me and I felt my mouth go dry and my cheeks heat up. I was really hoping that Harrison wouldn't call any more attention to me and just allow me a few days to settle in with these gruff-looking men before he mentioned anything about my being psychic. I understood the squad already knew about my background, but having it called out the first day was going to make me uncomfortable.

"Abigail Cooper joins our team with a rather unique set of skills. She's been invaluable to the Troy, Michigan, field office, and has assisted us in the resolution of several cases that would otherwise have gone cold."

I could feel every pair of eyes in the room on me and I held my breath, hoping Harrison would move on quickly.

"Ms. Cooper has been granted the official title of civilian profiler. By trade she's a gifted intuitive, and for those of you in this room who do not believe in psychics—let me assure you, there was a time when I was far more skeptical than any of you. She won me over. In fact, she blew me away. And I have no doubt that within a very short period of time, she'll do the same for you."

In any other situation I would have felt grateful for

Harrison's faith in me, but the polite silence was broken by a few mumblings and I knew these guys weren't going to discard their individual doubts just because the boss told them to.

Still, Brice's eyes narrowed at the reaction from his agents. "Let me also state, ladies and gentlemen, that I will not tolerate any disrespect for *any* member of this squad. Do I make myself clear?"

I nodded my head enthusiastically, but I was the only one who put a lot of effort into it. I had a feeling that I wasn't the only person who would have to work at gaining the agents' respect.

"Excellent," Harrison said, as if he hadn't noticed their reluctance. He then turned to the boxes lining the walls. "Behind you are the cold cases sent to us from Houston, Dallas, Corpus Christi and San Antonio. We'll be receiving El Paso's and Lubbock's cases in a few days."

We all turned and eyed the Bankers Boxes. They looked far too numerous for our little squad to tackle.

"I believe the best way to proceed is one box at a time per investigator," Harrison said. "CCS has been given the overall goal of a five percent solve ratio, but I'd like to push that closer to eight percent. If we audit at least one hundred files per month, I believe the six of you will be able to resolve five to eight of those cases. With the talent in this room I know we can achieve that goal."

There was a collective groan from several men in the room. I wondered why. Eight cases solved seemed like a really lowball number to me.

Harrison held up his hands to settle everyone down. "I know that's aggressive," he said, "but we've got a lot riding on our success rate. If we overdeliver, that could mean more resources and money for our budget, not to mention possible promotions for all of you. And remember, we have a year to accomplish that. It's going to take some time to get the momentum going, but I know we can do it."

My brow furrowed and I looked at Dutch to gauge his reaction, but he had his poker face on, so it was hard to tell if he was worried about hitting the goal or not.

Harrison then signaled to Katie at the back of the room and she began handing out several stapled pieces of paper to the investigators. "Mrs. Copperidge is passing out the audit forms for the files. I'd like you each to take a box, audit each file, and turn them in to me. Those files with the highest percentage will get assigned out first, but we won't assign an investigation into any case that does not score higher than a seventy-five. From there we can prioritize and decide which ones to focus on."

Katie appeared in front of my desk at that moment and handed me a thick stack of paper. "Here you go, Abby," she said with a smile.

"Thanks," I said, taking the pile and feeling a little overwhelmed by the volume of each individual form. I was also quickly realizing that I'd become the FBI's most recent paper pusher. Whatever illusions I'd had about my glamorous new job had officially flown out the window.

Dutch came over at that moment and stood close to me. "Don't worry," he said. "We'll do the first box of audits together. It's not so bad once you get the hang of it."

I leveled a look at him that said I sincerely doubted that, before switching my attention back to Harrison.

Our fearless leader was indicating the boxes by the filing cabinets again. "I'd like you all to select a box and begin the audit process. If you come across a case file that you personally worked on, please do not audit it. Bring it to me and I will do the audit for that file."

The agents in the room all moved in the general direction of the Bankers Boxes, and Dutch and I waited until most of them had collected theirs before I pointed one out to Dutch. "That one," I said to him, pointing to one close to us labeled "March thru May of 2008."

Dutch smiled. "You like that box?"

I nodded. "Feels lucky."

Dutch bent over and picked it up before motioning me to follow him to his office. "Bring the forms," he instructed.

I trailed after him and couldn't help but notice the raised eyebrows of the agents as we passed by.

I entered Dutch's glass office and placed my chair in such a way as to have those prying eyes at my back. "Gotta love the warm, fuzzy feeling I get off that crowd," I remarked sarcastically.

"They'll lighten up," he assured me before removing the lid of the box and peeking inside.

I sighed. "You never told me I was about to enter the riveting world of auditing."

Dutch extracted the first file. "What'd you think this was all about, Abs? Nine hours a day of shoot-outs with bad guys?"

"Well, I didn't think it'd be nine hours of impossibly dull paperwork," I snapped. I didn't really know whom I was more mad at: Dutch for not leveling with me about what the job was actually all about or myself for not asking more probing questions.

My S.O. sat down and regarded me soberly. "Having second thoughts?"

"No," I lied. "It's just that . . ." My voice trailed off and I looked at the box full of files and the stack of audits on Dutch's desk.

"What, doll?"

"Is this *really* the way you guys do this? I mean, do these audits even work?"

Dutch reached for one of the forms. "Not always," he admitted. "But it's the best system we've come up with so far."

"So how does filling out a bunch of forms ultimately indicate which cases to focus on and which ones to leave behind?"

"Well," Dutch said, flipping through an audit form, "we'll go through and answer the questions here and put down the pertinent information. All the answers are assigned a value, and at the end of the audit we add up the total and do a few more equations to arrive at a percentage. Those case files that score seventy-five percent or higher are likely candidates for us to focus our efforts."

"And how many files typically score that high?"

Dutch shrugged. "Usually only one out of ten or fifteen," he said. "Give or take."

I was starting to understand why Harrison had assigned us such a low resolve rate. "There has to be a better way," I muttered.

At that moment Dutch's phone bleeped. He hit the speaker button and Harrison's voice crackled loudly through Dutch's office. "Agent Rivers, I've got D.C. calling in for a status report. Can you please join me for this conference call?"

"Right away, sir," Dutch said, getting up and coming around to my side of the desk with the case file. "Here," he said gently. "Why don't you start this on your own and I'll be back to help you when I'm off the call?"

As soon as Dutch left, I opened the case file and stared at the most beautiful little girl with innocent brown eyes, caramel-colored skin, and a smile as big as Texas. The name under the photo read "Keisha LaSalle." She was a native of Dallas, had lived for a short time in New Orleans, then moved back to Dallas after Katrina. The file indicated that she had gone missing in May of '08. She was only nine years old at the time. My heart sank when I looked at the sweet smiling face because even though the case file was labeled "Missing Persons," I knew immediately that she was deceased. Her image appeared flat and lifeless to my third eye—and I also had the feeling that she'd been murdered in a most horrible fashion.

"Oh, sweetie," I said, running my fingers over the face in the photo. "I'm so sorry."

And that's when my natural instincts took over and I did what I do best. I closed my eyes and began to collect information out of the ether. At some point I opened my eyes and used the back of one of the audit forms to take notes, and after about five minutes I knew without a doubt this was one of the cases we might be able to resolve.

There wasn't much to the file; Keisha was reported missing by her older brother and guardian, Antoine LaSalle, who told police and then the FBI investigator who'd followed up that his baby sister had gone to school on a Tuesday morning and never came back home.

The neighborhood was canvassed, scent dogs were brought in, and a cursory check of all of Keisha's relatives was conducted, but all roads led to nothing. It was as if the poor little girl had vanished into thin air.

What I wrote on my notes was fuzzy at best. I kept coming back to images of paint cans and paintbrushes. I wondered if she'd been taken near a paint store, or if someone posing as a painter had grabbed her off the street. I also had a strong connection to a playground. I kept seeing a jungle gym in my mind's eye. And something even odder, I swore that when I concentrated very hard, I could smell the scent of gasoline, but try as I might, I couldn't put all these together to form a complete picture.

Still, I knew these were relevant clues; otherwise, my intuition wouldn't have brought them to me. So I wrote them all down and set the file aside, then leaned back thoughtfully in the chair and sneaked a glance through the blinds to the office next door, where Dutch and Harrison were still huddled over the phone talking to D.C. I looked again at the stack of audit forms on the desk, which I still felt were a complete waste of time, and made a decision.

Poking my head out of Dutch's office, I said, "Katie, could you tell me where I can get a legal pad to take some notes?"

Dutch finished with his conference call about an hour later. He found me in his office working on the very last file in the Bankers Box, and I had all the other files sorted into three stacks: Dead, Iffy, and Solvable.

The Dead group was by far the largest, but out of eighteen files in the box, I'd come across four that I felt we could solve. And only one of the others, the file on Keisha, got pushed to Iffy.

"What'cha doin', dollface?" Dutch asked, peeking over my shoulder while I scribbled "Dead" on the legal pad and placed it inside the last case file.

"Auditing the files," I told him.

Dutch chuckled. He thought I was joking and he moved around to take his seat. "Oh, yeah?"

"I'm serious."

Dutch cocked his head. "Okay," he said in that voice that suggested he was trying to tread carefully. "Did you make it through the form?"

"That form is useless," I said with an impatient wave of my hand. "Really, it's a total waste of time."

Dutch's brow furrowed. "So, *how* exactly have you been auditing these files?"

I tapped my temple wisely. "I've got my own system."

"Which is?"

"I've been pointing my radar at each and every file," I told him, picking up one in the solvable stack. "See? Like this one: The San Antonio Feds were investigating a series of homicides. Some guy was targeting taxicab drivers—robbing them, then shooting them execution-style. The MO was always the same; these were cabs that regularly picked up fares at the airport. Each dead cabbie was discovered within a day after they'd been reported missing; all of the cars were dumped in remote locations just off I-Thirty-five but within a mile of some other form of public transportation. According to the case notes, the theory was that someone posing as a passenger hijacked the cab, forced the driver to a remote location where they robbed them, then shot the cabbie at point-blank range.

"The case notes further suggest that an extensive surveillance of the airport's taxicab traffic yielded nothing concrete because of the heavy volume of departing passengers—there were just too many cabs to try and follow on any given night. And by the time surveillance cameras were installed to focus solely on departing cabs, the suspect must have gotten cold feet, because no more murders took place."

"Okay," Dutch said patiently. "What did your radar hit on?"

"I think there's a clue the bureau overlooked."

"A clue?"

I nodded. "The case notes say that all five cabs were wiped completely clean. No fingerprints were found, not even ones that belonged to the driver. But I think you missed one."

Dutch held out his hand for the file while I was talking, and I gave it to him with my finger tapping that note in the case file. "Our forensics units are top-notch, Abs," he said. "If there were any fingerprints in those cars, we would have found them."

I raised an eyebrow. "O ye of little faith," I said with a *tsk*. "There's a fingerprint on or behind a mirror. Have your guys go back over those cars and look around the cars' mirrors."

Dutch frowned. "Abby," he said gently. "This case is two years old. It's unlikely that we would have held on to the cabs. They've probably already been sent back to the cab company or to the junkyard by now."

But my radar insisted otherwise. "Okay, but will you please just check anyway?"

Reluctantly Dutch lifted the receiver on his phone and began dialing a number located in the file. It took some time, but finally he was put through to the head forensics manager in San Antonio. I overheard only half of Dutch's conversation, and by the sound of it the other guy wasn't too optimistic that he still had even one of the cars in question, but Dutch finally managed to convince him to go check.

After Dutch hung up, my stomach gave a low grumble. "Hungry?"

I smiled. "I could eat."

Dutch got up, grabbed his keys, and said, "We won't hear back from that guy for a while anyway. You can tell me more about your auditing system over lunch."

We found a wonderful little deli called Murphy's not too far from our office. My Reuben was amazing and the atmosphere delightful. "Okay, so I really think I'm warming up to Austin," I admitted.

Dutch laughed. "I knew it was always all about the food."

When we got back to the office, Dutch's message light was blinking. I watched his face while he picked up the voice mail. At first he looked surprised; then he reached for a notepad and jotted a few things down; then he locked eyes with me and gave me a thumbs-up. My knee bounced impatiently until he finished listening, and the moment he hung up, I asked, "What'd they find?"

"Two of the five cabs were sent back to their respective companies. Two more were shipped off to the junkyard, but one was never claimed and remained in the FBI's evidence yard."

I felt a little rush of adrenaline and I knew he had more to tell me. "And? *And?*"

Dutch beamed me the full grille. "And, supergirl, just to prove me wrong, the managing lab tech dusted all the mirrors on the car. Know what he found?"

"A fingerprint!" I exclaimed, jumping to my feet and pumping my fist.

Dutch laughed at my exuberance. "Yes," he said.

"He extracted two perfect prints from just behind the rearview mirror."

I raised my arms in victory. "I am awesome!"

Dutch laughed again. "And ever so humble."

I gave him a smart look and sat back down. "Is that it?" I asked him, sensing there could be more.

"No," Dutch said. "This is actually the best part: Turns out the prints he recovered matched one of the suspects on the list. A guy with a previous conviction for robbing taxicab drivers and who's currently in jail on a felony assault conviction. They were never able to confirm his alibi, but they had no forensic evidence to tie him to the cabbie murders. Until now."

My eyes widened. "So we solved it?" I asked. "We solved our first case?"

Dutch came around the desk and held out his arms to hug me. "We did, Abs. We sure did."

The next case we tackled from my Solvable pile was quite puzzling. The details of the investigation involved a bank manager named Donald Wyzinski who'd locked up his branch one night, and security tapes showed that he'd stolen over fifty thousand dollars in cash as he exited out the back. He was found dead the next morning, with the briefcase full of money still in his crumpled car, which was wrapped around a tree. Accident investigators took note of two pairs of skid marks on the road, and a foreign car's paint on the left rear quarter panel.

The FBI agent assigned to the case thought perhaps the manager had been involved in some illegal gambling, and owed someone a lot of money. Before he had a chance to pay off his debt, he was run off the road.

Still, there were several pieces that didn't add up: Donald had no criminal record of any kind, not even a traffic ticket. His friends and family all said he was a quiet, affable young man, who was shy around girls, was fiercely devoted to his family and his church, and donated his time and money to charitable causes.

Plus, his Web browser contained no history of any gambling sites, not even penny poker. He could have been betting the horses, but the nearest track was over seventy miles away from his home, so it seemed pretty illogical. No one could figure out how he'd gotten mixed up with what everyone assumed was the wrong crowd—and neither could I.

When I focused on Donald's energy, however, I kept coming back to one name on the contact list, Jackson Wyzinski—Donald's brother.

I had written his name down in my notes and showed it to Dutch when we moved on from the taxicab murders. "You need to refocus on this guy," I said as Dutch looked over the case notes.

"The brother?"

I nodded. "He did it. Bring him in and interrogate him, pronto."

Dutch laughed. "Hold on there, Sherlock. Let me just sort through this for a minute, okay?"

I crossed my arms and sat back in my chair while my foot bounced up and down. Dutch took his sweet time reading through the file, and I was about to get up and go visit the vending machines when he suddenly shifted forward in his chair. "Wait a second," he whispered as he came across something in the back of the file. "Donald had a one-million-dollar life insurance policy that was almost fully vested." Dutch glanced up and blinked at me.

"I'm assuming that's important?"

Dutch nodded. "If he needed money, why didn't he just dip into his life insurance fund, instead of risking his career and reputation, not to mention a felony conviction, by robbing his own bank?"

A slow smile crept onto my face. "Let me guess," I said. "The policy was paid out to the brother, right?"

Dutch glanced back down at the file, and his shoulders fell. "No. The beneficiary was Donald's mother, Estelle Wyzinski."

I frowned and shook my head. "Dutch," I insisted, "the brother's involved. And I know he had something to do with Donald's murder. Just make a call or something, would you?"

Reluctantly, Dutch picked up the phone and began to dial the number of the insurance company.

Two hours later he and I were high-fiving each other. We'd learned several key facts: One, Donald and Jackson's mother had suffered a severe stroke a few years before Donald's accident, and Jackson had been given power of attorney over her affairs. Estelle had died about six months after her son, but as far as we could tell, she'd died of natural causes.

As the only remaining heir, Jackson inherited what remained of the one-million-dollar life insurance policy.

Dutch was able to get a copy of the actual application form that Donald signed from the insurance firm, and when he compared it with Donald's signature from his driver's license, they didn't even come close to matching.

Dutch also pulled Jackson's credit report, and we were both shocked at the amount of credit card debt Jackson had run up prior to his mother's stroke and Donald's crash, over a hundred thousand dollars, in fact, which had been paid off almost exactly thirty-two days after Donald's crash. Dutch checked, and was able to confirm that the insurance money had been wired into Estelle's account on the thirty-first day, and because Jackson had power of attorney, he had control of her bank accounts, and had obviously paid off his debts using those funds.

Dutch had enough for a warrant, but quickly discovered through a public-records check that Jackson had moved to Florida. Dutch then had a buddy of his at the Tampa office pick Jackson up, and within twenty minutes, Wyzinski admitted that he'd taken out the insurance policy on his brother right after his mother's stroke without Donald ever knowing about it. He'd made sure to put down his mother's name as the sole beneficiary to avoid suspicion if his brother died of unnatural causes, and because he had been granted the power of attorney, he knew he'd have access to the money. He told the investigator that the purchase of the policy was prompted by his gambling addiction, which had started to get out of control, and he figured if he ever got into serious trouble, he could take out his brother and have enough cash to settle his debts.

Serious trouble had arrived when a bookie had sent a few muscled thugs to rough Jackson up and threaten him. Afterward, he'd called Donald and confessed that he was in debt to the mob, and that they were threatening to kill him if he didn't show up with fifty thousand dollars the night of the accident.

Donald didn't have that kind of cash on hand, but he did have a 401(k). He told Jackson that he would withdraw the funds from the bank's cash reserves, then start the process of liquidating the funds from his 401(k) the next day and replace the money in time for the end of the week's audit before anyone was the wiser.

He'd then agreed to meet his brother at a remote location with the cash, where Jackson was waiting to run him off the road, using a stolen car.

However, after Donald was sideswiped into a tree, Jackson had taken one look at his dead brother and he'd panicked. He'd left the scene without taking the money and dumped the stolen car in a nearby lake. A month later, when the funds arrived, Jackson had paid off all his debts and entered Gamblers Anonymous. As part of the twelve-step program, he'd been forced to take a hard look at himself and his actions, which had brought about a wave of guilt, and he was actually relieved to be picked up and clear his conscience with the Tampa Feds.

We listened on speaker as the agent in Florida relayed the confession, stunned that it had all come out so easily. Afterward, I got another huge hug from my main squeeze and we were able to put a big fat "2" up on the whiteboard under the heading "Cases Solved."

By the end of the day, Dutch and I were on a roll, and had put the clues together on one last case that closed more easily than even the first two.

After that, I was on one heck of a high and I couldn't help smiling gleefully at the other agents' stunned faces as Dutch erased the "2" and wrote in a "3." As one, they all turned to stare at me through the glass in Dutch's office. I waved all friendly-like at them, and didn't even mind when not one of them waved back.

Harrison also took note, and as Dutch was wiping his hands together and walking back, Brice looked over at me through the glass and crooked his finger. I got up and dutifully went to his office. As I entered, he shouted, "Rivers! You too. Please join us."

I knew we weren't in trouble, but Harrison had this way of making you feel like you could be. "Have a seat," he instructed.

I sat at once, my back rigid against the chair. Dutch came in and shut the door. "We're having a good day," he said cordially while he took the chair next to mine.

Harrison's eyes focused again on the whiteboard. "I see that. What are you two up to?" he asked, his tone flinty.

"Solving cases, sir," Dutch replied easily.

"I thought I directed you to audit files, Agent Rivers."

Dutch's easy countenance never wavered. "Yes. Abby's already finished a complete audit of an entire box of files, sir, and from that, we've managed to solve three cases in the course of the afternoon."

Harrison's steely gaze swiveled to me. "You've completed an *entire* box of audits?"

My mouth felt dry and I had to clear my throat before answering. "Yes, sir."

"Let me see," he said.

I glanced at Dutch and he nodded, so I got up and walked quickly back to his office, collected all the files, and brought them back to Harrison's office, where I grouped them into my three piles again. Only, as I set down the stack of solvable cases, I moved the three we'd already resolved to a fourth pile. "These are the cases Dutch and I were able to resolve."

Harrison grabbed one of the files in the "Dead" pile. He opened it up and saw the big yellow sheet of legal paper with my handwritten note across it that read simply, "Dead."

"What the hell is this?" he demanded, holding up the sheet. "Where's the audit?"

It was Dutch's turn to clear his throat. "Abby's been doing her own special kind of audit, sir."

Harrison's eyes came up to stare at us, his look incredulous. "Her own *special* kind of audit?"

I sat forward to explain. "I've been using my radar, sir. By concentrating intuitively on each individual file, I've been able to isolate which cases will eventually be solved, and which ones have no further energy."

Harrison blinked. "Come again, Ms. Cooper?"

I sighed. I hated all this "sir" and "Agent Rivers" and

"Ms. Cooper" crap, but it's what the office environment seemed to demand, so I reined myself in and tried again. "For me, thoughts contain energy. And if I ask a question in my head, something like, *Can the case that I'm focusing on be solved?* then that thought will either travel outward and feel like it has energy to it, or it will hit a proverbial big brick wall, and I know it's a dead end."

Harrison held up his hand in a stopping motion. "Hold on," he said. "Are you telling me that if you *think* a case can be solved, it can?"

I glanced at Dutch for help and he took the lead. "Consider it like this, sir," he said. "When Abby focuses on a case, she's looking into the future to see if there is a positive resolution to it. If she sees one, she knows that by working backward she might be able to hit on the clues that were missed in the initial investigation, and we can work off those to solve the case. But if she looks into the future and doesn't see it being resolved, she knows that it will remain a cold case."

Harrison sat back in his chair utterly dumbfounded. "You're shitting me," he said.

Dutch and I exchanged a look. "No, sir," I said meekly. "I'm afraid that's what we've been doing."

"And," Dutch said, his tone a little more firm, "that's what you hired her for, isn't it, sir?"

Harrison let out a laugh that caught me completely off guard. And he kept laughing until his face turned red and tears were leaking down his cheeks. In all the time I'd known him, I'd never seen him lose his composure like this, and I didn't know if I should go ahead and laugh with him or get ready to pack up my things and update my résumé.

And I could only imagine what the other agents in the office were thinking. Although my back was to them, I was fairly certain they were taking in everything that was happening in the boss's office.

When Harrison had finally sobered enough to speak, he looked surprised to see that Dutch and I hadn't joined him in the merriment. Wiping his eyes, he said, "I'm finding this all a little hard to take in."

I squirmed in my seat. "I know it's a little unconventional, sir."

Harrison chuckled again. "A *little* unconventional, Abby?"

The moment he said my first name, I relaxed and smiled. "Listen, if you really want us to waste time with these paper audits and number crunching and percentages, then fine, I'll cooperate and go along with that. But I gotta tell you, we'll get a whole lot further doing it my way."

Harrison's eyes moved back to the whiteboard and he shook his head ruefully. "Oh, of that I'm certain, Abby. It's the end of day one for this squad and you've already managed to get us halfway to our goal for the entire month."

"So," Dutch said, "should we carry on?"

Harrison picked up a stack of blank audit forms and dumped them into the recycling bin next to his wastebasket. "By all means," he said. "Beginning tomorrow, Abby, you will be the only person on audit duty, and you'll weigh in on which of our investigators should take the cases that require follow-up. I want to make sure that we give them to the right agent. Can you come in early tomorrow to get a jump start on another box so that we have enough cases for the entire squad?"

"I can."

"Excellent," he said with a broad smile as he reached out to shake my hand. It still threw me when Harrison was happy. I'd seen only glimpses of his lighter side and I almost didn't know how to react when he was anything but cool and reserved.

Dutch and I stood to go then and I was almost out the door when Harrison added, "Oh, and one more thing."

I turned back to him. "Yes?"

"I'd like you to start training the other agents to use their own intuitive abilities. Eventually I'd like them to audit these files using your techniques."

I opened my mouth to tell him there was no way I could turn his squad into a bunch of psychics like me, but I thought better of it. Why put limits when I wasn't sure how naturally intuitive these guys were? Maybe one or two of them would prove to be every bit as good as me.

Then again, maybe not.

Chapter Three

I arrived at the office at six fifteen a.m. It would have been closer to six if I hadn't gotten lost. Twice.

And no sooner had I made it to my desk than my cell phone rang. "Where are you?" Candice asked.

"At the office," I told her, trying to unload my purse, keys, sweater, and coffee without spilling the last all over my desk.

"It's six fifteen."

"Thank you, Madam Time," I said. "Are you going to give me the weather report next or are you all about the clock this morning?"

Candice chuckled. "Didn't we have a date at the gym in my building this morning?"

I did a mental head slap. "Crap on a cracker!"

That won me another chuckle. "Look'it who's gotten creative now that she can't use expletives."

"I'm really sorry, Candice. I forgot."

"It's okay," she assured me. "But what the heck are you doing at the office so early on your second day?"

"Brice piled a ton of work on my shoulders last night and I needed to come in early and get a jump start."

Candice was quiet for a moment before she said, "That man has tunnel vision when it comes to work. Do you need me to talk to him?"

I took a sip of my Starbucks, which was still delightfully hot. "No. Thanks, though. I don't really mind. And if I start minding, I'll come to you and you can beat him up for me, 'kay?"

Candice laughed. "Wouldn't be the first time I had to use a little muscle against him on your behalf."

I smiled as the memory of Candice forcefully pinning Brice against the side of a house to protect me floated to my mind. "Yeah, well, *hopefully* we can avoid revisiting those fun times."

Candice cleared her throat then and said, "I really did want to talk to you, Abs. Can I pull you away for lunch?"

Her voice sounded serious and I wondered what was up. My radar was hinting that I'd better say yes, so I did and we made plans to meet outside the building at noon. "But do me a favor," she said before signing off. "Don't tell Brice you're having lunch with me, okay?"

I thought that was curious, but I didn't probe because I was already pressed for time.

The minute I was off the phone with Candice, I turned in my chair and regarded the boxes behind me. They were stacked about three tall all along the filing cabinets arranged by date. One of the things that I noticed now that I hadn't before was that a vast majority of the boxes were dated 2005.

I also looked around to those boxes still remaining on the other agents' desks. I got up from my chair and wandered over to take a look at their progress. I had to smile when I realized most of these guys had gotten through only about six audits apiece.

I figured they'd warm up to me once they saw how much time I'd save them. Still, I wondered how Harrison was going to break the news to them that they'd be focusing their efforts only on those files I had a good gut feeling about.

With a sigh I headed back over to the boxes against the cabinets and stood there for a moment with my hands on my hips. My task seemed incredibly daunting. But standing around staring at a bunch of boxes wasn't going to get the job done, so with another sigh I reached for one of the 2005 boxes and trudged with it to my desk.

When I opened it, I was surprised at how many files it held. Most had precious little paperwork in them, and as I focused my radar on file after file that I eventually marked, "Dead," I knew why. The box was filled with reports that ran from late November 2005 to the end of January 2006. I noticed that in several of the cases either the suspects or victims had come from Louisiana after Hurricane Katrina.

Even though Katrina hadn't directly hit Texas, Houston, Corpus Christi, and San Antonio had all taken in a large number of former New Orleans residents and with the increase in population had come an uptick in crime.

It seemed that the FBI was handling a lot of the local-police overflow and the bureau itself had quickly become overwhelmed too.

So little follow-up was done on so many of the files that it was impossible for me to get anything from them.

By seven a.m. I'd gone through two more boxes from '05 and was seriously frustrated. Nearly all the files I'd focused my intuition at felt like dead ends.

I decided that it might be best to do what I'd done the day before, and point my radar at the boxes to feel which ones might contain the most bang for my buck. Immediately a set of three boxes from 2008 and 2009 caught my attention. With a bit of chagrin I saw that they had been sent over by the Dallas bureau, so whatever cases were in there were probably more thoroughly investigated.

I got up and began to cart these over to my desk and was just lifting the last one when the agent who had the desk next to mine entered. "Morning," he said.

"Hey," I said casually. These guys hadn't rolled out the welcome wagon for me, so I didn't think I was going to work too hard to win them over with my own sunny disposition.

The agent took his seat and set down his coffee. Something rang my radar and while I struggled with my box, I said, "Watch that cup. You don't want your coffee to spill."

The man eyed the cup, which was in the center of his desk and well away from the edge, then barely hid his disdain before shrugging out of his suit coat. As he moved to wrap it over the top of his chair, however, the sleeve caught his coffee cup, tipping it over, and black liquid spilled all over his desk.

I pressed my lips together firmly, working to conceal a smile, while he just stood there, dumbfounded at the mess on his desk.

I set the box down and hurried over to the credenza at the back of the room where Katie had arranged a coffeepot and various condiments and paper supplies.

Grabbing a handful of napkins, I rushed back and began to mop at the mess on the desk. "Thanks," said the agent as he took a few of the napkins I offered him and scooped the coffee into his wastepaper basket.

I left him with the napkins and retrieved a whole roll of paper towels from the ladies' room. After about five minutes we had the mess cleaned up and I handed him what remained of the paper towels. "Might want to keep these nearby," I told him. "Just in case."

He smiled sheepishly and surprised me by sticking out his hand. "Oscar," he said. "Rodriguez."

I took his hand and pumped it a few times. "Abby Cooper. Nice to meet you, Agent Rodriguez."

I moved to take my seat after our introduction, but he stopped me by asking, "How'd you know I was gonna spill the coffee?"

I laughed. "Haven't you heard? I'm psychic."

He cocked his head curiously at me, and I could tell he was trying to sum me up. "I heard," he said. "But no one believes it."

I shrugged and took my seat. "Yeah, I get that a lot. Still, there is the coffee"—I then motioned with my head over to the whiteboard—"and Agent Rivers and I did solve three cases yesterday. Er . . . using my sixth sense of course."

Rodriguez took his seat too and stared at me thoughtfully. "So, you're for real?"

"I'm for real."

"Okay," he said, leaning back in his chair, his eyes challenging me, "then tell me something about me that no one else knows."

"What am I, a circus act?" I snapped, shaking my head. I've had my fair share of people demanding that I prove myself with a little demonstration, and it always pisses me off that they think I should jump through hoops at the first snap of their skeptical fingers. "I don't do party tricks, Agent Rodriguez." And I focused on the box at my feet.

"Sorry," he said, in a way that suggested he clearly wasn't.

"Whatever," I muttered. "Who cares what you think?"

"You got a problem, lady?"

Our conversation was quickly heating up. I looked up, and glared at him. "Yes," I said. "I do."

He attempted to laugh. It was a hollow sound. "Why?

'Cause I'm not falling all over myself just because you told me my coffee might spill? Where I come from, we call that a coincidence."

My eyes narrowed a little more. "Of course it was. Just like it's a *coincidence* that I know you have a trip to South America coming up at the end of the month to visit with family. And it's a *coincidence* that I know that you own a silver car that you drive way too fast and that you recently got a ticket that you're using your badge to get out of.

"You'll get out of it all right, but the judge is going to let you know it's your last freebie. It's also a *coincidence* that you're going to need to see a doctor about that sore shoulder of yours very soon. And it's also a *coincidence* that I know your girlfriend recently broke up with you, but within the next week you guys'll get back together because she'll call and you'll tell her what a jerk you've been. What a jerk you *are*."

Rodriguez stared hard at me for a long time, but all he said in reply was, "I don't have a bum shoulder, lady." Then he got up and walked over to the coffee area at the back of the room to brew a fresh pot.

I sighed at his departing figure and got back to my own work.

Dutch came in around a quarter to eight and I'd gotten through two more boxes by then, but I hardly felt good about it. Instead, I had a raging headache and was hungry as hell. (Heck. I meant hungry as *heck*!)

"How's it going?" he asked, stopping by my desk with a fresh cup for me from Starbucks and a muffin.

I took the coffee and muffin gratefully, then pointed to the pile of several folders marked "Solvable." "It goes," I said. "But some of these . . ."

My voice trailed off and Dutch picked up the nearest file from the late fall of 2008. Opening it, he whistled low. "That's gotta sting," he said.

Unfortunately I knew exactly what he was looking at. The file opened to a picture of a decapitated corpse, lying prone on the side of the road with his head tucked gruesomely under one arm.

The case had come to the FBI because the killing had all the marks of a Mexican drug cartel's hit. Except that the victim, twenty-nine-year-old Jason Cushing, had a clean record except for two DUIs and a couple of drunk and disorderlies, including an incident where he'd been drunk enough to accept a dare from a buddy and had streaked across the stage of a huge Unity church during one of their live Sunday morning television broadcasts. How this prankster had ended up being the target of the Mexican Mafia was anyone's guess.

My notes on the file had been embarrassingly lacking in detail, but I couldn't let go of the feeling that the case could be solved. I felt deep in my gut that there was more than met the eye to Jason Cushing's murder.

"Fun stuff," I muttered, rubbing the back of my neck. After looking at so many crime-scene photos, I felt like I needed a shower and my head throbbed and I just wanted to eat a little something, then lie down for a while.

Dutch must have noticed because he asked, "You okay?"

I closed my eyes and rubbed my temples. "I'm fine. It's just a headache."

Other agents began filing into the office then and Dutch squeezed my shoulder before he headed off to his own office.

Harrison walked in promptly at eight a.m. and made sure to stop by my desk with a warm hello before strolling to his office with nothing more than a casual nod to the other agents.

For all the guff I gave Harrison, I had to admire his political savvy and how he looked out for me. He knew full well that I was the odd man out with this group, and by continually singling me out with a little extra attention, he was telling the group that I was special and they'd better be careful how they treated me.

About ten minutes later my desk phone rang. I jumped and picked it up quickly. "Hello?"

"Did I startle you?"

"No, sir," I said, peeking toward Harrison's office. He was smiling at me from behind his desk. "Okay, maybe a little."

"Candice says that you were in the office by six a.m. this morning."

Good ol' Candice. Giving me that extra fifteen minutes to make me look good. "She did?" I said. I wasn't about to correct her, but I didn't want to lie to Harrison.

"Yes," he said. "And I appreciate it. So, can I pull you

away for a minute so you can catch me up on your progress before our meeting?"

"Of course," I said, already getting to my feet. "Be there in a sec."

I gathered all the files and trotted into Harrison's office. Dutch was right behind me and he shut the door. "What have you got for us?" Harrison asked as I settled into a chair.

"Well," I said, picking up several files and handing them to Harrison. "Those definitely need some follow-up. I've made notes where I felt there were witness statements that weren't jibing or if it was more of a case of missing forensics, and that one just needs someone to go pick up the car." I pointed to the file Dutch was currently holding.

"You know where it is?" he asked me, pivoting the file around so I could see the crime scene. The case was a hit-and-run of a census worker who'd been canvassing a rural area in Waco.

I nodded. "The car was hidden right after the accident. All you have to do is haul it in and gather the forensic evidence. Then you can bring in the guy I've circled on the suspect list. I think he'll give you a full confession."

Harrison squinted at the photo "He will?"

I nodded again more vigorously. "Every time I focus on him, all I get is waves of guilt. He feels terrible about what he did."

The man I circled was one of several suspects who'd owned the make and model of a car that fit the description given by a witness, but the car had never been found, and the suspect had sworn that he'd given the car in question to a cousin who'd taken it back to Mexico several months earlier. Because the man had several cars on his property and a whole host of relatives that often drove his cars, it had been a difficult case to prove.

Harrison leaned forward looking keenly at me. "So where's the car?"

"It's in a pipe."

Dutch cocked his head. "A pipe?"

"Yeah," I said, pointing to the small sketch I'd drawn at the bottom of my notes. "See that? That's one of those big drainage pipes near a retention pond or something. There's got to be one near the suspect's home, and I believe he somehow managed to get the car into it."

Harrison made a few notes of his own and asked, "Any input on which agent we should give it to?"

I smiled. I could well imagine that the agent assigned would have to muck around in the mud and scrub to find the car, and I had just the candidate. "Rodriguez," I said. "He strikes me as just the kind of go-getter this case needs."

"Excellent. What else?"

I weeded through several more files for Dutch and Harrison until I got to the files left in my "Maybe" pile. One of them was Jason Cushing; the other was poor little Keisha. "These two I believe can be solved, but I'd like your permission to keep working on them for a bit until I feel confident I have something solid to hand one of your agents."

Harrison motioned for me to give him the files, and I

waited while he opened Cushing's first, grimaced at the crime photos, looked through the details, and landed on my notes.

I felt a little embarrassed about what I'd written, which was simply, "Not drug related," and left it at that.

"And this one?" Harrison asked, switching over to Keisha's file. "You think you know where this little girl is?"

"I think I might be able to narrow down where her body is, yes, sir."

Harrison's eyes came up to meet mine. "You're certain she's dead?"

"Yes."

Harrison sighed heavily. "Damn," he said. "She's a cute kid."

I nodded. "Yes, sir. She was."

"Okay," Harrison said, closing both files and handing them back to me. "Keep them as long as you need and let one of us know when you want to assign either of them out."

"Thank you, sir," I said.

"All right, then," Harrison said, getting to his feet. "Let's assign the cases we have so far. Abby, are you all right to continue with the file audits?"

I barely stifled a sigh. My noggin was still throbbing and I knew I was pushing the limit of what I could do intuitively in a day. "I believe so, sir."

"Excellent. After lunch you and I can discuss how best to conduct this training for the agents. I'll break it to them in the morning meeting that they'll need to make some time to join you in the conference room for your intuitive-development classes."

"Great," I said with all the enthusiasm I could muster—which wasn't much.

At the morning meeting more than a few eyebrows were raised when Harrison announced that the audit forms were being abandoned, and from now on, all cases would be run through me first and assigned if I found they had merit.

Harrison then handed everyone their case files with the notes inside before saying, "Last on my agenda is to tell you that Ms. Cooper will be conducting some lectures on enhancing your powers of perception, especially when it comes to the investigative process. Now, I'm not going to make attendance to her lectures mandatory"— Harrison paused to lock eyes with each member of the squad individually before he added—"yet. But make no mistake: Agent Rivers and I consider her an invaluable member of this squad and the *only* person we could not easily replace. So consider that before you dismiss her abilities and her willingness to make you better investigators. Clear?"

There were a few mumbled *Yes, sir*s from the group, but I could tell that even after that strong endorsement from the boss man, these guys weren't going to beat a path to my classroom's door.

Shortly after the meeting I attempted to get back to work. This was made all the more difficult for two reasons: First, I was acutely aware of the train of agents who one by one went in to talk to Harrison and Dutch. And while I couldn't hear what they were saying, given the amount of finger-pointing in my direction, I had little doubt that there were more than a few protests to this dramatic change in standard operating procedures.

The second reason was that, for some odd reason, I had a phrase swirling around in my brain that wouldn't allow me to concentrate. All the rest of the morning I kept hearing the phrase *Duck and cover* in my head. "You're not kidding," I said to my crew as the third agent got up and headed to Harrison's office.

Still, it was all most annoying and I was incredibly relieved when noon finally arrived. "Feel like grabbing some grub?" Dutch asked as I stood up and reached for my purse.

Oops. I'd forgotten to tell him I was having lunch with Candice. "Can I take a rain check? I promised Miss Fusco that I'd meet her for some girl talk."

"Sure," he said. "I bet she wants to show off her ring."

With a gasp I blurted out, *"Harrison proposed?"*

Several heads snapped in our direction and Dutch's eyes grew wide and I immediately felt bad.

"Sorry," I whispered. "I forget to use my inside voice sometimes. But did he?" I asked again. I couldn't believe Dutch would know before I would. I mean, I fully expected Candice to call me immediately to share the good news.

"I don't know," Dutch said. "I just assumed that he would have already popped the question, given your conversation with him the other day."

There was something odd reflected in Dutch's eyes, but now that he'd mentioned it, I was too anxious to get to Candice and see if she had a big honkin' diamond on her ring finger. "I'll let you know after lunch," I said to him, and leaned in to give him a kiss when we heard someone make a loud throat-clearing sound from behind him.

I peeked over Dutch's shoulder and saw Rodriguez giving us the evil eye. "Right," I whispered to Dutch when he looked uncomfortable. "No smooching at the office."

"And inside voices," he whispered with a wink, before squeezing my hand warmly. "Say hi to Candice for me, and give her my congratulations if the situation warrants."

The situation did not warrant. Candice appeared looking radiant and more relaxed than I'd ever seen her, but had no big diamond on her hand to show off. "Being rich agrees with you," I told her as she motioned me down the street.

Candice laughed. "Abby, I gotta tell you, being wealthy does not suck."

I chuckled too. "So my sister tells me." For the record, my sister, Cat, is the wealthiest person I've ever met. She's worth *bajillions*.

"And probably Dutch and Milo too, huh?"

I cocked my head at her. Now that she mentioned it, I realized I was surrounded by people who were very well-off. "Odd, isn't it? How many people I personally know who are worth some major bucks."

Candice nudged me with her shoulder. "I think you're our lucky charm."

That made me grin. "Yeah, and it would be my luck that I'd have that effect on everyone else but me."

"Government not paying what it used to?"

"No. And I think it's *always* paid on the low end."

We arrived at the restaurant and Candice held the door for me as we entered. "How goes it, by the way? Have you astounded any of your coworkers yet?"

"Oh, they're astounded all right," I said with a roll of my eyes. "If I had any expectations that I'd have an easier go of it here in Austin, I was dead wrong. Pretty much my crew's been telling me to duck and cover all morning."

Candice held up two fingers when the hostess asked her how many. "Is Brice standing up for you at least?"

"He is. I pinkie swear," I added when she looked at me skeptically.

We were shown to a table and given menus and it was a moment before Candice picked up the conversation again. "Can I ask you something?"

"Of course."

"Has Brice seemed a little . . . off, lately?"

That surprised me. "Off?"

Candice's radiant glow seemed to dim a little and she squirmed in her seat. "I think he might be having some regrets," she admitted, and to my astonishment she also began to tear up. "I think he's about to break it off with me."

"Oh, Candice," I said, reaching out to squeeze her hand. "Sometimes you can really be an idiot—you know that?"

Candice's jaw dropped and she half laughed and half sobbed in reply.

"Are you two ready to order?" asked a waitress who'd suddenly appeared at our table.

Without letting go of Candice's hand, I said, "Can you bring us both some water with lemon and give us a minute?"

The waitress appeared to notice Candice's rather fragile appearance then and she hastily moved off.

Once she'd departed, my friend dabbed at her eyes with her napkin. "So you don't think he's having second thoughts about us?"

"No."

"But he's been acting all weird lately," she insisted. "Every time he's around me, he gets fidgety and uncomfortable. I swear to God I think he's reconsidering our relationship."

I smiled. If she only knew just how much he was reconsidering it and thinking about taking it in a whole new direction. "So you want to know what my radar has to say?"

Candice reached for the glass of water that a busboy set down for us. "Yes," she said softly. "And please tell me the truth. I can take it."

"I think there might be a few changes ahead for you guys. And at first those changes may cause some issues between you, but eventually it feels more like you'll end up moving forward as a team, not as individuals going in your separate directions."

Candice's eyes watered again. "Really?" she asked in a squeaky whisper.

"If there is one thing I know with absolute certainty, Candice, it's that Brice Harrison is head over heels in love with you."

Candice took another sip of water and worked to collect herself. Our waitress came back then and we rushed to look at our menus and order just so she'd leave us alone for five seconds. After she'd gone away again, Candice said, "I trust you, but I swear to God there's been a shift in his demeanor."

We were starting to get into dicey territory here. If she kept probing, I had no doubt that I'd probably slip and tell her what Brice was up to, so I worked to put an end to her insecurities. "I know you like him more than you've ever liked any guy," I began.

"No, Abby," she said quickly. "I love him! I mean, I know that sounds crazy. I've only known Brice for what? Four months? But I love him. I mean, it's like there's this deep connection we have, and I don't know what I'd do if he left me."

I looked her dead in the eyes. "He's not leaving you."

Candice closed her lids and another set of fresh tears leaked its way down her cheeks. "God, I hope you're right."

The moment I got back to the office, I marched

straight into Harrison's office and shut the door. "*What* are you waiting for?" I demanded.

"Please come in, Ms. Cooper," he said drolly.

"I'm serious," I said, crossing my arms and tapping my toe impatiently. "Do you know that I just spent the last hour with my heartsick friend, trying to reassure her that you aren't as dumb as you look?"

Harrison's brow furrowed. "Have you been drinking?"

I sat angrily down in a chair. "Ha-ha," I said drily, and was shocked to see he didn't seem to be kidding. "I'm completely sober!"

Harrison just stared at me and blinked. He looked like he might be on the verge of calling Dutch in for backup.

"I'm not joking," I said evenly. "You have to do something!"

Harrison tossed his hands in the air. "I have no idea what or whom you're talking about."

I took a deep breath and tried again. "Candice has noticed a change in your demeanor. She thinks you're having second thoughts about the two of you and she's really worried that you might be getting ready to break up with her."

"*She what?*"

"You need to pop the question, and you need to do it pronto, because the last guy Candice suspected was about to break it off with her was dumped before he ever had a chance to say, 'I think we should talk.'"

The color drained out of Harrison's face. "She's going

to break up with *me*? Just because she thinks I might be ready to break up with *her*?"

"Yep."

"But . . . but . . . ," he stammered. "I've just been waiting for the right time!"

I made a big show of tapping my wristwatch. "I'd say that time is riiiight about now, sir."

Harrison sat back in his chair and stared at his desk. Finally, looking up at me, he said, "Okay."

I raised an eyebrow. "Okay?"

He nodded. "I'll do it tonight."

"You look a little pale," I remarked. "You okay?"

"Yeah," he said. "I mean, I've never asked anyone before."

"You haven't?" That surprised me. Harrison was in his late thirties. I was sure he'd had at least one proposal in his life, if not a walk down that aisle. "Really? No one?"

Harrison shook his head and let out an uncomfortable laugh. "I don't even know what to say," he admitted. "Should I put the ring in some champagne? Or take her out to dinner? Maybe I should rent a sailboat and take her out on the lake?"

I made a face. "Dude," I said. "Candice doesn't need any of that. She's pretty simple. Just sit her down, tell her she's the one, and show her the ring." I then had another thought. "You *do* have a ring, right?"

The color returned to Harrison's cheeks and he blushed. "Yes."

I sat forward eagerly. "Can I see it?"

Harrison considered that for a second before he reached into his drawer and pulled out a small black box. With great care he opened the lid and held it out for me to see, and at that moment, Rodriguez opened the door and stuck his head in. "Oh!" he said, seeing Harrison and me with the ring between us. "I . . . uh . . . I didn't mean to interrupt. I can see you're busy."

He quickly closed the door and I fell into a fit of giggles. "Ahh," I said as Harrison put the ring quickly away with a mortified look on his face. "I can't *wait* to hear what rumors start swirling around the office after that!"

Chapter Four

It turned out that the reason Rodriguez had come into Harrison's office was that our boss had told him to. What Harrison hadn't had a chance to tell me was that because there had been such a stink raised about using me to determine which cases to reopen, Harrison had decided to send me with Rodriguez to help locate the car that had hit the census worker.

"It's the only way to prove to these guys that they should take you seriously," Harrison argued after telling me his decision. "If you lead Rodriguez right to that car, then there's no way he or anyone else on the squad can doubt you. Especially since the previous investigators did such a thorough search of the area."

"You want us to go today?" I asked, looking again at my watch. It was already one thirty, and I needed to collect my thoughts before the lecture I was planning on giving to the agents later that afternoon.

"That's for the two of you to work out," Harrison said. "But you're right. It is a little late to make the trip up to Waco. If you want to wait until tomorrow morning, that's fine with me."

I brightened. Here I'd thought I'd be stuck in the office for the next month doing the taxing work of sorting through case files all day. "Okay," I agreed. "I'd love a chance to play bloodhound."

"Excellent. Now, if you'll excuse me," he said, clearing his throat, "I have a speech to prepare."

I shook my head and got up to leave. "Keep it simple, Brice. Just stick to those four little words and you'll be good to go."

I opened the door then, but Brice stopped me. "What four words?"

I turned back to him and smiled before answering. "Will you marry me?"

"*Excuse* me?" said a deep baritone right behind me.

I think I jumped a foot. "Dutch!" I gasped, glancing over my shoulder to see his rather stunned expression. Lowering my voice, I explained, "I was just helping Brice for an important discussion he's having later."

Dutch crossed his arms and that something that I'd noticed earlier flashed again in his eyes. "Uh-huh," he said, and I was surprised to see him looking irritated.

I forced a smile and pointed to my desk. "Better get back to work." I bolted then for the other end of the room.

An hour and a half later I was in the conference room waiting nervously for my class. I'd sent a general e-mail out to the group that we'd be meeting at three o'clock and the lecture wouldn't go longer than an hour. Dutch and Brice had already let me know that they wouldn't be able to attend this first lecture because of a conference call they had with D.C., but that if their call ended early, they'd pop in.

I watched the clock on the wall and kept telling myself that it was okay if the agents showed up late, as long as they showed up. But by three ten, when no one came through the door, I knew I'd been stood up. "Crap," I said after sticking my head out of the conference room and seeing all the empty desks.

Katie walked by at that moment carrying several shopping bags filled with office supplies. "Hi, Abby," she said as she passed.

"Do you know where everyone is?"

Katie set one of her bundles down and turned to look at the empty room. "Out working the cases you gave them, I believe."

My eyes bugged. "All of them?"

"Except Rodriguez," she said. "He stepped outside to take a personal call."

I sighed heavily. "Great. Just great."

Katie gave me a sympathetic smile. "Don't let them get to you. I've heard nothing but amazing things about your abilities, and I'm sure you're every bit as gifted as they say."

I eyed her skeptically. "You've heard about me?"

Katie smiled. "I was Bill Gaston's administrative assistant when he first came to the bureau, before my husband was later relocated to Round Rock. We've kept in touch over the years, and when he heard that the CCS was going to be located here in Austin, and that you'd agreed to join the team, he contacted me directly and made me apply for the office-management position. He raves about you, you know."

Hearing about Bill Gaston's faith in me lifted my spirits and I was able to put the fact that I'd been summarily dissed by the other agents in perspective. "I'm a big fan of Gaston's," I told her.

"He's a good man," Katie agreed. "And when he says someone's the real deal, I tend to believe it. Give it time, Abby. These guys'll come around."

I hoped Katie was right, but it felt like a kick in the gut as I packed up all my supplies and notes from the conference room and headed back to my desk. By now I was really tired and I didn't know how I was going to get through the last hour of the day having to tune in on files. My radar felt weak and thready, and that headache had never really gone away even though I'd popped a few Excedrin.

As it happened, I was saved when Dutch stuck his head out of Harrison's office and asked, "Is the lecture over?"

"It never started."

Dutch eyed the room and sighed. "Give them time, Abs," he said, coming fully out of the office to walk to my desk.

I nodded but didn't say anything else. Dutch looked down at me with sympathy. "Why don't you head home?"

I eyed the clock. "But it's only three thirty."

"Weren't you here at six?"

"Umm . . . more or less."

"That's still a full day," he said, moving a lock of my hair behind my ear. "Go. You look beat. I'll be home by six and I'll bring some dinner."

I glanced around at the empty room and its lack of prying eyes and ears and kissed him. "Have I told you lately that I rilly, rilly love you?"

Dutch smiled. "No. You rilly haven't."

"Well, then, consider your cute butt notified."

Someone cleared his throat from behind me again.

"Oh, sheep!" I whispered. "We've been caught again, haven't we?" I sneaked a look over my shoulder and Rodriguez was standing there with a disapproving look on his face. I knew he wouldn't say anything directly to Dutch—who was his superior—but I could only imagine the earful Harrison was going to get the moment I left.

"Good night, Ms. Cooper," Dutch said formally as I backed quickly away. "Drive safe."

The next morning when I walked into the office, I found Harrison snoring on the small leather couch in his office. I knocked loudly on his door and he sat up with a start. "Morning," I said as he blinked blearily.

"Morning," he said, his voice croaky. "What time is it?"

"A little after seven. What time did you get here?" I figured he had come in really early, got tired, and was taking a catnap before the squad showed up.

Harrison stood, stretched, and rubbed the sleep out of his eyes. "Midnight."

"Midnight? What brought you back here at midnight?"

He gave me a crooked smile. "Your friend Candice."

"Huh?"

"She kicked me out."

"She *what*?"

"She needs time," he said dramatically.

"Time for what?"

"Time to think." Harrison was now pacing his office and I could see that whatever had gone on between him and Candice the night before was still bugging him.

I held up my hand. "Hold on a sec. Can we back up? What happened between you two?"

Harrison sat down on the couch with a heavy sigh. "I took your advice, and it backfired."

I thought back through the advice I might have given him and remembered the conversation we'd had about the proposal. "So, you asked her to marry you?"

"Yeah."

"And she kicked you out?" None of this was making sense. Especially given how broken up Candice had been about the thought of Brice leaving her.

"The kicking-out part came later."

I came all the way into Harrison's office then and pulled a chair up to the couch. I then handed him my

Starbucks coffee and ordered him to drink it. "Maybe after you wake up a little, you'll start making sense."

He smiled ruefully, took the cup and a big swig of java. "When I got home last night, I found Candice crying on the balcony. At first she wouldn't tell me what was wrong, so I thought I'd just give her some space and go hang out in the bedroom. But then she accused me of walking away, so I went back to try and find out what was wrong. I finally managed to get it out of her that she thought I was having second thoughts and wanted out of our relationship.

"I tried to tell her she was crazy, but somehow we got into an argument and I sort of shouted the proposal at her, only I realized that I'd left the stupid ring here. And of course she then accused me of only proposing to her because she was upset, which I vehemently denied and I swore to her that I'd been planning this for a while but forgot the ring at work. She didn't believe me and kicked me out."

"Whoa," I said when he took another sip of coffee. "What're you gonna do?"

Harrison looked at me in disbelief. "What am *I* gonna do? Are you serious?"

My brow furrowed. "Uh . . . I thought I was."

He shook his head and handed me back the coffee. "I'm not doing anything, Abby. *You* need to talk to her."

That surprised me. "I do?"

He nodded vigorously. "Yes. Tell her about the ring. Tell that I bought it a week ago and that you saw us engaged in a vision or a dream or something. Tell her that she's overreacting and being an idiot and to let me come home for Christ's sake!"

I was suddenly regretting my decision to stick my nose into Candice and Brice's personal business. "Okay," I said meekly. "I'll talk to her. But give me the day, all right? When Candice is really upset, she doesn't listen so well."

"Tell me about it," Brice muttered. He then looked at his watch and stood up. "I gotta get cleaned up before the rest of the squad shows up. And do me another favor: don't mention to anyone that I slept here, okay?"

"No problem," I assured him. One look at the rumpled clothing he was wearing and they'd be able to figure that out all on their own.

Rodriguez arrived at eight a.m., and without even looking at me, he said, "You ready to head to Waco?"

"Yes," I said, suddenly remembering that I'd left my iPod at home. I could only imagine what fun a two-hour joyride with Agent Ice Cube would be without my tunes.

On our way out we passed Dutch, who had no idea I was going along for the ride to find the missing car. "Wait a second," he said, grabbing my arm. "You're going out in the field?"

His face was lined with concern, so I tried to reassure him. "Harrison approved it. And we're just going to try and locate the car used in that hit-and-run of the census worker. It'll be perfectly safe."

"I'll take care of your girlfriend, sir," Rodriguez said,

and the way he said "girlfriend" made it clear that he didn't approve that the boss's main squeeze worked on the squad.

Dutch took one step forward, real anger in his eyes. "Her name is Ms. Cooper, Agent Rodriguez. I'll thank you to remember that. We clear?"

Rodriguez swallowed, lowered his eyes, and looked chagrined. "Crystal clear, sir. My apologies."

Dutch backed off and regarded me. "You stick close to Agent Rodriguez, understand? I don't want to hear about you wandering off on your own and getting into trouble. And no interviewing suspects, Abby. You're not cleared for fieldwork yet, and I don't want you in any potentially hostile situations, *capisce*?"

Dutch knew me a little too well. "I promise," I said. "I'll be good. We're only going to sniff around for the car."

Dutch's cold stare swiveled back to Rodriguez. "She gets so much as a bug bite and I'm holding you personally responsible."

"I'll keep her safe, sir," Rodriguez assured him.

I didn't exactly appreciate Dutch's intimidation tactics. He wasn't doing me any favors by bullying these agents into working with me. "Let's go," I said, and hurried out the door.

Rodriguez and I rode in silence for the first hour of the trip. I figured he wasn't going to be much of a Chatty Cathy, so I'd managed to grab a few new files to work on before leaving the office.

One file from March of 2009 caught my attention,

and it was eerie, because much of it read like a file I'd keyed in on the day before.

The paperwork was light—not much follow-up had been done—but the things I made note of were that it involved the beheading of a young Hispanic male named Felix Lopez from a south Dallas suburb who'd had a long list of minor criminal convictions. It looked like he'd spent far more time in prison than out in his short twenty-one years for things like assault, robbery, criminal trespass, driving while intoxicated, driving under the influence of narcotics, and the list went on and on.

He'd started his criminal career early, in fact, when he'd been tossed in the can at just seventeen for attempted rape of a fifteen-year-old. But what I couldn't figure out as I sorted through the various other convictions for drugs, assault, and robbery was how this fairly small-town punk had ended up decapitated in a similar fashion as Jason Cushing—the almost unmistakable mark of a Mexican drug-lord hit.

The agent assigned to the case had documented the presence of Los Zetas, which later became La Familia Michoacana, in the area. Los Zetas was a well-known and particularly violent Mexican drug cartel. I remembered newscasts from the previous year describing a major FBI and local law-enforcement sting that had taken down many key members of La Familia.

This particular cartel were infamous for their style of killing. Their victims were usually beheaded and the bodies dumped in open fields or by the side of the road—and more often than not, their heads were discovered in separate locations—adding to the cartel's ruthless reputation.

Back in early 2009, information about the cartel was still being gathered, and indications that La Familia was about to split off was evidenced by the infighting within the Los Zetas ranks, and the deaths of a few of their less loyal members.

The investigators determined that somehow Felix had ended up on the wrong side of one of those members during that surge in violence.

I wanted to connect these two murders, but there were quite a few discrepancies that didn't make that connection obvious. To begin with, Felix was murdered four months after Jason. And Felix's body wasn't found on the side of a road, but in an abandoned warehouse, and his head was never recovered. He'd been identified through fingerprints. It looked like he'd been bound and murdered, then decapitated. At least I hoped he'd died before he'd been made into a headless horseman. And while Felix was Hispanic, Jason was not. It could have been that both men were killed because of some unknown connection to Los Zetas, but every time I tried to confirm that through my radar—I couldn't. The idea of Jason and Felix being taken out by the Mexican Mafia kept bouncing back at me—as if it was a false statement that I needed to reexamine.

And I was fully convinced that Felix and Jason were connected. Other than the possible Mexican Mafia connection, there was nothing in the files to indicate how—but when I thought about that possibility, it felt right—like two pieces of a puzzle you're convinced don't go together, but only because you haven't discovered how they fit into the bigger picture yet.

Felix's case was one I thought we might be able to solve—it had that completion energy about it—but no further clues came to my intuitive mind, so I didn't have anything to recommend other than something about this file seemed very off, as in it felt unreal. I even wrote down the word "forgery" on my legal pad, but I didn't know what was forged or what wasn't real.

After ten more minutes of trying to come up with something else to jot down, I gave up and set it aside with a sigh, settling for staring out the window at the passing scenery.

"You really think we're gonna to find this car?" Rodriguez asked into the silence, and I jerked a little at the sound of his voice.

"Yep," I replied without looking at him.

He was quiet again and I didn't try to make conversation. I'd pretty much had it with these testy FBI boys and their skepticism. I'd learned by now that you couldn't tell them—you had to show them.

"My girlfriend called me yesterday," Rodriguez said, again interrupting the solitude of the car. "Well, my *ex*-girlfriend called me yesterday."

I couldn't help it; I turned to look at him. "You don't say?"

The corner of Rodriguez's mouth lifted a little. "She broke it off with me about two months ago. We'd been together since high school, you know? It was rough."

I wanted Rodriguez to get to the good part, because I fully remembered telling him that he'd hear from his ex. "What'd she say?"

Rodriguez allowed himself to smile a little more. "She misses me."

"Gee," I said lightly. "Where've I heard that before?"

The smile vanished and the agent next to me shifted in his seat. "Yeah, well, I gotta give you credit. That was way too freaky to be just a coincidence."

"What'd you tell her?"

Rodriguez's eyes swiveled over to me, then darted back to the road. "I told her that I'd been a real asshole and that I missed her too."

I smirked. "Good boy," I said. Then my radar kicked in and I knew how the rest of the conversation had gone. "You need to let her take her time," I told him. "I know you were expecting to get back together right away, especially since she was the one who called you, but she needs to make sure you've changed and that you're going to respect her enough to give her a little breathing room."

His eyes zinged back to me in surprise. "That's almost exactly what she said."

"Dude," I said seriously. "I'm no amateur, okay? I actually do this for a living. Well, I used to do this for a living before the economy went to pot."

Rodriguez laughed. "Yeah, okay. I hear you. So maybe I'm a little less skeptical of you now."

"Yippee," I said woodenly. "Just the enthusiastic endorsement I was looking for."

"Hey, you gotta cut us some slack, okay? How do we know you're for real unless we see it with our own eyes?"

"Oh, I understand, Agent Rodriguez. It's just, you have to remember, there are millions of skeptics out there, and only one of me. After a while, proving myself just gets old."

Rodriguez nodded. "I get it," he said. "And if we find this car today, I'll tell everyone back at the squad room you're for real."

"Get your endorsement speech ready, then, buddy, because we are *so* finding that car!"

An hour later we were standing at the bottom of a dried-up riverbed at the opening of a huge pipe that carried runoff water away from a megasized subdivision a half mile away. Parked inside the huge pipe was one heck of a dirty, rusted-out car with noticeable fender damage that fit the description of the hit-and-run vehicle to a tee.

There were no plates on the car, but the VIN matched the one registered to our suspect. "I love it when I'm right," I said to Rodriguez, who was peering inside the dirty windows.

He wiped his hands on his jeans and sent me another smile. "Okay, okay," he said. "I've been converted. You're psychic and I'm willing to tell everyone how good you are from now on."

"Excellent. Now, do we haul this guy in or what?"

Rodriguez pulled out his cell phone and began to dial. "No way. You heard what Agent Rivers told us. No interviewing suspects with you in the field."

I bounced my eyebrows and said, "He didn't say we couldn't haul him in, though, now, did he?"

But Rodriguez wasn't biting. "We'll have the car towed to the FBI yard for them to do their forensics and gather as much evidence as we can. I don't want to arrest this guy until we're one hundred percent positive it's his vehicle and we know we've got a solid case against him."

"But I already told you, if you just bring him in, he'll give you a full confession." I felt that in my bones.

"I'm not doubting you," Rodriguez was quick to say. "But let's make sure we have a reason to bring him in before we jump the gun, okay?"

I checked my radar to see if there'd be any harm in waiting, and it didn't feel like there would be, so I let Rodriguez have it his way.

He called for the FBI's tow truck and we waited for nearly an hour and a half before it showed up. The driver apologized, saying he'd had to come all the way from Dallas.

After the old car had been towed away, Rodriguez motioned for us to be on our way. "Hungry?" he asked.

I sighed in relief. I'd been famished for over an hour. "I am. And I hope you can find me some junk food, because Dutch has been on this health-food kick lately and I think it's killing me."

We found a Chipotle restaurant in downtown Waco and while I was chowing down on a burrito, Rodriguez slid a folder toward me. "What's this?"

"It's a cold case," he said. "Something I was working when I was with the bureau in Dallas."

"Did you pull it from one of the boxes?" I asked carefully. I remembered Harrison saying that the investigators weren't supposed to audit their own files.

"No. Agent Cox pulled it and gave it back to me after he did the audit."

I looked at the score at the top of the lengthy form. "Ooh," I said. "It failed."

"It failed the old audit," Rodriguez corrected. "Which didn't surprise me, because my old partner and I worked that case into the ground. We just came to a total dead end."

I hadn't opened the folder yet. I was still weighing what I should do with it. "What's the case about?"

"Two kids named Wendy Hayes and Tyler Harvin were a couple of runaway seventeen-year-olds. They lived in Oklahoma and their parents were neighbors who'd never gotten along and forbidden the kids from seeing each other. The folks even had a lawsuit over the property line between their land."

"Sounds like Romeo and Juliet," I said.

"Something like that," Rodriguez said. "Anyway, the parents wanted Wendy and Tyler to break up. But the kids had other plans, and they stole Wendy's mom's car and tried to drive it to Houston. They thought they could get lost in a big city like that. The problem was that the car broke down here in Waco. Tyler phoned the local auto repair, a shop called Clady's, run by this sweet old guy Russell Clady.

"Anyway, Russell was the one that notified the authorities the day after he fixed the kids' car. He said he just didn't buy that they were nineteen and on their way to visit relatives in Corpus Christi. He said that he'd called the number they'd given him once he'd made the repairs, but they never showed to claim the car. When the local sheriff discovered that the car was stolen, he went to the hotel where the kids were staying. Wendy and Tyler had checked in, but hadn't checked out, and when the sheriff went to their room, he found their luggage there, but no sign of them.

"He then contacted us when he learned the kids were missing from Oklahoma and we'd have jurisdiction."

I opened the folder and stared at the two photos of Wendy and Tyler. They both had soft doughy complexions and Wendy was a freckled red head. Tyler had eyes that were too small for his face, and a broad flat nose. The effect was that it made him look suspicious.

"They're both dead," I told Rodriguez. "They were abducted and killed someplace else."

Rodriguez took a pull from his Dr Pepper. "You really think they're *both* dead?"

"Yes."

This seemed to unsettle Rodriguez.

"You thought they were alive?"

He shifted in his chair. "We thought they might have argued, and that Tyler could have killed Wendy, and hidden her body somewhere, then taken off without claiming the car to make it look like they might both still be alive."

I shook my head and focused again on the photos in the file. "No. That's not how it went down, although I'm sure there was a struggle. A third party killed your teens."

"Who?" Rodriguez pressed.

I closed my eyes to concentrate, calling out to my crew for assistance.

"Was it the motel manager? He passed a polygraph, but I never believed that guy was telling the truth. I've always thought there was more to the story than he was telling us. He's a creepy-looking dude, too. We did a background check on him and—"

Annoyed, I opened one eye. "Shhhh," I whispered. "Psychic at work."

Rodriguez looked chagrined. "Sorry."

I closed the eye again and focused. My mind flooded with the image of the tow truck that had come to pick up the car from the pipe. I frowned.

"What's the matter?" Rodriguez whispered. I could feel him watching me very closely.

"Nothing," I said. "My brain's just jumbled with too much input from this afternoon. Hang on a minute."

I took a deep breath and tried again. *Hey, guys,* I thought. *Help me out here. I need to see who took Wendy. Show me who killed her.*

Again the tow truck barreled into my thoughts, and it was too intense this time to dismiss. I snapped my eyes open, knowing I had the answer. "Agent Rodriguez, when Wendy and Tyler broke down, did they call a tow truck to take their car to be repaired?"

Rodriguez cocked his head. "I think so. My partner worked the case alone in the beginning—I was on vacation when it first came in." Motioning for me to give him the file, he flipped through the pages after I'd handed it to him, and said, "Huh."

"What?"

"Jeff didn't note it."

"Would that Russell Clady guy remember who towed the car?"

"He might," Rodriguez said, pulling out his cell phone and dialing the number for the shop. After several rings I heard him say, "Hey, Russell, it's Agent Rodriguez calling. I know we haven't talked in a while, but I have a few quick follow-up questions on the Wendy Hayes and Tyler Harvin case. Give me a shout as soon as you can, please."

Rodriguez left his return number and hung up. He then eyed me curiously. "How would you feel about going to Clady's?"

It was my turn to shift in my seat. Dutch would be royally ticked off if he knew we were following up on a lead. "I'm not supposed to interview suspects, remember?"

Rodriguez smiled broadly and began to pile our left-over wrappers onto the tray. "Russell's not a suspect, remember? He called the authorities. Plus, the old man's harmless. He's got to be eighty with a bum hip. I'm pretty sure he couldn't hurt a fly."

Still, there was an unsettling feeling in my stomach and I didn't say anything for a long moment, trying to decide what to do.

"Maybe meeting Russell would help your sixth sense figure out more about the case," Rodriguez suggested. And that's what really helped make the decision. Sometimes, all I need is to interact with someone who's got a personal connection to a missing person and I can pull even more clues out of the ether.

"Okay," I said, getting up. "I'm in."

We arrived at Clady's Ace Car Repair about twenty minutes later. The place wasn't so "Ace," though. It was more like a dump.

All manner of decaying and rusty cars were scattered about a large fenced-in lot with a small garage in the middle. There was dirt, grease, and oil everywhere, and lots of litter too. Old tires, oil drums, car seats, and smaller car parts were strewn about everywhere. It was like an elephant graveyard where the jackals had come to spread the bones.

"Nice," I said as I passed through the narrow gate to the small dirt road leading to the garage.

"Watch your step," Rodriguez warned as he parked a few yards from the entrance and got out of the car. "There's probably all kinds of small scrap metal that could pierce your shoe."

"Lovely," I muttered, wrinkling my nose. The place smelled heavily of oil and gas. We approached the front door and saw the sign in the window that said that the owner was out to lunch and would return by one. I looked at my watch. "It's quarter to."

"I think we should wait," Rodriguez said.

"Okay," I agreed, really hoping Russell wasn't going

to be late getting back from lunch. I didn't like this place. It gave me the creeps actually, and I wanted to leave.

While we waited, Rodriguez called in to check on the car retrieved from the pipe, while I moseyed around and used a big stick I found to poke at stuff in the grass. I must have wandered farther than intended, because the next thing I knew, I felt a very subtle slashing sensation around my neck. It was so slight that I almost didn't notice it, but it was still enough to make me stop poking the ground and look around. That's when my crew practically burst into my head in alarm.

My head whipped up as I tried to find the source of the intuitive feeling of something slicing across my neck. What the heck was I picking up?

I was at the back of the garage and there were two large oil drums resting against the building. Both were sealed and rusted, but as I approached, something foul tickled my nostrils, and it wasn't petroleum.

My heart began hammering in my chest and I realized that I was breathing really hard. Wendy and Tyler were in the drums. I knew it like I knew my own name. I called out to Rodriguez, but he didn't appear. I could barely pull my eyes off the containers, but I had to get him, so I hurried through the tall grass, watching my step, to the other side of the building.

"Agent Rodriguez!" I called, seeing him still on the phone by his car. He held up his finger in a give-me-a-minute gesture, but I was too wound up to be ignored. *"Agent Rodriguez!"* I shouted.

I saw his eyes flash to me with irritation, but he quickly

realized something was wrong because he ended his call abruptly and hurried over to me. "What's the matter?"

I grabbed his wrist and tugged him toward the back of the building. "I've found them," I said, my voice shaking.

"You've found who?"

"Wendy and Tyler!"

Rodriguez didn't ask me anything else until we'd dashed around the building. He stopped then and looked around. "Where are they?"

I gulped and pointed to the drums. "In there."

Cautiously, Rodriguez approached the rusty metal containers. He stopped when he was about five feet away and sniffed. He looked back at me and asked, "Are you sure?"

Anxiously, I pumped my head up and down, my stomach threatening to give up the burrito. "They're both in there."

Rodriguez moved in and began turning and twisting the right drum out from against the wall. Something clunked around inside and a wave of the most awful odor hit me like a ton of bricks.

My stomach bunched and I turned away, gagging and trying desperately not to toss my lunch—but it was useless. The smell was too intense and the horror of the scene was just too much for me. After I'd recovered myself, I looked back to see Rodriguez eyeing me critically. "You okay?"

I wiped my mouth with my sleeve. "Fine," I croaked.

He seemed to take me at my word and left it at that.

"There's a label on the drum. It reads, 'Clady's Ace Towing and Car Repair.'"

"He was the tow truck driver," I gasped, and put my arm over my nose.

Rodriguez wiped his hands together and moved away from the drum. "Come on," he urged, heading back to the front of the building.

"Where're we going?" I had to run to keep up with him.

"We need to get you out of here and I have to get a warrant."

"You're just going to *leave* them there?"

"I can't open the drums without probable cause, and right now, as far as the law is concerned, you and I are trespassing. We gotta do this by the book, so let's get out of here before Russell comes back and sees us snooping around. The last thing I need him to do is move that drum away from here before we have a chance to get back with a warrant."

"Good thinking," I said, trotting along beside him. But as we rounded the corner, we both came up short. Parked in the middle of the dirt road, blocking the exit was a large tow truck with CLADY'S ACE TOWING imprinted in large gold lettering on the doors. A tall, greasy fellow with thick arms and salt-and-pepper hair leaned his head out of the truck and eyed us suspiciously. "Can I help you?" he asked, his Texan drawl prominent.

"Afternoon," Rodriguez said, with an easy smile. "We were looking for Russell Clady."

The man's eyes narrowed a fraction. "He's dead," he told us. "Died last spring."

Rodriguez appeared surprised but recovered quickly. "Can you tell us where the owner is, then?"

"That'd be me," said the driver. "I'm Russell's son, Darrell."

Rodriguez appeared to be processing that while my crew was repeating the words *Duck and cover!* over and over in my head.

I leaned in toward Rodriguez and whispered, "We've got to get out of here."

Darrell spat some chew on the ground. "What is it you two want, exactly?"

Rodriguez's eyes moved from the exit, which was blocked by the tow truck, to his car, parked near the building, and all the while the air filled with tension. "We were having some car trouble and we were hoping you could take a look at it for us," Rodriguez said casually.

Darrell chewed his tobacco thoughtfully, but I could tell he didn't buy that for a second. "What kind of trouble is she giving you?" he asked, motioning with his head toward our car.

"I've been hearing a rattle in the engine," Rodriguez said.

There was a long pause while Darrell continued to stare at us with his cold, suspicious eyes. Finally he turned off his engine, leaving the exit blocked, and climbed down from his truck. I could see he was a big man, maybe six four or six five, and he carried himself with a sense of confidence that made me incredibly nervous. I knew Rodriguez carried a gun, which was good, because in a wrestling match, this guy would have made mincemeat out of him.

He passed us on his way to the garage without saying a word and moved to unlock the garage door. Rodriguez leaned close to me and whispered, "While he's working on finding that rattle, I'll call for backup and a warrant."

I relaxed a teeny bit. Thank God he had a plan.

When the garage was unlocked, Darrell motioned to Rodriguez. "Why don't you start her up and pull her in here so I can take a look?"

Rodriguez moved over to the car and I followed, sticking close to him. "Where're you going?" he asked me.

"I left my purse in the car," I said loudly when I realized I might look stupid getting in with him because he was only going to pull it forward a few yards. "And I need to get my files from work." Rodriguez nodded; he registered that we didn't need the man seeing those and realizing we were FBI.

We got in and I pushed the seat back to get at the files on the car floor. One had fallen under the seat far enough that I practically had to bend myself into a yoga pose to get at it.

"What are you doing?" Rodriguez whispered while he started the car.

I grunted. "There's a file way under the seat," I explained, straining to get my arm into the right angle to grab it.

"Why don't you get it from the backseat?" he asked me.

I stopped straining and blinked stupidly. "Good thinking," I said, and started to withdraw my hand, but the phrase *DUCK AND COVER* bolted so loudly into my brain that I winced. I sat there frozen for a moment, wondering what the heck that was all about when in the very next instant there was an explosion of glass right above my head.

I screamed. Rodriguez swore. A moment later another explosion and more glass tore our world apart.

Chapter Five

Rodriguez's body hit me like a ton of bricks, pinning me down on the floor of the car. Something splattered wetly across my face, and shards of glass clattered and clinked against the dashboard.

I screamed again and tried to cover my head with my arms. "My gun," I heard Rodriguez say hoarsely. "Get my gun!"

I stared at him while adrenaline rushed through my veins, causing my palms to sweat and my breathing to intensify. My brain was having a really hard time absorbing what was happening, but certain things were starting to click. We were being shot at. And by the amount of red stuff pooling on the seat by Rodriguez's right shoulder, I knew he'd been hit.

"I can't move my arm!" he growled angrily, while his left hand struggled to free the gun at his right hip.

I reached over to help him as another round hit our car and a small hole opened up in the seat right above my head. I bit down on my lip hard, trying not to scream again, and tugged Rodriguez's gun free of its holster.

I tried to put it in his left hand, but he wouldn't take it. Instead, he laid his left hand over my own and whispered, "Shoot him!"

I stared at him in disbelief.

Another explosion shattered the back window and more glass flew. I felt a shard slice my cheek and I winced.

"Shoot him!" Rodriguez hissed.

"I don't know how!" I mouthed.

"You don't need to do anything more than point and shoot," Rodriguez growled through clenched teeth. "He's going to come out here any second to make sure we're dead. When he gets close, take him out."

I had never shot a gun in my life. And, up to that moment, I'd never even held one. At home, whenever Dutch set his gun down, I avoided it like the plague. The truth is, firearms scare the sheep outta me.

But this was life or death, and as terrified as I was of the big black object in my shaking hand, I was even more afraid of those approaching footsteps.

"Hold the bottom of the handle with your left palm to steady your right," Rodriguez whispered quickly. "Then, just stare down the sight and point at his chest.

Fire as many shots as you can. Once you start, don't stop."

Just like Rodriguez had predicted, outside we could hear the distinct sounds of slow-moving footsteps crunching on gravel. Darrell was heading to finish us off.

The footsteps on the gravel got closer and I tried to hold the gun steady in my sweaty trembling hand. I didn't want to take the shot too early, but if I waited too long, I'd never get the round off.

Crunch . . . crunch . . . crunch, came the footsteps.

I looked to Rodriguez for courage. He leveled his gaze at me and nodded. Then, ever so carefully I twisted and slid over Rodriguez's waist, angling myself toward the driver's-side window, which had been completely blown out. Keeping my head and torso low and wedged up against the steering wheel, I tried to hold the awkward position. I leveled the gun, closed one eye, and stared down the sight, and when a blurry shape came into view just a few feet away, I squeezed the trigger.

The gun reacted like a small bomb in my hand. It recoiled and something shot out the side and hit the dashboard before striking the side of my neck. Whatever hit my neck was hot and I winced, but I was so focused on following Rodriguez's instructions to keep firing that I didn't pay attention to anything else but firing the gun over and over.

I shot again, and again, and again, and each time the gun bucked in my hands and metal casings pinged off the dashboard, striking me in the arm, cheek, and neck.

My nostrils filled with the sharp acrid scent of gunpowder and my mouth went completely dry. I pulled that trigger until the magazine was empty, and kept pulling it reflexively until I felt Rodriguez's hand on the muzzle.

"Did you get him?" he asked urgently.

I was breathing so hard that I had a difficult time forming words, and my brain didn't want to catch up to the massive input on all my senses. "Yes," I finally managed, recalling that blurred shape in front of the gun sight recoil backward two or three times as I shot at it. I also recalled the loud *whump* as the blurry shape hit the ground. "But don't make me look."

Rodriguez groaned. He was clearly in pain. "You have to," he told me. "If he's still moving, you have to take him out."

I clutched the gun with both hands. "I'm out of bullets."

"There's another clip in the glove box," he said. "Get it out and I'll help you reload."

I twisted again in the seat and slid back to the passenger side, keeping low. It was difficult to open the compartment and extract the extra magazine in the cramped space, but I managed okay. I wiped my hands on my pants and followed Rodriguez's instructions to change the clip, but it was much more difficult than I thought it'd be, and all the while I kept imagining that at any moment Darrell would pop up and take us both out.

Finally I got the new magazine in. "Slide the top back to load the chamber," he said.

I didn't know what he meant, and when I looked at

him, I saw how pale he was and how much blood was leaking onto the seat. Rodriguez seemed to recognize I didn't understand, because his left hand came up again and landed heavily on the top of the gun. "Pull this back," he instructed. I pulled, but it wouldn't move. "Pull harder," he urged, his words jumbling together like he was tipsy.

I gripped the top firmly and pulled hard. The top of the muzzle slid back, then zipped closed. "It's ready to shoot," Rodriguez told me. "But be careful." As he said this, his eyes fluttered. I knew he was about to lose consciousness and I had to do something quickly to make sure we were safe before we could call for help.

Sliding over Rodriguez and keeping my body low, I inched toward the window. Holding the gun with both hands again, I carefully eased my head over the top of the door window and looked out.

Darrell lay flat on his back, his eyes wide open in surprise. There were three big holes in his chest and one more in his abdomen. The giant revolver he'd fired at us was lying on the ground about three feet away from him.

The reality of what had happened and what I'd done hit me like a freight train. I began to tremble in earnest and tears welled, then dribbled down my cheeks. "Did you get him?" Rodriguez asked.

I moved away from the window and back to the wounded agent. "He's dead," I said, and I couldn't help it—a small sob came out with the words.

Rodriguez's eyes fluttered. "Call for backup," he mumbled before he passed out.

What felt like an eternity later I found myself sitting on a gurney enclosed by a green curtain. Someone emitted a small moan in the bay next to mine and I drew my legs up to hug them and close my eyes. In my arm an IV dripped saline and glucose while I was treated for shock.

I was having a hard time keeping it together. Rodriguez had been rushed into surgery and I'd collapsed as I'd gotten out of the ambulance. It was the oddest thing—my knees had just buckled and I'd hit the pavement hard.

Someone—probably an EMT—had lifted me up and helped me inside. The sheriff followed close behind me, and one was right now stationed on the other side of that curtain.

Rodriguez hadn't regained consciousness when the sheriff had shown up, and I wasn't sure they believed my story, but I could hardly blame them. Until Rodriguez woke up . . . if he woke up . . . I was the only witness to what had gone down.

Abruptly the curtain was pulled aside and a man in a yellow dress shirt and green tie said, "You Abigail Cooper?"

I nodded dully.

His head disappeared again around the curtain, but I heard him say, "She's in here, Agents."

Footsteps approached and the curtain was summarily ripped aside and Dutch's pale face, creased with worry, appeared. "Jesus!" he said when he took one look at me before he moved quickly to my gurney only to scoop me up into his arms and hug me tightly.

The waterworks began again in earnest and I clung to him for dear life. I was so overwhelmed by all the emotions that had been storming through me that all I could do was cry, and cry.

My sweetheart held on to me, rocking us gently while stroking my hair and whispering, "It's okay. You're safe. I'm here, dollface. Everything's going to be all right."

Eventually I calmed down and I was able to take a breath without shuddering. Dutch cupped my ears and tipped my head back to look earnestly into my eyes. He seemed to want to say something to me, but his own eyes were moist and I was amazed that he seemed so emotional. Instantly I wanted to reassure him. "I'm fine," I whispered.

He closed his eyes and leaned his forehead against mine. "What was Rodriguez thinking?" he growled. "I'm gonna kill that son of a bitch when he gets out of surgery."

"It wasn't his fault, Dutch," I said, gripping his wrists. "Really. We were there just to check a few facts from the old owner, who wasn't even a suspect. We never dreamed we'd be in trouble until we found the oil drums and the owner's son started shooting at us."

Dutch backed his head off mine and his features were hard again. He'd put on his cop face. "Start from the beginning," he ordered.

Behind him another voice said, "And don't leave anything out."

I looked past Dutch to see Harrison, his shirt damp and pressed against his chest. "What'd you do, run here?" I asked him, and somehow, making a wisecrack helped more than anything to ease the terrible tension gripping my insides.

"We were worried," Harrison said, pointing to Dutch. "And I tend to sweat when I'm worried."

The corner of my mouth lifted. "Attractive," I said drolly. "That Candice is one lucky lady."

Dutch made a sound like a half cough, half laugh, and when I looked back at him, I had some hope that I could in fact bounce back from this terrible day.

Forty-five minutes later I'd given them the whole story about all the events leading up to my arrival at the hospital. I'd been interrupted only once, when a deputy from the crime scene had arrived to let us know that they'd found two decomposing bodies in the two oil barrels behind Clady's.

"The vics are Wendy Hayes and Tyler Harvin," I told Harrison, jumping slightly ahead in my story. "They're part of a missing-persons case Rodriguez and his partner had worked when he was with the Dallas bureau."

We also learned that when his father was still alive and running the shop, Darrell did most of the heavy lifting and drove the tow truck. While Russell was indeed a sweet old man who'd never hurt a fly, his son was a different character altogether.

Darrell had a record of domestic abuse. He'd put his wife in the hospital more than a few times and she finally left him in 2006, when he'd done two years in the can for assaulting her.

But since he'd gotten out of prison in 2008, he'd stayed low under the radar working at his father's garage until Russell died, and Darrell took it over. Why had he killed the teens? Maybe it was because he found Wendy attractive, and wanted to rape her, but needed her boyfriend out of the way. Maybe it was for another reason altogether. The only thing I knew for certain was that sociopaths don't always need a reason—they just need an opportunity to cause harm.

Once the nurse freed me from the IV, I sat with Dutch and Harrison in the waiting room until we heard news from the surgeon operating on Rodriguez. I'd been given a mild sedative, which was starting to kick in, and it was making me drowsy. Still, I was really surprised when Candice burst in through the automatic doors and dashed straight for me.

Just like Dutch had done, she pulled me up to her and hugged me fiercely. "I got the message an hour ago that you'd been in a shoot-out and were in a Waco hospital. I drove like a maniac to get here. Are you okay? Are you hurt? Can I do anything?"

She said this all in a rush and she was squeezing me so tightly that I could barely take a breath big enough to answer her. "I'm fine," I reassured her, but she only tightened her grip. "Okay, so my ribs hurt," I added with a squeak.

Candice immediately released me and placed her hands gently on my side. "Where? Which ones? Has a doctor seen you? Have they taken X-rays?"

Harrison stood and moved over to us. "Hey," he said softly. "She's fine. Just a few abrasions and she's been treated for shock."

Candice acted as if he didn't exist. "Where does it hurt, honey?" she asked me again.

I blinked at her. She didn't get that I'd tried to make a joke. "I'm fine. Honest, Candice. I'm okay."

My friend stepped back to give me some space, but then seemed to rethink it and reached forward to clutch my hand in hers. She then closed her eyes and swallowed hard. "Don't you *ever* do something like that again," she whispered. "I nearly had a heart attack on I-Thirty-five."

I shuffled forward and hugged her this time. After hearing her take a nice deep breath, I coaxed her to the chairs and noticed that she made sure to sit on the other side of Dutch, which was three chairs away from Harrison.

I saw the muscles in Brice's jaw bunch, but he wisely chose not to push the issue.

Just as we all sat down, the surgeon came out to tell us that Agent Rodriguez came through the surgery just fine. He'd lost a fair amount of blood, but after several transfusions his vitals were all good.

"He was shot with a hollow point," the doctor told us. "It did some damage, nicked his lung and took out some muscle tissue, but there was nothing we couldn't repair or any permanent injury done to the shoulder or any of the surrounding tendons, so with some good physical therapy he should make a full recovery."

I felt another huge chunk of tension leave me and exhaustion began to take over. I leaned against Dutch and held his hand. "Can we go home soon?" I asked.

Harrison spoke before Dutch had a chance. "Take the car," he said. "I'll wait here until I can take Rodriguez's statement."

"I can drive you," Candice said quickly, and I realized she didn't want to get stuck taking Harrison home.

If I'd had even an ounce of energy more, I would have told her she was acting like an idiot, but energy was something I was in short supply of. In fact, as the three of us headed out to her car, I couldn't get my legs to work right and I kept tripping. Dutch must have noticed because he scooped me up and carried me the rest of the way. I think I even fell asleep before he loaded me into the car.

The next day Dutch gave me the news over breakfast. "You're going to have to meet with Internal Affairs this morning."

"Internal Affairs?" I gasped. "Why do I have to meet with Internal Affairs?"

Dutch took a deep breath and let it out slowly, something he always did before telling me news he thought I wasn't going to like. "Abby," he began, "you have to understand. You shot a man yesterday."

I recoiled as if he'd physically slapped me. "In self-defense!"

He held up his hand in a stop motion. "I'm well aware," he said calmly. "This is just procedure. You'll go in and give your statement to them—"

"I already gave my statement!"

Dutch took another deep breath and let it out. "Yes," he said. "We got that. So all you'll have to do is repeat what you told us, and they'll investigate to make sure the shooting was justified."

I sat back in my chair and looked at him critically. "What aren't you telling me?"

His eyes met mine. "Yesterday was a very bad day," he said softly.

"Duh," I snapped. I'm not my most congenial in the morning.

Dutch ignored that and continued. "And IA is going to take issue with several things, so be warned."

I glared hard at him. "Would you just tell me, already?"

My sweetheart closed his eyes for a moment. I could tell I was trying his patience, but as a kid I'd always been terrified of being sent to the principal's office. "First of all," Dutch began, "the fact that Rodriguez wasn't following protocol by investigating a case that should have been assigned by Harrison is an issue."

"For God's sake, Dutch! He was the original investigating agent!"

"Yes, and a year ago he had declared the case officially cold. When it showed up in our office, it should have been audited by you or one of the other agents, and given to Harrison, who then would have had me follow up with the lead."

"But it scored so low that you guys would have tossed it out!"

"Not if you had audited it," Dutch argued. "You're the one who got the tow truck connection, right? You would have determined there was a lead to follow up on and it would have gone to me or Harrison to investigate."

I folded my arms across my chest and pouted. Stupid smart boyfriend making his usual stupid good point. "Fine. What else will they have an issue with?"

"Well," he said, and I could tell his patience was wearing thin, "Rodriguez was told not to take you out in the field except to find the car in the hit and run. Once you guys found that car, he should have taken you back to Austin immediately. In other words, he disobeyed a direct order from me."

"We were only going to *ask* a harmless old dude a question! We didn't even know Clady's *had* a tow truck! Don't you think if we'd known that particular fact, Rodriguez would have dumped me off back home and taken another agent with him?"

"It doesn't matter what you *thought*, Abby!" Dutch shouted, finally fed up with me. "It only matters what happened. And yesterday, what happened is that Rodriguez disobeyed protocol, took a civilian profiler with *no* field experience out to interview a possible suspect, and subjected them to a shoot-out where that civilian profiler then had to shoot a man in self-defense!"

Dutch's voice cracked a little as he finished shouting, and I didn't think I'd ever seen him so angry in all the time I'd known him. Wisely, I waited until he composed himself again to say, "It wasn't Oscar's fault, Dutch. I swear to God, it wasn't."

But he didn't seem even remotely convinced. "Rodriguez put you in danger, Abby. It's only a miracle that you weren't killed. And I can't let him off the hook for that. I'm sorry, but I just can't."

I reached out for his hand, but he pulled it away and stood up. "Come on," he said gruffly. "We'll be late."

An hour later I was thrown to the lions. And, just like you would imagine having a fun little romp with hungry man-eating beasts would be, I came out on the losing end.

The lions in question were two stern-looking IA Feds with no sense of humor and what I could only assume was a severe case of constipation caused by the giant stick up their butts. And they made it clear: Everything I told them was probably a lie. They even had me take a polygraph . . . the bastards.

They also kept me all day with only one break for the ladies' room. By four o'clock it was obvious that even with the polygraph they didn't believe me. They kept asking me the same set of questions over and over and over. It was really annoying.

But at last I figured out how the game was played and I crossed my arms and refused to answer any more questions. I also threatened to get an attorney. I didn't know if I was allowed one or not, but I think I might have played that just right, because they stopped asking me questions and wrapped up the interview.

I was left alone for another hour when Dutch opened

the door of the conference room and said, "Can you come to Harrison's office?"

I tried to read his expression for any sign of what IA had determined, but he had his cop face on, and there was no telling. "I'm thirsty," I said. "And I have to go to the bathroom."

A crack in the granite appeared and his eyes softened. "I'll get you something to drink, and you can hit the ladies' room on your way to Harrison's office."

I got up wearily and moved to the door. "If you can also locate some cookies or chips to go with that drink, I'd owe you."

"I'll see what I can do," he promised.

When I made it to Harrison's office, a Coke and a bag of Oreo bite-sized cookies waited for me. "Thanks, cowboy," I whispered as I took my seat. I then popped the lid on the Coke, drinking thirstily for a moment before diving into the cookies. I wanted to eat and drink as much as I could before I lost my appetite, because I was pretty sure I was about to get fired.

"You've been suspended," Harrison said.

I sighed and set down the bag of cookies. I'd gobbled down only two. "Gee, Agent Harrison, don't beat around the bush or anything. Please, tell me where I stand."

"It's not my choice, Abby," he explained, and I was grateful for the kindness in his eyes at least. "It's standard operating procedure whenever there's an agent involved in a shooting."

"But I'm not an agent."

"Yes," he said, "but for these proceedings, we're going

to act as if you are. You'll be suspended with pay until IA clears you."

"How long will that take?"

"Given the amount of forensic evidence found at the scene, including the two bodies in the oil drums, the amount of ammo we pulled out of your car, and Rodriguez's shoulder, I'd say two weeks to a month at the most."

"And Rodriguez?"

"Also suspended."

I looked from Harrison to Dutch and back again. "So . . . what? I'm just supposed to go home and sit around waiting for those bozos to decide if I acted in self-defense?"

Harrison looked me square in the eye. "Yes."

My shoulders drooped. I felt like my parents had just grounded me. "Well, that sucks."

Dutch looked at me sympathetically. "At least you're being paid while you're away from here," he offered.

I had an idea then and I asked, "Can I at least take a couple boxes home and audit some files for you guys?"

Dutch and Harrison exchanged a couple of uncomfortable glances. "No," Brice said. "I'm afraid you can't touch any new case until you're cleared by IA."

I turned in my seat and regarded the whiteboard behind me. There were now five cases in the "Solved" column. In barely a week I'd gotten us almost all the way to our goal. "Seems like we were just starting to get some momentum," I muttered.

"We still have those cases you gave us to work on until

you return," Brice said confidently. "And two weeks isn't so bad. You'll be back here before you know it, Abby."

"Fine," I said, feeling like all the wind had been taken out of my sails. "I've got some files at home. Do you want me to go get them?"

Dutch smiled. "That's okay," he said. "I can bring them back tomorrow."

Harrison stood then, effectively ending the meeting. "I'll call you as soon as we hear from IA. In the meantime, try not to worry. I'm convinced you acted appropriately given the situation you found yourself in."

Dutch walked out with me, and we headed for home. Or so I thought.

I was really so worn-out from the afternoon with the jerks from IA that I didn't notice where we were until gridlock hemmed us in and we slowed to a crawl. Looking around, I asked, "Is this the right way?"

"We're taking a detour. I'm treating you to something I think you need."

I smiled. "Got something special in mind, hmm?" What a great boyfriend I had. Taking me out for a nice dinner and, hopefully, a humongous glass of wine.

Dutch pulled off onto an exit without elaborating. I continued to think nice, happy thoughts about him right up until we pulled into the parking lot of Red's Indoor Range. "Pit stop?" I asked as Dutch parked and shut off the engine.

"I'm going to teach you how to shoot."

I blinked at him stupidly. "Excuse me?" Where was my fancy dinner and that giant glass of vino?

"Abby, there are times in every relationship when a man has to decide if his girlfriend is a magnet for trouble. And you, dollface, are like trouble's Mecca."

I felt heat sear my cheeks. "I am *not*!"

But Dutch just inhaled deeply, let it out slowly, and said, "Excluding what happened to you yesterday but within the relatively short time that I've known you, you've been attacked by a serial killer, kidnapped by the mob, stalked by a madman, shot by a psychopath, trapped in a prison riot, pursued by a renegade agent, and just four months ago, you barely escaped being a deranged killer's science project."

Crap. Stupid smart boyfriend had another stupid good argument. "None of that was my fault!" I yelled defiantly.

"Exactly my point, sweetheart."

I folded my arms across my chest and glared angrily at Dutch. "I do *not* want to learn how to shoot a gun, Dutch."

"Why not?"

My jaw dropped. Did he not know me at all? "Because they kill people!" I said, and without warning my eyes filled with tears. "I hate them, okay? I've seen too many people get shot, including me. As far as I'm concerned, we should repeal the Second Amendment and learn how to get along!"

I was treading on dangerous territory here. Dutch was a proud card-carrying member of the NRA and I was fairly certain he voted Republican. "We're not talking politics here, Abby. We're talking about safety. If you're ever in a position again where you have to shoot or be shot, I want you to have that option with some sense of confidence."

"I shot just fine yesterday," I reminded him.

"You did," Dutch admitted. "And you have no idea how relieved I am that Rodriguez was conscious and alert enough to talk you through it. But what if he hadn't been? What if that bullet had taken him out? What do you think would have happened to you?"

I wiped the tears off my cheeks and sniffled loudly while looking down at my lap. Into the long silence that followed his question, I finally shrugged and mumbled, "Dunno."

Dutch lifted my chin with his fingers and those gorgeous midnight blues pinned me to my seat. "I do," he whispered. "And that's what scares me. It's also why I won't take no for an answer. Now, we can continue to argue about this, or you can come in with me and get it over with."

For the record, we did a little of both. The argument continued into the gun shop, through the fitting of earplugs and earphones, into the range—where Dutch tried to educate me on the various parts of a gun, how to load the bullets, how to hold a firearm properly—and all during the placement of the paper target.

In the end I got off eight rounds, noticing with satisfaction that seven of those shot nice round holes into the paper target. I then set the gun down and refused to continue. All of Dutch's efforts to make me feel more comfortable and confident around weapons were just too close to the trauma I'd been through the day before.

I tried to explain that to him on the way home, but he was surprisingly unsympathetic. "Then we'll get you a therapist to talk about what happened in Waco, but you're still going to the range with me on a regular basis."

I believe I broke my no-swearing rule at that point with a few colorfully worded expletives that I'd kept in case of emergency, and after that, we stopped speaking to each other altogether.

When we got home, I didn't even go inside with Dutch. Instead, I was so pissed off that I got in my own car and headed to Candice's.

When I got close to her condo, I thought it might be best to call ahead. "Hey," I said when she answered the phone. "Can I share in your I-hate-my-boyfriend misery?"

"Aww, Sundance, what's up?"

"Dutch is being an asterisk." I was already feeling bad about the explosion of expletives from earlier.

Candice chuckled. "And you called to talk about it?"

"Actually, I'm about a block away from your condo. Can I hang out with you tonight?"

There was a pause on the other end of the line and it suddenly occurred to me that Candice might already have made up with Harrison. "Um . . . ," she said. "Sure."

My shoulders drooped. "No," I said, already turning on the blinker for a U-turn. "That's okay, honey. I can sense you have company, and the last thing I want is to be a third wheel."

Candice chuckled again. "It's not what you think, Abs. Come on over. We'd love to see you."

I struggled with whether to accept her invite now that I knew she wasn't alone. I hated to intrude, but I had nowhere else to go and I really did need a shoulder to cry on. "Okay," I said. "If you're positive I won't be in the way."

"You won't. Plus, I have wine and snacks from the restaurant downstairs."

"See you in two minutes." Good old Candice knew just what I needed after a terrible day. I made a mental note to get her to instruct Dutch on how to treat my stressed-out self.

I made it over to Candice's condo and up to her floor in record time. I pressed her bell and waited. In short order the door was opened and I found myself staring into the twinkling eyes of the last man on earth I expected to see there. Without a second thought I threw myself forward and tackled him to the ground.

Chapter Six

"Milo!" I shouted as we tumbled to the ground. "Ohmi-god! What're you doing here?"

"Well," he said awkwardly as he tried to get up while I hugged him fiercely. "Right now, I'm hoping you didn't break my back."

"Sorry!" I said, scrambling off Dutch's best friend. "I've just missed you!"

Milo wheezed his funny laugh and got up stiffly. "You saw me last week."

I took a step back. "Really? It's only been a week?" He nodded. "Good God!" I said. "It feels like so much longer."

Candice came out from the kitchen holding a beautiful goblet of red wine. "Here," she said, placing it in my hand. "Drink first. Catch up later."

I took a huge sip and closed my eyes in delight. It was a smooth seductive vintage. "That is amazing," I said, opening my eyes only to have an egg roll placed in my free hand.

"Eat," she ordered.

I popped the egg roll in my mouth. It was light and buttery and slightly spicy. "Jesus," I whispered. "I may never go back home."

Candice motioned us toward the living room, and Milo and I took our seats while Candice fussed over us with plates and dips and hors d'oeuvres. Only after she took her seat did I say to Milo, "Dutch never told me you were coming to town."

Milo's eyes shifted to Candice. They exchanged a look and I knew there was something going on here. "Spill it," I ordered.

Milo smiled and ducked his chin. "You'd just tune in on it anyway, so, okay, Abby, I'll tell you; Candice invited me here."

Now, for the record, Candice and Milo haven't always been the best of chums. In fact, there had been many a moment when they'd been downright testy with each other, so this was quite a surprise. "She did?"

"I heard the news through a friend of mine," Candice explained.

"News? What news?" Why was I always the last to hear about stuff?

Milo looked uncomfortable and he played with the egg roll on his plate. "I got laid off," he said.

"What?"

"Now, don't get all excited, Abby," he warned. "It's a blessing."

"The Royal Oak PD laid *you* off? Why? When? *Why?*" I was repeating myself, I knew, but Milo had been such a good and decorated detective that I couldn't imagine the reasoning behind letting him go.

"In the end, it came down to budget cuts and politics," Milo said, lifting his wineglass and swirling the contents thoughtfully. "Given the fact that I'd be the least affected financially, my commander came to me and asked if I'd like to volunteer for the layoff."

"Jerkwad!" I shouted.

Milo smiled and winked at me. "Yes, but he was also right. Thanks to you and those lucky numbers you gave me, and the security business Dutch and I run on the side, I'm set for life. And if I could save the livelihood of a younger detective, then it was the least I could do."

"Does Dutch know?" I couldn't imagine my sweetheart keeping that kind of news from me.

"No," Milo admitted. "He doesn't. You guys had so much going on these past couple of weeks that I didn't need to add my stuff to your plates."

"Does he even know you're here?"

Milo smiled wickedly and took a sip of wine. "Not until you tell him."

He had me there. I was terrible at both keeping a secret and lying to my boyfriend. I'd probably spill it the moment I saw him. "You mean you were just going to come into town, hang out with Candice, and not even see us?" I was a little hurt that Milo wouldn't tell us he'd come to Austin.

He was quick to reassure me. "Abs, you guys were next on my list of places to visit. Candice heard that I'd been laid off and invited me down here, which meant that I needed to see her first."

"So what are you going to do?" I asked. "I mean, I know you and Dutch have the security business to manage, but is that enough for you?"

Again Milo and Candice exchanged a look. "He's going to work with me," she announced.

"Maybe," Milo corrected. "I haven't made up my mind yet, remember?"

I blinked and shook my head. "Hold on," I said firmly. "Will one of you please explain what the hello-dolly is going on here?"

Milo chuckled. "She's still not swearing?" he asked Candice.

Candice laughed too. "Oh, she's still *trying* not to swear. I'm not convinced that she's given up completely."

I felt my cheeks flush, especially after what I'd let loose in Dutch's car. "Don't change the subject. Tell me what's going on!"

"I've applied for a PI license down here," Candice said. "I'm going to open up my own office, and I've asked Milo to be my partner."

I felt my eyes widen and a little hurt entered my heart. "I thought I was your partner," I said meekly.

Candice cocked her head. "Honey," she said. "You're working with the FBI now, remember?"

I frowned. "Maybe not for much longer."

It was Candice's turn to look surprised. "What's happened?"

"I got suspended." I then explained to Milo what'd happened in Waco and how I'd spent the day being grilled by IA only to be told by Harrison that I was on paid leave until Rodriguez and I were cleared.

"For Christ's sake," Candice spat. "Brice needs to grow a friggin' pair and stand up for you!"

"He did," I said. "I swear he did, Candice. But it's a little out of his hands."

Candice didn't seem convinced, though, and I remembered Brice's request to have me talk some sense into her. I figured that with Milo around maybe I'd wait for a time when she and I had a little more privacy. "So, anyway, after I got the third degree from IA, Dutch takes me to the shooting range!"

Milo's eyes widened. "He what?"

"Oh, yeah," I said, getting worked up all over again. "His idea of helping me to relax is to put a gun in my hand and order me to shoot."

Milo shook his head back and forth and wheezed. "For such a smart guy, he can really be stupid about women."

"Right?"

But Candice wasn't convinced. "Sorry, Sundance, but I'm with Dutch on this one. You do get in a lot of sticky situations. And you really do need to learn how to properly handle a gun."

My jaw dropped. I couldn't believe she was taking his side. "Are you serious?"

Candice got up to retrieve the wine bottle from the kitchen counter. "I am," she said, coming over to pour more into my glass. "And you do."

"Traitor," I sniffed.

"What if I taught you?" she asked kindly. "Would that help?"

I rubbed my temples. All this talk about guns and shooting was giving me another headache. "I don't know. Maybe."

Candice sat back down and crossed her legs, looking at me in that way that suggested she was just as determined as Dutch to make me into a deadly weapon. "'Kay," she said easily. "You think about it and we'll head out to the range when you're ready."

I looked to Milo for help, but his expression suggested that he was now also on Candice's side. "You really do get into a lot of trouble. And once you've used a gun a few times, you realize they aren't so scary."

I narrowed my eyes at them. "We need to change the subject. All this talk about guns and shooting people is a total buzzkill."

That night I slept on Candice's couch. Both she and Milo had convinced me to at least send Dutch a text message letting him know where I was.

He didn't text back.

Which was fine by me.

Okay, so it wasn't, but . . . whatever.

Maybe we both needed a little break from each other anyway.

Still, by the time Milo left to go knock on our door

and surprise Dutch, I was already feeling bad about giving him the cold shoulder.

The next morning Candice woke me with the most delicious-smelling coffee ever made. At least, to my nose it was. "I will take an entire pot of *that*," I said, sitting up and rubbing my eyes.

Candice placed a nice steaming mug of java into my hands. "What's on your agenda for today?"

I hugged the mug and inhaled deeply. "A whole lot of nothing much," I said. "I'll probably just go home, unpack a few boxes, and mope."

"That sounds like all kinds of fun."

"What's on your docket?"

"I was going to look for office space. Care to ride along?"

"You're really hanging a shingle down here?"

"I am."

"I thought you were going to take it easy. Enjoy life. Hang with your boy toy."

Candice stared into her cup, circling the rim with her finger. "Things change."

I took a sip of coffee, which was smooth and creamy, then set down the mug and focused on my friend. "He'd been planning it for a while, you know."

Her eyes shot up to meet mine. "Who'd been planning what?"

I smiled and leaned back against the cushions. "You know who. Brice. He'd been planning on proposing to you for a while."

"Did he tell you to tell me that?"

I laughed. "No. Well, at least he asked me not to say anything until he had to get me to say something because you kicked him out."

"Huh?"

"I picked up on the whole engagement thing last Sunday when Dutch and I came over to visit you guys. My radar plucked it out of the ether while we were all having drinks on the balcony."

Candice turned to stare out the large sliding glass door. "Was that why he acted all funny and pulled you into the kitchen?"

I winked at her. "Yep."

A mixture of emotions crossed Candice's face, but eventually she seemed to soften. "He really *was* planning to ask me to marry him back then?"

I nodded. "You should see the ring, honey. It's awesome."

"There's a *ring*?"

"Of course there's a ring! He's had it in his pocket for like a week, trying to work up the courage to ask you. And the other day after we had lunch, I sort of tore into him and told him to propose already because you were getting mixed signals from him, only he forgot the ring at his office and . . . well, you know the rest."

"Oh, shit!" Candice said, jumping to her feet. "I have to call him!"

I got up myself. "Yes, you do," I told her. "And I need to boogie. Call me later, after I get a shower in and change my clothes, and we'll go hunt for some office space."

I left Candice twirling in circles as she considered what to say to Brice. My friend wasn't so great with the apologies, so I hoped she kept it short and sweet and that the two of them got back together quick.

Dutch was gone by the time I got home, and Milo must have tagged along with him to work because there was a rental car in our driveway, and a suitcase in the spare bedroom, but no sign of our good friend.

I did a preliminary search of the kitchen for any sign of a note from my S.O., but I was S.O.L. on that one. "Love you too, cowboy," I groused as I headed upstairs to take a shower.

A little later as I was working on unpacking a box in the living room, Candice called to say that she was on her way to pick me up.

While I was waiting for her, I decided to gather all the files I'd brought home over the past few days so that Dutch could take them back into the office, which he must have forgotten to do that morning.

There was a small stack of new files on the kitchen table, and I couldn't help it—I opened the top one, just to take a quick peek.

I got a small shock when I saw a smiling, beautiful young girl with ebony skin, brilliant white teeth, and pigtails held by Pokémon bands.

The file was labeled "Missing Persons" and belonged to a nine-year-old named Fatina Carter. She'd gone missing from a south Dallas suburb in January of 2009. Her grandmother said that Fatina had left home early one Saturday morning to visit with a friend one street over. She never made it to her friend's house and she was never seen again.

Her image appeared flat and plastic to my intuitive eye, and I knew better than almost anyone else what'd happened to her. I looked through the file quickly, which was easy considering there was precious little there.

By the case notes I discovered that an extensive search of the area around Fatina's home had been conducted, along with interviews with family, friends, and neighbors. No one knew anything; no one saw anything. Fatina had vanished into thin air.

Closing my eyes, I focused on her file with my radar and immediately I saw the image of paint cans and a roller. I opened my eyes again and stared at the beautiful little girl, certain that whoever had taken her had also taken someone else.

I got up and began rummaging around in my pile of files, searching until I found the one on Keisha. I opened it and used my finger to scroll through the pages, searching for any connection the two different agents had made to these nearly identical cases—but no link had ever been made, even though both investigations had been handled by the same bureau in Dallas. "Rat bastards," I said, angry that no red flags had gone up with two missing girls of similar description and age.

A knock on the door startled me and I hurried to let Candice in. "You ready?" she asked.

"Yeah," I said. "Just give me a sec."

I ran around for a bit, making sure Eggy and Tuttle

got the opportunity to water the lawn one last time before I grabbed my purse, my keys, and, after a quick second thought, the two files on Fatina and Keisha.

"You're bringing work along?" Candice asked when she saw the files.

"Yeah. Do you mind?"

"No. Of course not."

We got in her car and buckled up. As she pulled out of my driveway, I asked, "How'd it go with Brice?"

Candice made a derisive sound. "He can be such a prick, sometimes."

My eyes widened. "I take it your discussion did not go well?"

Candice gripped the steering wheel and was quiet for a moment, gathering her thoughts. "I called him and told him that I wanted to talk, and could he get away for lunch? He said he was too busy to get away, and could he call me later?"

I waited for the rest of the story, which would reflect Brice's obvious "prick"-ness, but nothing more followed. "That bastard!" I finally said with a giggle.

"I'm serious, Abby."

"Oh, I have no doubt you are, which makes it all the more hilarious."

She cut me a look. "It was all in his tone," she explained. "He can be a really cold SOB sometimes."

I couldn't help it. I started laughing in earnest. "Oh, honey, we all know *that*. It's his warm fuzzy side most of us can't find."

Candice sighed. "I don't know what's going on with

us lately. It's like, no matter what the other person says or does, it hits the wrong chord."

"Yep," I agreed. "Dutch and I have been having a little of that too lately. I think it's astrological."

This won me a smirk. "It's the planets' fault, huh?"

I turned in my seat to face her. "As a matter of fact it is. I read in my horoscope the other day that Uranus is being a bully lately, and since he rules innovation and rebellion, he's causing massive changes for all of us, which is why so many close relationships are being affected."

"Uranus," Candice said derisively. "He's such an ass."

"Har, har!" I mocked. "Try the veal. You'll be here all week, right?"

Candice bounced her eyebrows. "Just until Tuesday."

We spent most of the rest of the day looking at commercial properties. I thought it was incredibly sweet of my friend to point out in several locations where I might be able to host clients. "You'll get your clientele back up and running before you know it," she assured me. "You're just too good not to be successful again, Abs."

I was also quite surprised at the reasonable rates being charged for office space. The rents were nothing like they were up north. "I can't get over how cheap everything is here," I remarked as we left yet another location.

"I know. And have you seen the crime rates?"

"No. Are they bad?"

Candice laughed like I'd actually said something funny. "I was researching the stats right before Brice and I moved, and two years ago there were only like twenty murders in Austin, compared to over four hundred for Detroit."

My jaw dropped. "Twenty murders for a whole *year*?"

Candice nodded. "Uh-huh."

I gazed at the gorgeous rolling hills dotted with bluebonnets and wildflowers. "I could totally get used to living here."

"I know exactly what you mean. Hopefully, the number of spouses cheating on each other is higher than the crime rate." I gave her a curious look. "A girl's gotta eat," she explained. "Those cases are my bread and butter."

"I thought your inheritance was your bread and butter."

"My inheritance is my nest egg. The PI business is my meal ticket."

My stomach grumbled and I looked at Candice pleadingly. "Speaking of meals, can we please find some food soon?"

"What do you feel like eating?"

I smiled. She'd walked right into that one. "Oh, man, could I go for a Coney dog and some chili cheese fries."

Candice eyed me sympathetically. "Sorry, honey. There are no Coney places down here."

"Nuh-uh!" I lived for Coney Island hot dogs and chili cheese fries.

"That's a Michigan thing," she explained. "Or a New York thing if you want to get technical."

"But I can't live in a place that doesn't have Coney Island!"

"Well, it's a little late to go back now. After all, you're already moved in and everything."

I slumped low in my seat and muttered moodily for the rest of the drive.

I wasn't pouty for long. Twenty minutes later Candice and I were seated on one of the picturesque balconies of a restaurant called the Oasis. The famous eatery was built right into a cliff's face some three hundred feet above the crystal clear waters of Lake Travis, offering some of the most breathtaking views I'd ever seen.

As we sipped our margaritas and snacked on chips and salsa, I leaned back in my chair and sighed happily. "This place rocks!"

Candice adjusted her sunglasses. "I know it's not a greasy spoon overlooking Woodward Avenue, but I thought it might come in a close second."

I smiled happily and munched on a tortilla chip loaded with spicy salsa. "It works."

We sat for several moments in silence, enjoying the ambience, when I noticed Candice eyeing the files I'd brought with me from the car. "I can't believe you thought you'd work on those here."

I smiled. "Yeah, well, they're heartbreaking cases, and I was hoping with a little alcohol and some nice atmosphere my radar might give me a few more clues."

Candice picked up one of the files and opened it. "Aww," she said. "She's a cutie."

I didn't know if she was referring to Keisha or Fatina and it really didn't matter. "She was murdered."

Candice's head snapped up. "Oh, no! Are you sure?"

I nodded. "Along with this girl." I pushed the other file at her. She opened it and her face fell. "What's your radar saying?"

I shrugged. "That we're probably looking at a serial child killer."

"Anything else?"

"There's a connection to paint."

"Paint?"

I took another sip of margarita. "I think the killer is a professional painter."

"You're talking about the kind that paints houses and not the kind that paints canvases, right?"

"Right. I think it gives him a really good cover when he's in these neighborhoods to scout for possible victims."

Candice considered the photo again and was silent for a long time. "I want to help you find this bastard," she whispered finally.

I smiled. Candice had a big heart. "Those are FBI files," I told her. "And truth be told, I'm not even supposed to be working on them. I'm suspended, which means I should officially butt out."

"You've never been good at that."

"There you go, stating the obvious," I replied, selecting another chip from the basket. "The point is that I have to give those back to Dutch and I'm not supposed to even think about them again until IA clears me."

"But of course you'll be thinking about them," she said, reading me easily.

"Yep."

Candice flipped through the notes in the file she was holding. "We can solve this, Abby," she whispered, as if someone might overhear her and report it back to the bureau.

I raised one brow skeptically and she continued her argument. "You know me, Abs. I've worked a half-dozen missing children's cases in my career."

I was well aware that at the big PI firm Candice left before going it alone, she'd handled all their missing and exploited children's cases—and done most of those pro bono. "Candice," I said, shaking my head. "I think it's a bad idea."

Candice swiveled the photos of the two girls at me. "How can you say no to these beautiful faces, Abby?" she demanded. I was beginning to think the alcohol had gone to her head. "Don't their families deserve closure?"

"But, honey," I countered, "these are *FBI* jurisdiction! We can't take these cases away from them."

Candice pointed to the dates on the files. "Yes, you're right. The FBI should continue its investigation because they've done such a sterling job locating these girls so far."

I sighed heavily. I didn't think I was going to win this argument, but there was little I could do about it. Brice wanted his files back, and I was already in deep doo-doo with the bureau. I couldn't see that I had a leg to stand on by telling him that I wanted to keep the files—especially since he'd already said no.

So I pressed my lips together and just waited Candice out. Eventually, she pulled her intense stare away from me and sat back in her chair, turning her head to look out at the view. "Fine. Then hand them back to the bureau, but let me make a copy of the folders."

And something inside me suddenly shifted. I reached out and laid a hand on her arm. "Why is it so important to you to work these two cases?"

"Because I feel like I've lost a little bit of myself ever since I let my PI practice go. Sure, the move and the new condo and the security of my inheritance are all nice, but I need to do something important again, Abby. I need to get back to what I do best. And investigating cases like these is what I do best."

I thought about that for a minute, and about the two little girls that had done nothing to provoke the horrible death I knew they'd suffered. "Okay," I told her, giving in at last. "I'll make us a copy."

"Us?" she repeated.

"Yes."

"You'll work it with me?"

I smiled. "What else am I gonna do for the next few weeks? Sit around and eat bonbons? I don't think so. Besides, this is what we do. We crack cases. Just like old times."

Candice lowered her sunglasses to eye me thoughtfully. "Won't that get you in trouble with your current employer?"

"I'm already in trouble with my current employer."

"Good point. Okay, we'll work it together, but whatever you do, don't let on to Dutch or Brice, okay? Our relationships are in enough trouble without letting them know what we're up to."

"That's a no-brainer. Speaking of troubled relationships, shouldn't we head back and confront ours?"

My partner frowned. "Sometimes, Sundance, you can be a real killjoy."

Candice dropped me at my house half an hour later and I walked up the driveway sniffing the air hungrily. There was grilled steak wafting from around back, so instead of going through the front, I followed my nose. "Milo!" I sang when I entered the backyard.

"Hey, Abs," he said, holding up a juicy-looking cut of meat. "You hungry?"

"Aren't I always?" Belatedly I saw Dutch sitting on a patio chair enjoying a beer. "Hey," I said to him.

"Hey."

"How was work?"

"Fine."

"Good."

"Uh-huh."

"I was out with Candice."

"Okay."

I sighed. "Well, I tried," I said to him. "Obviously you're still in a mood or something."

Dutch didn't answer me. Instead he got up and walked inside. I stared after him and felt tears sting my eyes. In all our time together he'd never just dismissed me like that, and in front of company too. "Yeah, fork you too, Dutch," I muttered.

Milo swung an arm around my shoulders. "He'll get over it," he said.

"What did I do that was so terrible?" I asked. "I mean, seriously, Milo? What's he so pissed off at me for?"

Milo gave me a brief hug before letting me go and returning to the steaks. "It's not you," he said. "It's him."

"Of course it's him!"

Milo chuckled. "He's working through something, Abby. Give him a little time and he'll come around."

I sat down in a patio chair and stared openmouthed at Milo. "He told you what's bothering him?"

"He did."

"Tell me!"

"I can't."

"Why not?"

"Because it's not my place, and it's not really any of my business."

"Is this about the stupid shooting range?"

"No."

I threw up my hands. "Then *what*?"

"Ask him."

I scowled and folded my arms across my chest. "He won't tell me."

Milo closed the lid to the grill and reached into a

small cooler nearby. Retrieving two beers, he uncapped them and handed both to me. "Take him a beer and give it a shot anyway."

With a tremendous sigh I stood and took hold of the beers. I found Dutch in the living room watching the news. I knew he'd heard me come in, but he didn't turn his head or look in my direction, so I set one of the beers down in front of him on the coffee table, picked up the remote, and turned off the television. "Milo told me what's bothering you," I said.

Dutch set down his nearly empty bottle and reached for the fresh one. "He did, did he?" There was a fair amount of skepticism in his tone, but I thought I'd better stick with my story if I had any chance of finding out why Dutch was so ticked off.

"Yes. And although I hardly think it's *all* my fault, I can see your point. So allow me to just state for the record that I'm sorry."

Dutch actually laughed. "Nice try. Milo told you bubkes, toots," he said, reaching for the remote.

I slapped it off the table and sat down in front of him. "What's up with you?" I demanded. He avoided my eyes, so I leaned in really close and repeated, "Seriously! What?"

Finally, Dutch's eyes swiveled to mine. "Do you want kids?" he asked.

It took me a full minute to reply, but that could be because I had to pick my jaw up off the floor first. "Do I *what*?"

"Kids. Are they in your game plan somewhere down the line?"

I leaned back and took a (very) long sip of beer. "Where is this coming from?"

"Answer the question."

"I can't," I said flatly. "Until you tell me why you suddenly need to know, I can't answer that."

Dutch took a deep breath and let it out slowly. "I'm not sure I do," he whispered. "I'm not sure I want kids, I mean. Maybe it's because of all my time in law enforcement, but I'm just not that into the idea of raising kids in this crazy kind of world."

In the back of my mind, I was relieved. I'd had a terrible childhood with incredibly dysfunctional and often abusive parents. I had never wanted children, mostly because I was terrified I didn't know how to be a good parent. Still, I shook my head and said, "Okay . . ."

"Does that change the way you feel about me? About us?"

"No!" I replied quickly. "Of course not."

"But what if someday it did?"

"It's never going to change the way I feel about you," I said honestly. "Seriously, cowboy, you're starting to freak me out here. Are you pregnant?"

I'd meant to interject a little levity, but Dutch wasn't finding it funny. "Where do you see us in five years, Abby? Do you think we'll still be together?"

And that's when my radar took over, probably because asking me a question like that triggers an automatic response from my intuition, and I knew exactly what our future held. Or what it probably held. A vision of the future is never a sure thing. Still, I was going to communicate the vision that had crystallized in my mind as if it were already a certainty. I set my beer down, leaned in again, and grabbed the sides of his head with my hands. "Do you really want to know what I see, Dutch? Where I see you and me five years down the pike? Because I can tell you if you really, *really* want to know."

He nodded, his beautiful midnight blues staring straight into mine, and I held both the fear and the love I saw in them even as I closed my eyes to focus on what our future held. "I see our new home," I whispered. "And it's beautiful. A two-story Tudor the color of cream with blue shutters, tons of windows, a red clay tile roof, and ivy creeping up the sides. Out back there's an amazing garden and a gorgeous view of the surrounding hills. Inside, we'll have a little breakfast nook facing east so that we can watch the sunrise over coffee. And our den will face west, so that we can watch the sunset over ice cream. Eggy will be a little old man by then, and Tuttle will completely rule our house, so that won't change."

I opened my eyes again and saw that I still had Dutch's full attention. "Above the garage we'll each have a home office. I'll see a few clients a week, and you'll work your security business, and we'll enjoy the heck out of our lives. Together. 'Cause that's what we do, cowboy. We stick together, no matter what."

For the first time in my life I saw something reflected in those magnificent blue eyes that stunned me. Real tears. Dutch wasn't just misty; he actually welled up and teardrops leaked down his gorgeous face. I leaned in to kiss him softly and sat back after he'd had a moment to collect himself. He then cleared his throat and looked down at his lap. "Do you remember that mole I had removed on the back of my neck?" Dutch had mentioned that on the advice of the doctor that gave annual exams to all FBI agents, he'd seen a dermatologist here in Austin right before we moved to have a mole removed.

I felt the hairs along my arms tingle. "Oh, sheep," I mouthed.

"The lab says it's malignant." I felt my stomach drop to my toes. "The dermatologist called two days ago to tell me. I have to go back in tomorrow to meet with him."

I used my radar to scan his energy carefully. I'm not a medical intuitive, but after reading for thousands of clients, my radar has become really adept at picking up major medical conditions like heart disease, high blood pressure, diabetes, and of course cancer. When I focused on Dutch's health, I did pick up the tiniest hint of malignancy on the left side of his neck, and it was so subtle that it was no wonder I'd missed it. Quickly, I moved over to sit in Dutch's lap and wrap my arms tightly around him. "You're going to be okay," I reassured him, so relieved that I felt deep in my bones he'd be fine. "Really, honey. I've seen you in that house with me five years from now. This is nothing to worry about. You're going to come bouncing back from this, no problem."

"I'll have to go in for additional surgery," he said. I couldn't tell from his voice if he believed me when I told him he'd be okay.

"Surgery?" I asked. This was sounding like a bigger deal than what I'd felt intuitively.

"It's outpatient. They want to make sure they've gotten all of the malignant tissue, and there are a few other moles that he wants to remove from my back, just to be safe. Hopefully, I can schedule it in the morning and be back to work right after lunch."

I eyed him skeptically. "I think you can take a sick day, tough guy."

"Anyway, they'll excise the cells, then schedule me for some topical radiation therapy."

"It's early," I insisted, using my sixth sense again to feel my way along Dutch's diagnosis. "You caught it in time. This is nothing, cowboy. Nothing. You'll be right as rain in no time."

He kissed me on the forehead. "You're sure?"

I smiled and backed up a little to look straight into his eyes. "I pinkie swear."

"I was afraid to ask you."

"I didn't even pick up on it," I admitted. "Seriously, it's such a small spot and so early that I had no heads-up about it at all."

"Sorry I've been taking all my stress about it out on you, Edgar."

"S'okay. Just don't take me back to that shooting range anytime soon, all right?"

Dutch gently gripped my chin with his fingers. "I have

to know that you can take care of yourself, even if I'm not around."

"Sugar, if there is one thing I know how to do by now, it is call for help. And there are plenty of people like Candice and Milo who have answered that call. But we don't need to worry about that, because you're always going to be around for this particular damsel-in-distress, sweetie. Always."

That got him to smile. "If you say so."

I stood up and held out my hand. "Come on. Let's go out and talk Milo into trading in his Motown collection for a cowboy hat and a pair of spurs."

"I've been working on that all day."

I tapped my temple. "Yeah, well, my radar says he's going to hold out unless we keep at him."

"He seems to like the beer down here," Dutch said, wrapping an arm around my waist. "Let's get him drunk and convince him it was his idea in the first place."

Chapter Seven

Milo left Austin a few days later. As we saw him off to the airport, I still wasn't sure we'd convinced him to move—mostly because it would mean relocating his family from the only home they'd ever known. Still, I knew that the door to his relocating to Austin would remain open for some time, and that was a positive thing at least.

Dutch compromised with my suggestion to take a sick day by working in the morning and scheduling his procedure for later in the afternoon. He kept reassuring me he wasn't nervous about it—but I saw right through him. "I got you some snacks for later," I told him. "I'll pick you up from the office at three, and drive you over to the clinic. They said they'd get you in and out by five, and I'll be in the waiting room the whole time."

"Thanks, doll."

"You're going to be okay, you know."

"If you say so."

"Seriously. You are."

"Okay."

"I mean it."

"I know you do."

I scowled at him. "God! Are you a stubborn son of a peach or what?"

"What'd I say?"

"Dutch!" I yelled angrily, using my hands like a bull-horn. "You're going to be fine! Do you hear me?! F-I-N-E!"

He just turned and looked at me in that wide-eyed way that suggested he'd woken the beast without meaning to. "Of course I am," he said very carefully. "I know I will. I'll be fine. Ducky even. Okay?"

"Bah!" I snapped, crossing my arms and turning away. "I give up. You're impossible!"

Dutch parked in front of the office, gave me a very quick kiss on the cheek, and hurried inside. I frowned at his departing figure, moved into the driver's seat, and drove over to Candice's. We were heading to Dallas to begin our discreet investigation into Keisha and Fatina's disappearance.

"Ready?" Candice asked, meeting me at the door to the parking garage.

"Yep." I followed her to a shiny new canary yellow Porsche. "Subtle," I said, pausing next to the car.

"It was a toss-up between this and candy apple red," she admitted.

"No one will *ever* notice you running surveillance from this puppy. It's so nondescript!"

Candice gave me a smart look. "Get in, Sundance. We're already running behind."

If we'd been running behind, we made up time very quickly. And, for the record, Porches are super-*duper* fast, just in case you didn't already know that.

To take my mind off the scenery flashing by at lightning speed, I casually glanced over at Candice's left hand.

"It's still in the box," Candice said before I even had a chance to ask.

"Have you seen it?" I'd heard from Dutch that Brice had moved back to Candice's, and I'd hoped that meant that the two had patched things up and were now engaged.

"Yes."

I waited for more, but Candice wasn't talking. "Don't force me to use my radar on you," I told her. "Come on, girl! I want details."

The corner of Candice's mouth lifted in a sideways grin. "We sat down and hashed it all out."

"Annnnnnd?"

My partner squirmed in her seat. "Well, after discussing our feelings, we both decided that we've been moving pretty fast, and maybe it's better to slow down and give this thing some time. See if we both feel the same way in a few months and then move it to the next level. We agreed to take all the pressure off—you know, just go really slow and easy. We even talked about seeing other people if the mood fit."

I gaped at her. "*While* you're living together?"

Candice shook her head. "Brice is going to look for his own place next week."

"So you two are splitting up?" I couldn't believe it.

Candice shook her head. "No. We're just stepping back and giving this thing some room to breathe."

"Oh, so now your relationship is a bottle of wine?"

"It's the right thing to do, Abby. I mean, Brice and I have clearly rushed into this. Three months ago we couldn't stand each other and now we're living together and talking marriage? That's not smart. So we've agreed to go back to casual dating, and if in six months we're still together and want to move things forward again, then okay. But giving it some time makes sense."

I raised a skeptical eyebrow, mostly because I'd switched my intuition on anyway and my radar was insisting that a big ol' diamond would soon find its way to Candice's left ring finger.

But it was none of my business, so I vowed to stay out of it. Using all my willpower, I turned in my seat without saying another word and stared straight ahead, repeating the vow to butt out.

To distract myself, I flipped on the radio and tapped my toe to the music.

Five minutes later I took out a pen and notebook and jotted down a grocery list.

Three minutes later, I pulled out the paper from my purse and played Sudoku.

Two minutes later, I gave up on Sudoku and leaned my head back to take a quick nap.

One minute later I opened my eyes and snapped, "You know, maybe it's me, but most of the succsessful relationships I know don't come equipped with a day planner and a stopwatch." (Vow of silence—eleven whole minutes.)

Candice sighed. "Here we go," I heard her mutter.

I swiveled in my seat again. "I'm serious!"

"Oh, I know you are," she said. "So, go ahead. Get it out of your system, Abs. Lay the lecture on me."

I ignored the sarcasm and dove in. "It's just that when I look intuitively at you and Brice, you work. As in, for the long haul. It's like you guys have known each other for years, and I don't know what six months of waiting and pretending to adore each other less than you actually do is going to accomplish. And agreeing to date other people is just ridiculous! You don't want to see anyone other than Brice, and he doesn't want to see anyone other than you, and I know that the moment he moves out, both of you are going to feel miserable without the other. You're fooling yourselves with all this bullsheep of slowing down. What you two *really* need is some assurance from each other that you're in a committed relationship. You guys *love* each other, Candice. And the sooner you own that and just say, 'I do,' the better. For you. For Brice. And for the rest of us faced with six months of looking at your sad little faces."

Candice didn't say anything for the longest time. And I figured that she might be mad at me for speaking my mind, so I turned again and went back to staring out the window.

"You know what?" she asked abruptly.

"What?"

"You're right."

"Duh."

That won me a smile. "So what do I do now, Abs? I mean, he and I already had *the talk* and all."

"You tell him how you honestly feel. You throw that big bag of caution you've carried around with you all these years out the window, and you tell that man that you love him, you don't want him to move out, and that you'll marry him anytime, anywhere."

Candice swallowed hard. "That'd be taking a mighty big risk, don't you think?"

I grinned. "Since when have you ever stepped away from taking a risk?"

"Point taken," she said.

"And, Candice?"

"Yeah?"

"I hear Key West is a great spot for a quickie wedding."

Candice laughed and pushed my shoulder playfully. "Stop, okay?" she giggled. "Just stop."

"I'm just sayin'."

We arrived in south Dallas about twenty minutes later. I resisted the urge to fan my underarms, as screaming down the highway at dizzying speeds tends to make me sweat like a gorilla. "You okay?" Candice asked when we got out of the car. "You look a little pale."

"I will be once we find the spot along the route where I lost my stomach."

Candice ignored me and looked at the house we'd parked in front of. It was a lovely home painted olive green with shiny black shutters and a beautiful white porch all along the front. The flower garden was well tended and fuchsia crape myrtles gave the porch some colorful shade. "Nice," Candice said as we walked up the driveway.

"Whose house is this?" I asked.

"Fatina's grandmother's. Since Fatina went missing last, I thought it best to start here where the leads might be a little warmer."

We approached the front door and Candice rang the bell. "Did it ring?" she asked.

"I didn't hear it."

We waited another few seconds; then Candice knocked. From inside we heard a dog barking and footsteps clomped across a wood floor. The door was then opened by a woman with gray hair, big sad eyes, and hunched shoulders. She put her foot out to stop the inquisitive nose of a small white dog before addressing us. "May I help you?"

"Mrs. Carter?" Candice asked.

"No," the woman replied, her sad eyes turning suspicious.

Candice pulled out the folder she'd tucked under her arm. It was a duplicate of the one I'd given back to

Dutch. "I'm so sorry. Yes, of course. You must be Mrs. Dixon. Your daughter was Mrs. Carter and your granddaughter was Fatina Carter."

At the mention of her granddaughter, the woman physically flinched, and those sad eyes returned. "What's this about?" she demanded.

Candice flashed a badge. I don't know what the badge read. And I didn't want to know what it read. My partner in crime wasn't yet a licensed PI here in Texas, so there was no telling who she was claiming to be. "I'm Candice Fusco and this is my associate, Abigail Cooper, a civilian profiler with the FBI." Candice nudged me and motioned that she wanted me to flash my ID card. I dug around in my purse for a minute, located it, and held it out for Mrs. Dixon to inspect. While she was doing that, Candice continued. "I'm working with the FBI on a joint investigation into the disappearance of your granddaughter."

Again Mrs. Dixon flinched, and her hand moved up to tug at the collar of her housecoat. "My granddaughter's been missing over a year now, miss, and six months ago the FBI told me they didn't have a clue what happened to her and until some new evidence showed up, there wasn't nothin' more to be done to find her. So I can't see why you-all would be interested in her again now."

I decided to speak up. "Mrs. Dixon," I began. "I was hired by the bureau specifically to audit some of their cold cases. I bring a unique set of skills with me and those have led us to the conclusion that Fatina was likely abducted. I believe a predator took your granddaughter right off the street on the day she disappeared."

"You ain't tellin' me nothin' I don't already know," Mrs. Dixon said, bending at the waist to pick up the white dog, who was determined to get past her foot and come out to sniff at us.

"Yes, well, I also believe we'll find her abductor."

Mrs. Dixon snorted derisively. "I heard that before."

For whatever reason, I wanted to convince her. I felt it was important that I have her on our side and so I flipped on my radar, and my focus went to the dog in her arms. "That was Fatina's dog, wasn't it?" I asked.

Mrs. Dixon hugged the pooch and in her eyes, mixed in with the sadness and irritation, was a bit of surprise. "Yes," she admitted.

"She's named after the weather?" I asked, puzzling over the intuitive clues now sorting through my mind.

Again Mrs. Dixon looked surprised. "Her name's Snowy. How'd you know that?"

"I told you, I bring a unique set of skills to the table, Mrs. Dixon. On the day she went missing, your granddaughter almost took the dog with her, didn't she?"

Mrs. Dixon's expression became stricken. It was as if I'd slapped her. "I never told no one that," she whispered.

"Her abduction was not your fault," I said to her gently. "She would have been taken even if she'd had the dog with her."

But Mrs. Dixon didn't look convinced. "Snowy was

very protective of Fatina. She would have fought any-one who meant my grandchild harm."

I shook my head. "You're wrong. The man who took Fatina would have gone after the dog first, and forced Fatina to cooperate to try and save the puppy she loved. He's a devious psychopath, ma'am. And this wasn't the first time he'd taken a little girl against her will."

I wasn't thinking when I said these words. They sort of fell out of my mouth as I was speaking, and they stunned me as much as they did the two other women. "Another girl was taken?" Fatina's grandmother asked.

"Yes." My radar was telling me that Fatina's abductor was a serial killer, and I had the distinct impression that he'd killed more than just Fatina and Keisha. I didn't mentally dwell on it, because at the moment, I needed to focus on Fatina.

Mrs. Dixon fixed her stare on me, and I could see her mulling her next question over, as if my answer would give her some insight into my character. "Do you think my grandchild is still alive?"

I didn't even hesitate because I knew that she was looking for someone—*anyone*—to tell her the truth. "No. I'm so sorry, ma'am, but I believe your grand-daughter died the same day she was taken."

Mrs. Dixon let out a long slow sigh, as if she'd been holding a little of her breath since her granddaughter went missing. "That's what I believe too." She then stepped back from the door. "Come on in."

We gathered in her living room, which was an assortment of colors and styles, none of which matched, but the overall effect was actually quite interesting. "What did you want to know?" Mrs. Dixon asked plainly.

Candice looked at me as if suggesting I should take the lead. I nodded slightly and turned to Mrs. Dixon. "One of my theories is that Fatina was abducted by someone who knew this area well. They might not have lived here, but they knew the neighborhood. I believe that it could have been a worker or contractor."

Mrs. Dixon's brow furrowed. "A contractor?"

I nodded. "A plumber or a handyman or painter or an electrician. Someone who wouldn't have been suspected driving a van and someone who could come and go without calling a lot of attention to himself. So my question to you is, was there a hired hand in the neighborhood at the time of Fatina's abduction?"

Mrs. Dixon's head swiveled to the front hallway. "No," she said slowly. "But about two weeks before she went missing, I'd had the house painted."

Candice looked sharply at me, and she mouthed, "Painter."

"What was the name of the company you hired to paint your house, ma'am?" I asked.

Mrs. Dixon wiped her hand down her face and rocked in her chair. "Wasn't no company," she said. "Was just a man. I don't even remember his name. I saw his poster at church, and tore off his number and called him. He was real cheap and he done a good job."

"Do you still have his number?"

Mrs. Dixon sighed, and I thought her thin shoulders

slumped even farther down, like she carried the weight of the world on them. "No," she admitted. "I had it tacked to my fridge for a time, but I remember throwing it out after he'd finished the job."

"Did you pay by check?" Candice asked.

I crossed my fingers because that would be a great way to track him down. "No," Mrs. Dixon said. "He wouldn't take a check. He asked for cash only."

"And you don't remember his name," I repeated, "not even his first name?"

Mrs. Dixon sighed and rubbed her eyes. "Dan?" she said, as if she were asking a question. "Or Don, maybe? It was one of them easy-to-forget sorta names."

Candice leaned forward. "Can you describe what he looked like?"

Mrs. Dixon took a deep breath and tilted her chin up as she thought. "He was light skinned, probably twenty or twenty-five years old. He was a little husky too, you know. . . . He had some meat on his bones."

"How tall?"

"Oh," she said, tapping her chin with her finger. "I'd say about five feet eight or nine. He wasn't no six feet, and I know that 'cause my husband was six feet tall and I used to come up to his collarbone. This man was shorter than that. I could almost look him in the eye." And then something occurred to her and she let out a tiny gasp. "You know what's funny, though?"

"What?" Candice and I asked in unison.

"He never did look me in the eye. I thought that was odd, 'cause he was always so polite and all. I don't like people who won't look you in the eye, but I made an exception for him 'cause he had good manners and always answered me 'Yes, ma'am' or 'No, ma'am.' But maybe he wasn't so nice as I thought. Maybe he was a bad man and couldn't look me in the eye 'cause of that."

"Is there anything else about him you can remember?" I asked. "Did he have any facial hair or any tattoos or piercings?"

Mrs. Dixon shook her head. "No," she said, and I could tell she wished she could give us more. "Do you think he was the one that took my Fatina?"

"I do."

Candice eyed me in that way that told me I shouldn't have said that, but I couldn't help it. I knew I needed to be straight with this woman.

Candice jumped to the next topic by asking, "Can you tell us about how you came to be Fatina's guardian, Mrs. Dixon?"

Again Mrs. Dixon's eyes turned sad. "Fatina is my daughter's child," she said. "And Fontana was my only child. She wasn't a bad person, but she fell in with the wrong crowd when she was about fifteen or so. It was right after her daddy died, in fact, and next thing I knew, my daughter was pregnant and on drugs. I done everything I could to get her to stay clean, but that pipe was too powerful for her.

"When Fatina was born, they found traces of crack in her blood and they took her away from Fontana. I fought for custody and won, and I promised that as soon as Fontana kicked the drugs, she could come live with us and help raise Fatina.

"Last time I saw her was when my grandbaby was still a toddler. Fontana said she was working to get clean and I believed her. Then she showed up here strung out and I told her not to come back, and I never saw her again. One of her druggie friends moved up to St. Louis, and Fontana went with him. I used to hear from her twice a year every year at Christmas and on Fatina's birthday, and then four years ago she didn't call and I knew she was dead."

"Did the police in St. Louis ever notify you of that fact?"

Mrs. Dixon shook her head. "No. They got some dead homeless black woman off the street, and they don't do nothin' to try and find the next of kin. And I didn't really want to know, truth be told. I was afraid of what I would have to tell Fatina."

Candice opened the folder and looked at the notes taken by the investigator on the case. "It says here that the agent assigned to the case thought there was some evidence that Fontana had taken her daughter."

Mrs. Dixon waved her hand dismissively. "Oh, that's a bunch of bull," she said. "That FBI man wasn't interested in finding my grandchild! He just wanted to close his case and be done with it, so he found one of Fontana's old boyfriends, who said he heard my daughter say that someday she was gonna come here and just take Fatina away."

"But you don't believe that's what happened," I said.

"No," Mrs. Dixon said with a shake of her head. "Fontana wouldn't do that to me or to Fatina, and besides, Fatina went missing several years after those phone calls stopped. I know in my heart that Fontana was already dead by then."

"And what about Fatina's father?"

Mrs. Dixon scowled. "That heap of garbage went off to meet his Maker right before Fatina was born. Died of a drug overdose. He was the one that got Fontana hooked on the pipe in the first place. And he only married her 'cause I threatened to turn him in to the police if he didn't. Fontana was a minor when he started havin' relations with her."

"How old was he?" Candice asked.

"Twenty-two," she replied with disgust.

"And there were no other relatives that might have been interested in taking over custody of Fatina?"

I knew Candice wanted to be thorough, but my mind was already made up that a family member hadn't abducted the little girl. "There is no one else but me," said Mrs. Dixon. "I got no one left, miss. Just this dog and this house. My sister died some ten years ago, and my husband's family is all dead too. Me and Snowy is all alone in this here house. Ain't no one to care 'bout us no more. And ain't no one for us to care for neither."

Mrs. Dixon's eyes watered and my heart broke for her. She appeared to be a gentle, good-hearted woman who'd had so much tragedy in her life. And I couldn't imagine going through all of that and finding yourself almost completely alone.

No one spoke for the longest time; it was as if we were observing a moment of silence for all the people in Mrs. Dixon's life that had been lost. Finally, however, Candice asked, "Mrs. Dixon, could I perhaps ask you to part with a photo of your daughter?"

The older woman sniffled and dabbed at her eyes. "What for?"

"I want to bring you some closure, ma'am. I know your heart is suggesting that your daughter and granddaughter are both deceased, but it must still tug on you a bit not to be absolutely certain."

Mrs. Dixon stroked Snowy's fur. "It does."

"Then loan me a picture and let me investigate. I'll do my very best to find out the truth for you."

"I ain't got no money to pay you," Mrs. Dixon said warily.

"That's perfect," Candice said with an easy smile, "because today, I'm not charging."

Mrs. Dixon regarded Candice for a moment before she got up and moved over to a sofa table where several photos were displayed in a variety of frames. Selecting one from the group, she brought it over to Candice. "This one's my favorite," she said, turning the frame around so that we could see the image.

In the photo, Fontana looked bone thin, but there was some light in her eyes and she had an easy smile. Next to her was Fatina, hugging her mother fiercely, although the little girl couldn't have been older than three or four.

I noticed with a heavy heart that both mother and daughter appeared flat to my intuitive eye, confirming to me at least that they were both dead. Candice took the frame from Mrs. Dixon and pretended to study it while sneaking a sideways glance at me as if to ask me if there was any hope. I frowned and subtly shook my head.

"Thank you, ma'am," Candice said, removing the photo from the frame carefully. "I promise to take very good care of it and return it to you just as soon as I find something out."

Mrs. Dixon looked unsure, and I suspected she was wondering if we were making legitimate promises or if this was some sort of elaborate scheme to bilk her out of what little money she had. "Here is my card," I said, reaching into my purse to pull out my new business cards embossed with the FBI logo. "That's my office number," I told her, "but I'll be in the field for the next few weeks, so if you need to get ahold of me, call this number." I then quickly wrote my cell number on the card.

Candice too reached into her purse and pulled out her own business card. Like everything else about my good friend these days, it looked expensive and classy. "Call me anytime as well, Mrs. Dixon. And if I could have your number to keep you updated as we get information, that'd be great."

Mrs. Dixon appeared overwhelmed by all the contact information coming at her. It made me wonder how the

original investigator on her granddaughter's case had
treated her. After giving Candice her phone number,
she walked us to the door, where we shook her hand
and headed to the car.

Once inside Candice asked, "What'd you think?"

"Intuitively?"

"Yes."

"That she's had one heck of a tragic life and we've got
to do everything in our power to give her some closure."

Candice smiled and started the car. "Funny," she said.
"I was thinking the same thing."

As we cruised away from the neighborhood, I was
grateful that Candice was controlling her speed better
on these suburban streets, and I allowed myself to simply look out the window at the passing houses. We came
to a stop sign and Candice focused her attention on the
navigation gizmo built into the dashboard, while also
checking the next address from one of the files.

As she was fiddling with that, I happened to glance
up at the street sign. "Pecan Valley Drive," I whispered.
Where had I seen that street name before? Or *had* I
seen that name before? Sometimes it's difficult for me
to know if my radar is giving me a clue, or if I'm simply
remembering something I've seen somewhere else.

I scanned the area carefully. The charming street
name was a misnomer. There was nothing appealing
about this neck of the woods. "Where are we?" I asked
abruptly.

"Hmm?" Candice hummed, still poking at her GPS
gizmo.

"Seriously, Candice," I said, laying a hand on her arm. "Where exactly *are* we?"

Candice pulled her eyes away from the dashboard. "About halfway between Fatina's house and Keisha's."

My radar was buzzing at me and my eyes kept roving to the street sign. There was something about it that I was missing. Something important. "Can you go down this street for a minute?"

Candice squinted out the window, then eyed me oddly. "For real?"

"Yeah."

"Abs," she said seriously, "this isn't exactly the kind of neighborhood where one drives a brand-new Porsche around."

She was right of course. There were lots of vacant and boarded-up homes on the block, and I also noticed that we'd caught the attention of a group of young men about two hundred yards away. "Okay," I reluctantly agreed. "You're right. Let's go."

Candice moved away from the stop sign and Pecan Valley Drive, and the farther away we got, the more convinced I was that I'd just missed something like a major clue, but for the life of me I couldn't puzzle out what it was. Still, just to make sure I wasn't missing something obvious, I took the two folders on Fatina and Keisha and searched the ink for any trace of Pecan Valley Drive, but found no reference to that street.

I had to put it out of my mind just a few minutes later when we pulled up in front of Keisha's house, which was a small but tidy little ranch with thick stone steps leading up to a wrought iron gate across the front door. There were also bars across the windows. I looked around at the other houses nearby. Most of them had the same detail on the windows and doors. At least there weren't any boarded-up houses on the street, but I did see plenty of curtains move to the side as people spotted Candice's shiny new Porsche. "Why do I think this visit is going to be the talk of the neighborhood?" I muttered as we got out.

Candice subtly glanced up and down the street, probably determining if it was safe to leave her car unattended. She clicked the button on her keys and the Porsche made a chirping noise. "Locked and loaded," she said with a wink to me.

We approached the door and I let Candice take the lead. She pushed the doorbell and this time we definitely heard it echoing from inside. We waited several seconds before Candice tried again, but clearly there was either no one home or no one willing to answer the door.

"What do you think?" she asked me.

I pointed my radar at the house. "I think no one's here."

Candice walked down the steps and moved over to the driveway. "Doesn't hurt to be thorough," she said over her shoulder. "Stay by the car. I'll be right back."

I moved to the Porsche and let my side fall against it with a tired sigh. Immediately it began to make a huge racket as the horn sounded, lights blinked, and an alarm blared. "Gah!" I shrieked, spinning away from the car.

Candice came running back from around the corner.

"What happened?" she shouted right before she pressed a button on her key again.

"Your freaking car is possessed!" I yelled. Then I realized the noise from the car had stopped, and I lowered my voice but flushed with embarrassment as several doors opened and people came out to see what all the racket was about. "All I did was lean against it."

"The alarm's a little sensitive," she admitted.

"Gee, Candice, *ya think*?"

My partner moved over to the driver's side. "Come on," she coaxed. "He's not home and you look like you could use some lunch."

At the prospect of food I let go my indignation and got right in. Buckling my seat belt, I asked, "When you say 'he's' not home, who're you talking about exactly?"

"Keisha's brother. He had custody of his baby sister when she went missing. Didn't you read the file?"

"Yes, I read the file," I told her. "But some of the details may have gotten lost because I read at least a hundred files last week."

"Ah."

"Was that the house Keisha lived in when she was abducted?"

"Yes."

"And her brother still lives there?"

Candice nodded. "According to public records, he does."

"I take it we're going to eat, then swing back by again to see if he's home?"

"Yep."

"He won't be," I told her, feeling that intuitively. "In fact, I don't even think he's in the area right now. Does he have some connection to the military?"

Candice smiled wide. "You sure you don't remember reading that in the file?"

I held up my hand like I was taking a vow. "Scout's honor."

"Okay, I believe you. Antoine LaSalle is in the army. He's a lieutenant currently stationed in Killeen."

"Killeen?"

"It's about forty-five minutes southwest of here."

"Why didn't we start there?"

"Way too many security checks to clear. 'Who are you? Where are you from? Who are you there to see? Why?' It's a royal pain in the butt just to deliver a pizza."

"We're delivering a pizza?"

"No. But trust me, I once tried to run some surveillance by posing as a pizza-delivery girl at a military base and let's just say it did not go well."

"Ah."

"If he's not there when we swing back by, then we'll leave him a note and my card and hope he calls."

"Then what?"

"Then we'll run you home so you can take care of your man, and then I'll try and find out if Fontana Carter ended up in the St. Louis morgue."

I remembered with a jolt the intuitive feeling I had that Fatina and Keisha weren't the only victims of our serial killer. "I think you should also do a search of other missing little girls who fit Fatina and Keisha's description from this area."

Candice eyed me. "You think there are more victims?"

"I do."

"Shit."

"There could even be a file on the other victim in one of those boxes back at the office and I just haven't come across it yet," I told her.

"Well," she said, "if there is a file on another missing little girl, then you're not going to be able to see it until IA clears you—which could take a while."

That got my attention. "You think they're going to take a long time to clear me?"

Candice shrugged. "IA investigations within local police departments are bad enough; I gotta believe that they're ten times worse when they're part of the FBI."

I gulped. "Great. Just great."

Candice shifted gears and bumped my arm with hers. "Don't sweat it, Abs," she said. "You did what you had to do in the moment, and if there's anyone who's to blame, it's that Rodriguez guy. You should be cleared no problem."

"But I *like* that Rodriguez guy."

"Oh. Well, then, we'll just hope for the best, okay? Now, where did you want to go for lunch?"

"The nearest Coney Island hot dog joint."

Candice gave me a sympathetic smile. "No such luck round these parts either, partner."

"So drive me back to Michigan," I said grumpily. "Where things used to make sense and I could get a decent hot dog with the works and an order of some chili cheese fries."

"I wouldn't do that even if I could," Candice said flatly.

"Why not?"

"Have you ever smelled your breath at the end of one of those lunches? Trust me, the box of Altoids you pop doesn't even cover it."

I felt my cheeks heat and I sank down in my seat, totally embarrassed. "So I like onions!" I snapped.

Candice laughed. "Oh, honey," she said sympathetically. "I know you love them. It's just that they don't really love you. Now, how about a nice bowl of soup and salad, hmm?"

Chapter Eight

We ate the most boring, lifeless lunch ever and I bought a pack of wintergreen gum the first chance I got. We also made our way back to the LaSalle residence, but just like I'd predicted, Antoine wasn't home, so Candice left him a note and her card and we headed back to Austin.

After retrieving Dutch's car from Candice's parking garage, I zipped over to pick him up, noting that I was running just a teensy bit behind. I found my S.O. leaning against the building, looking all manly and gorgeous. I also found that any frustration I'd had with him earlier seemed to melt away. "Hey, cowboy," I said, pulling to a stop at the curb. "Can I give you a lift?"

Dutch moseyed over to the driver's side and opened my door. "How about letting me drive?"

I shrugged and gave up the wheel. The moment we

pulled into traffic, he started in. "I called your cell a couple of times this afternoon."

Oops.

"Sorry. I didn't hear it ring." Nervously I took it out of my purse and squinted at the screen. "Ah, I see. You called all right." For the record, it's hard to hear a cell phone ring above the roar of a Porsche's engine.

"Where ya been all afternoon?" Dutch pressed.

"Hanging out with Candice."

"Where?"

Uh-oh . . .

"Here and there."

"More there than here?"

I sighed tiredly. Dutch had been with me long enough to never trust it when I didn't answer my phone. It was the first sign that I was up to something. "We had a spa day," I said quickly. "We got massages and pedicures."

"Really?" he said in that voice that told me he didn't for one second believe it.

"Yep." I was sticking to this story if it killed me.

"What was the name of the spa?"

"Pecan Valley Salon and Spa." Wow. I'd rattled that off without a moment's hesitation. Maybe I was getting better at this whole lying thing.

"Pecan Valley?" he repeated. "Where's that?"

"Not sure. Candice drove and I mostly kept my eyes shut."

Now, this he actually bought, because he cracked a smile. "I hear she got a new car."

"Porsche," I told him. "Canary yellow."

"Subtle."

"That's what I said!"

While Dutch had his outpatient procedure, I paced the lobby of the clinic right next to the hospital. I wasn't worried until the clock read five thirty. Dutch's doctor had told me when we'd met with him two days earlier that he'd be out no later than five p.m.

By six I'd worked myself into a small tizzy. The receptionist told me that sometimes these things ran a little long and just to be patient, but I kept having the feeling that something wasn't quite right, and when we got to six fifteen, I blew a gasket. All those coping skills I'd learned in my anger management classes went right out the window and I started to pound my fist on the counter like Shirley MacLaine in *Terms of Endearment*.

A nurse bolted out of the back and grabbed my arm, pulling me to a chair and insisting that I calm down.

I insisted she tell me what the f-bomb had happened to Dutch. "He's had a little trouble with the anesthesia," she admitted. "But he's doing much better now and he's almost ready to go home."

Through clenched teeth I repeated, "Trouble with the anesthesia?"

The nurse kept her voice low and level. "Besides the section on Mr. Rivers's neck there were several more moles on his back that Dr. Cassidy wanted to remove. They both decided to go with a variant on a general anesthesia rather than several locals. This particular drug still has a tendency to put patients to sleep, which is what happened with Mr. Rivers, but during the end of the excisions, his breathing became very shallow and his blood pressure dropped significantly."

My hand moved to cover my mouth. "Oh, God!"

The nurse held up her hand as if she wanted to tell me to remain calm. "It's not that uncommon a reaction," she said. "We've seen it before and we got it under control very quickly." I continued to gape at her and she added, "I promise you, he's fine, just very queasy and a little light-headed."

"I want to see him."

"He'll be right out," she assured me.

I stood up and with unveiled agitation I said, "I'm not waiting out here a minute longer. You can either take me to him, or I can cause another scene."

The nurse's eyes widened. "All right," she said tersely. "Come with me."

I followed her through the door and along a corridor to one of the recovery rooms. Dutch was lying on a gurney with his feet propped up on pillows and a cold compress on his head along with another one against the back of his neck.

I moved right to his side and picked up his hand. He looked pale as hell and my heart skipped a beat. "Hey," I said when he opened his eyes.

"Get me out of here."

I turned to the nurse. "Bring me his clothes, please."

"He really should lie still for a little longer, ma'am."

I turned back to Dutch. He shook his head no.

"We're leaving right now. Please bring me his clothes."

At that moment, the doctor finally poked his head in. "How's our patient?" he asked jovially.

I turned on him with narrowed eyes and a whole lotta attitude. "Why didn't anyone tell me what'd happened to him?"

Dr. Cassidy immediately came to my side and laid a gentle hand on my shoulder. "I'm so sorry," he admitted. "I've been short staffed this week. One of my nurses went on maternity leave early and I got caught in a bind. I needed all my staff with me to make sure Agent Rivers got the attention he needed, and it wasn't until just a few minutes ago that we were confident he was stable."

More than anything, his apology helped to chill me out. "I was worried."

"I know. I'm sorry."

Crap. I could hardly be mad now. "It's okay. But he really wants to leave. Can I take him home?"

"Of course." Turning to the nurse, he said, "Megan, please bring Miss Cooper here Agent Rivers's clothing."

It took a long time to get Dutch dressed and down to the car. He was still very groggy from whatever drugs they'd pumped into him, and he couldn't seem to focus on helping me put his pants or his shirt on. I also cursed myself for not bringing along a pair of his sweats, as it would have been much easier than trying to get his dress slacks on.

By the time we got home, it was well after seven and my phone was lit up with voice mails from Candice, Brice, and my sister, Cat. I realized with regret that I hadn't spoken to Cat since landing in Austin—something I was sure to be lectured about when we did finally speak.

Still, Dutch was my top priority that night, and his neck and back were so sore and he was still so wobbly on his feet that getting him upstairs to bed was out of the question. Instead I sat him carefully in a chair and made up the couch.

He was asleep almost as soon as I got him settled and covered with a blanket.

I then fed poor Eggy and Tuttle, who were practically starving by then, and nuked some leftovers for myself.

The phone rang just as I burned my tongue with the first bite. "Ow! Hewo?"

There was a pause, then, "Abby?"

"Hi, Candwice."

"Why are you talking funny?"

"I bewned my tongue."

I fished an ice cube out of my water glass to hold on my tongue while Candice processed that. "What're you eating?"

"Leftovews."

"How's Dutch?"

"He's aw wite. A wittle qweasy."

There was a chuckle, then, "You nurse that tongue, Sundance, and I'll do the talking."

"Owkay."

"I did some follow-up online going back through the *Dallas Morning News* and I found an article about a little girl who went to the same school as Keisha who also went missing in March of two thousand eight."

Removing the ice cube, I said, "Two months before Keisha?"

"Yes."

"How old was she?"

"Ten."

"Any trace of her since?"

"Yes."

I felt a heaviness grow in my chest. "She came up dead." I knew it before Candice even told me.

On the other end of the line, my friend sighed sadly. "She was found in a retention pond less than a mile from her home about six weeks after she went missing. The body was so decomposed that no cause of death could be determined, and the coroner eventually ruled it an accidental drowning."

"But we know different."

"Do we?" Candice asked.

"I'm sorry. What?"

"What I mean is, do you intuitively feel there's a connection between all three of these girls?"

"What's the little girl's name?" I was already switching on my radar.

"Patrice Walker."

I closed my eyes and focused on the little girl's energy. I got the same image of a van with a ladder and paint cans littering the ground, but this time I also flashed on something else. I saw the street sign for Pecan Valley Drive. "Weird," I said.

"What?"

"I swear I see . . ." My voice drifted off as I remembered something.

"You see what?"

"Candice?"

"Yeah?"

"Did that little girl live on a street called Pecan Valley Drive?"

There was a gasp; then she said, "Man, Abs! You are good!"

I sighed tiredly, not much in the mood to feel good about the hit. "The three girls are connected. Patrice was the first victim."

"Feel like heading back to Dallas tomorrow?"

I leaned out of my chair to eye my S.O., who was fast asleep on the couch. "Maybe not tomorrow," I told her. "Dutch had a rough go of it at the doctor's office. I'm thinking he's going to be calling in sick tomorrow."

"Did you want me to let Brice know?"

"He's there?"

"He's in the living room watching basketball. I'm in the bedroom with the door closed. I didn't want him to overhear our conversation."

"Have you two had the follow-up talk?" I asked.

"Not yet."

I frowned. In my opinion, Candice was wasting time being miserable in her relationship when she and Brice could be celebrating at that very moment. Still, I knew I'd probably stuck my nose far enough into her business.

"Yeah, if you could tell him that I'm calling Dutch in sick, that'd be great."

"You got it. We'll pick this up the day after tomorrow."

"As long as Dutch is well enough to go back to work and doesn't need me," I added.

I could hear Candice's soft chuckle through the line. "Okay, Nurse Nightingale. Get some sleep and tell the cowboy I hope he feels better soon."

Dutch bounced back very quickly, and he would have gone to work the day after his surgery if I hadn't taken the added measure of hiding his car keys before I went to bed the night before. He was pretty grumpy about the fact that I'd called off for him, but as the day wore on and he worked to find a comfortable position to sit in, I could tell that he was actually glad about it.

I spent much of the day unpacking the boxes that still remained from the move and by five thirty p.m. our little Texas rental was all nice and tidy-like.

Cat called me twice during the day, once to give me a pretty terse lecture for not calling her in a week, and the second time to apologize for the lecture. She also suggested that she was coming out to visit very, *very* soon and I'd just have to deal with it, as she missed me and she wanted to make sure I was taking care of myself.

I took a shower after all that unpacking, and was just coming down the stairs considering a pizza when the doorbell rang. "Abby!" Dutch yelled from his seat on the couch.

"I'm right here," I said, coming around the corner.

"Can you get the door?"

I smirked at him as I walked toward the front hall. "Are you expecting company?"

"No."

I opened the door and took a step back, completely surprised. "Dave!" I shouted.

Our handyman and good friend, formerly from Michigan, was standing on my front porch holding a mammoth take-out bag with an ART'S RIBS logo on it. "Hey, Abs," he said jovially. "You guys hungry?"

I ushered him in with a quick hug, completely forgetting how much his showing up at dinnertime used to drive me crazy. (And I will admit this change in attitude was likely because Dave actually brought dinner this time.)

Dutch looked pretty happy to see our old friend too, and he managed to get stiffly off the couch to offer his hand. "Great to see you, buddy," he said.

Dave seemed to notice Dutch's hunched-over posture. "You okay?"

"Had some moles removed from my back and my neck yesterday. Still a little sensitive."

"Oh, man," Dave said. "That's rough. I know the thing to take the edge off."

"A beer?"

"No, but now that you mention it, a nice cold one really does sound good. Especially since I brought Art along."

Dutch looked around. "Who?"

Dave held up the big bag so that Dutch could see the logo. "Best ribs in Texas."

We ate like kings that night. Dave was right; Art's ribs were the best I'd ever had. And it was so great to catch up with him too. He looked good in a way that I hadn't ever noticed back in Michigan. It was as if the secure job he'd found down here working for his brother-in-law had given him a boost in confidence and taken some of the worry out of his eyes. "Me and the old lady are picking out a floor plan," he told us, referring to his wife the way he always had, even though I knew he worshipped the ground she walked on. "We're finally going to buy our own place."

Dave's brother-in-law was a builder, and he'd given Dave a job as construction supervisor. "Buddy, that's fantastic!" I said.

My friend puffed out his chest and beamed a wide-toothed smile. "Feels good not to have to worry about money all the time," he admitted. "And the old lady's working now too."

"She is?" Dutch and I said together.

"Yep. She got a job in some boot store in Georgetown. Sells more cowboy boots than any other salesperson in the store."

"Which store?" I asked a little too quickly. It was well-known that I'd been trying to find out Dave's wife's actual name for the past couple of years, and he'd always managed to keep her and it from me.

He caught on right away. "Not tellin'."

"Fine," I said with a sneaky grin. "Georgetown's not

too far away, you know. And how many boot stores can there be?"

"Enough to take up an entire afternoon," Dave said smartly.

"Hey, Abby," Dutch interjected, right when I'd thought up a snappy retort.

"Yeah?"

"You feel like going for ice cream?"

I looked at him. "Honey, I really think you should take it easy tonight. Going for a drive is a little ambitious, don't you think?"

Dutch blanched. "Uh," he said, turning those big midnight blues on me. "I was thinking maybe you could go get us some and bring it back?"

"Oh! Um . . . I guess. I mean, sure. Sure I can."

As I hurried to get my jacket and keys, I had the distinct impression that Dutch and Dave were waiting for me to leave so that they could talk privately about something I wasn't supposed to know about.

I considered using the old radar to figure out what they were up to, but then thought better of it. It had to be hard on Dutch at times to date someone like me, and I don't just mean for the mood swings and the severe handicap I present in the kitchen. There wasn't much that he was able to keep from me. If I wanted to know something, he could do little to stop me from figuring it out.

So I decided to take the high road and keep my intuitive nose out of it, which, for the record, was *really* hard. Especially since when I got back, Dave asked to take his ice cream to go and made a rather nervous and hasty exit.

Still, I kept my mouth firmly shut, and cleaned up the dinner dishes. Dutch got out of his chair and came to stand next to me while he ate his ice cream. "Thanks for getting this," he said, motioning with the bowl in his hands.

"Sure."

Dutch cleared his throat a little. "So, you probably used the crew to figure out what we were talking about, huh?"

I set a plate in the dishwasher. "Nope."

"Nope?"

I turned to face him. "Is it hard living with me?"

Dutch seemed surprised by the question, but he quickly recovered. "Impossible," he said with a smile.

I bit my lip. I knew he was kidding, but that still stung, so I turned back to the dishes and began to scrub in earnest.

"Abs," he said, but I wouldn't look at him. Dutch set the bowl down on the counter and reached across to pull my shoulder around to face him again. "Sweethot, I love living with you."

I blinked as unexpected tears sprang to my eyes.

"Hey," he said, seeing the waterworks. "Edgar, what gives?"

I took a deep breath and tried to collect myself. "I think it's all this stuff with Candice and Brice. They're crazy about each other—I mean, really in love—and they'll tell everyone else their true feelings except they won't tell each other."

"How are we like them, exactly?"

"In the car on the way to get the ice cream, I realized that anytime I want to know what's going on with you, I use my radar, and that can't be fair. So I don't want to resort to that anymore. If I need to know what's going on inside your head, or inside your heart, I'll ask, but you have to promise to tell me."

The corners of Dutch's mouth lifted in a grin. "Do you have any idea how much I love you, cupcake?"

The tears that I'd managed to tamp down came back in earnest. "I'm hoping it's a lot."

Dutch shut off the water and pulled me into a fierce embrace, even though I knew the move must have really hurt his back. Kissing the top of my head, he said, "It's *way* more than a lot, Abigail. It's so much, it's obscene."

Chapter Nine

I took Dutch to work the next morning because it was raining cats and dogs, and with his range of motion still a challenge, I didn't want him to try to drive in foul weather.

I was also glad it was Friday, and that he'd have the weekend to rest and make a full recovery.

After dropping him at the office, I shot over to Candice's because we'd agreed to make another trip to Dallas. Candice met me in the parking garage. "Do you want me to drive?" I offered. Hopefully, she'd let me, because I definitely did not want to scream down the highway in this weather with her Porsche.

Candice eyed my MINI Cooper skeptically. "That's okay," she said, and motioned me over to her car. "I promise to take it slow and easy today."

With a groan I rolled up the window and parked, then hurried over to the Porsche. I clicked the seat belt as we pulled out of the garage, grateful that at least my friend was going to try to stay within range of the speed limit.

And for most of the trip, she did really well. But that could have been because of the weather. "Jeez, it is really coming down!" I said, peering out at the torrential downfall that seemed to worsen the closer we got to Dallas.

"I've heard that Central Texas can experience crazy periods of intense drought or torrential rainfall," Candice replied, her hands gripping the steering wheel firmly.

I knew that she hated driving in heavy rain. Candice and her older sister had been involved in a very bad accident during a terrible storm, and Candice's sister had been killed. "You should have let me drive," I muttered.

Candice sat forward a little more to squint out the windshield. "It's okay," she assured me. "I'm fine."

It took almost twice as long to finally get to south Dallas, and for some reason the navigational system in the Porsche wasn't working. "I have to take the car back to the dealership tomorrow so they can fix it," she remarked. I could tell she was irritated. And I didn't blame her; if you're going to plunk down a huge chunk of change for a shiny new Porsche—it'd better work.

Candice had to rely on the turn-by-turn directions from her iPhone, which got us lost. Twice.

"Stupid app!" Candice snapped after she pulled over

in front of a mall, which the iPhone swore was the right address. "I knew I should have purchased the other one."

I knew not to talk to her when electronic gizmos failed. Candice could handle a big beefy bad guy holding a gun with cool aplomb, but have her cell phone or computer freeze up, and she'd lose it for sure. "Maybe I should ask for directions?" I offered after several minutes of listening to her mumble expletives.

"Gimme a minute," she growled.

I gave her five.

"Okay, I think I got it working now." Candice turned the face of her phone toward me and I smiled big and gave her two thumbs up. She looked at me and grinned. "Sorry for being so grouchy."

"It's okay," I said, taking the phone from her so that I could hold it while she drove.

We finally made it to Antoine's and I was surprised that we were starting with him again. "I thought we were going to Patrice's house."

"She's next," Candice assured me. "Right after we check in with Antoine to see if he's home."

I grabbed my umbrella off the floor of the car, and braced myself to get wet. The rain was still coming down really hard, and I wondered if the umbrella would make a lot of difference, as the wind was blowing in big wet gusts. Candice and I did our best to dodge puddles and hurry up the steps to the front door, which opened just as Candice raised her fist to knock.

I let out a tiny gasp when I caught a glimpse of the

man framed in the doorway, mostly because he was so tall and imposing.

Antoine LaSalle was easily six five and he was built like a brick sheep house. I think he had muscles on top of muscles, but my radar suggested he wasn't all brawn. There was a fearsome intelligence to his eyes, which flashed back and forth between me and Candice, and I knew he had our number right away. "Yeah?"

"Antoine LaSalle?" Candice asked.

Our host crossed his massive arms and set his feet shoulder width apart. "Who wants to know?"

Candice broke out her badge with one easy flick of her wrist. "I'm Candice Fusco and this is my associate, Abigail Cooper, with the Cold Case Squad of the FBI."

One eyebrow lifted on Antoine's face. "Cold Case Squad?" he repeated. "This about Keisha?"

"Yes," I said. "We're looking into her disappearance."

Antoine fixed his intimidating stare on me, and as he did so, I found it very hard not to turn around and dash back to the car. There was something about him that genuinely frightened me, and it wasn't just his size and imposing manner.

"You two are about two years too late, don't you think?"

"We've recently come across some information, Mr. LaSalle, that we believe might lead us to a description of a suspect."

Antoine's features showed interest. "Suspect? You guys found a suspect?"

I thought it pretty clever of him to simply repeat the

general facts we were giving him and wait for us to expand on them. I think Candice caught on to the tactic too, because she sidestepped that by turning slightly to look out at the rain. "Might we be invited in to discuss the details with you?"

LaSalle appeared to mull that over for a minute, and I guess he decided we were on the up-and-up because he stepped to the side and casually said, "Come in, ladies."

Now, I'll be honest here: The last place in the world I wanted to go was into the den of this particular lion, but as Candice walked right on in without a care in the world, I decided I couldn't very well let her go it alone.

Once we were out of the rain, I looked around curiously. Okay, so I took in the location of the closest exits just in case things got dicey, but I made a show of eyeing the decor and nodding in approval.

Actually, the house kind of surprised me, because Antoine had gorgeous taste. His house was a mixture of light-colored wood, soft linens, and cool angular furniture. It was also extremely neat and organized. Hardly an item out of place, save for a large duffel and some military boots poking out of the hallway.

Antoine seemed conscious of these items, because he pushed them back with his foot. "Just got back from a tour in Afghanistan," he remarked as we walked past.

He then motioned us to the sofa on the far side of the room, while he took a chair directly across from us. I couldn't help but notice that his back was to the only available exit and he'd probably purposely positioned us up against the back wall.

The subliminal message was clear: We might think we were there to interview him, but he was going to control the conversation.

Candice sat gracefully on the couch and pulled out her notepad from her leather shoulder bag. Flipping to a clean white sheet, she said, "Can you tell us about the day Keisha disappeared?"

Antoine didn't move a muscle from his relaxed position in the chair across from us, and yet I swore he'd stiffened. "What can I tell you that you haven't already read in her case file?"

"Sometimes things are lost in translation, Lieutenant. I've read the agent's account of what happened to your sister on the day she disappeared, but I'm interested to hear it directly from you."

"Why?"

"Because there might be a relevant clue that got left out of the notes."

Antoine was silent for so long I thought he wasn't going to answer. "I saw her off to school that morning, same as I always did. I went to work. I came home. She wasn't here. I called around to all of her friends, searched the neighborhood, and alerted police, and we never saw her again."

I was watching Antoine closely, using my radar to detect anything of importance out of the ether, but I couldn't get past this image of him as a crouching tiger, ready to pounce the moment our guard was down.

"What time did you arrive home that day?"

"Sixteen thirty."

Candice scribbled on the notepad, and I had to do a little mental math to figure out he was talking about four thirty p.m. My partner then flipped back a few pages and said, "We know from the original investigation that Keisha was in school that day and that several students saw her walking home by herself around three fifteen in the afternoon. No one noticed anyone strange following her. Are you sure that Keisha didn't come home and then leave again to go somewhere else? Like, maybe to a friend's house?"

"Positive."

Candice looked up. "How can you be so sure?"

"She had homework to do."

"Can you elaborate on that, please?"

"The rule in this house was that Keisha was to come straight home from school and do her homework. My sister was a very bright girl, and she knew that in order to get ahead in life, she would have to study hard and get good grades. She wasn't allowed to visit with friends until all her homework was finished." Candice opened her mouth to ask a follow-up question, but Antoine beat her to it by saying, "I checked with her teacher. Keisha had been assigned both math and history homework. If she had made it home, she would still have been working on it when I arrived."

Candice toyed with her pen as she looked back at La-Salle. "And yet, you mentioned just a minute ago that when you arrived home and found Keisha missing, you immediately called around to her friends to see if she was with them."

"I didn't know at that time that Keisha had assignments to complete."

"Lieutenant," I said, interrupting the conversation that was getting us nowhere. "Had you had any work done to your house in the weeks prior to Keisha's disappearance?"

LaSalle's dark eyes pivoted to me. "Work done?"

"Yes, sir," I said. "You know, construction, or home improvement. A new paint job perhaps?"

Again I felt LaSalle's energy stiffen, but he answered my question easily. "No."

I leaned forward. "How about anyone in the neighborhood? Did you notice any contractors at any of your neighbors' houses?"

"I don't stick my nose into other people's business, ma'am."

My radar dinged. LaSalle was lying. "Really?" I asked him. He stared at me with a blank expression. "Because I think that you're someone who might notice everything."

LaSalle's lips peeled away from brilliant white teeth. "You do, huh?"

"Yes," I said, using my radar to try to figure him out. But there wasn't much I could pull out of the ether that wasn't already obvious. He was a big guy. He was a soldier. He liked to intimidate people into giving up information. And he loved his sister—of that, I was positive.

But why he wasn't cooperating was a real mystery, and my attempt to goad him into revealing more failed.

He simply nodded and turned his attention back to Candice, waiting for her next question.

"Is there anything more you might be able to share with us that perhaps you didn't have a chance to tell the original investigators?" she asked.

"No."

From the corner of my eye I watched Candice inhale and exhale slowly. If LaSalle was holding on to information, we weren't about to get it out of him. "Okay, then," Candice said, tucking her notepad back into her purse. "We'd like to thank you for your—"

LaSalle interrupted our attempt to end the discussion by asking, "What new lead have you discovered?"

Candice hesitated before answering. "She was abducted and murdered on the same day she went missing by a predator, likely a pedophile, who knew this neighborhood well."

LaSalle's lips pressed together. "*That's* your big breakthrough?"

"No," she said. "Our big breakthrough is that we've talked with the grandmother of another missing little girl of the same age as Keisha. The circumstances surrounding her disappearance are quite similar to your sister's, in fact. After interviewing the girl's grandmother, we discovered that she went missing within two weeks of their house being painted. We think the man who worked on the house might have some knowledge about what happened to the little girl. And perhaps he also has some information about what happened to your sister."

"Her house is within one mile of yours," I added.

"You're talking about Fatina," LaSalle said. "Yeah, I know about her."

"Did you also know about Patrice Walker?" I asked.

LaSalle drummed his fingers softly on the arm of his chair. "No."

"She disappeared from a house halfway between here and Fatina's."

"When?"

"March two thousand eight."

"Have you identified a suspect?" LaSalle asked again.

"No," Candice admitted. "But we have the description of a person of interest."

"The painter."

"Yes."

LaSalle inhaled deeply. "I don't know how I can help you. My sister's been missing for almost two years. That's a long time for the trail to go cold."

I frowned and looked at Candice. She mirrored my expression. LaSalle had given us nothing, and we'd pretty much told him all we knew. The guy was a smart son of a peach, I'd give him that.

Candice stood and pulled out her card from her bag. "If you think of anything that might help us in our investigation, would you please call me?"

LaSalle took the card, which he studied before saying, "I'd appreciate it if you'd keep me in the loop, Ms. Fusco."

"Of course," Candice assured him, but her tone was clipped and flinty. "We'll be just as forthcoming as you've been with us."

LaSalle and Candice then had a little stare down, and for a long time no one spoke or moved. Finally LaSalle nodded and motioned us to the door, which he opened for us, and we ducked through and hurried to the car.

The rain had not let up. "My God," I said when I was buckled in again. "Does it always pour like this around here?"

Just then there was a bright flash, followed by a loud clap of thunder. I jumped and Candice turned the engine over. "I'd like to call it a day, but we're not far from Patrice's place. I say we brave the elements and track down her mother."

I nodded. "Sounds like a plan. Hopefully she'll give us more than LaSalle."

We arrived at Patrice's last known address just a few soggy minutes later. A young man who looked about fifteen or sixteen answered the bell. "Wha?" he asked.

"Hello," Candice said formally. "Is your mother or father home?"

"We don't want nothin'," Obviously he thought we were saleswomen.

Candice did her thing with that magic badge and the boy barely looked at it. "My name is Candice Fusco. I'm a private investigator looking into the disappearance of a little girl from this area two years ago. I understand your sister also went missing a few years back?"

The boy looked confused. "You mean my cousin?"

Candice blinked. "Your cousin was the little girl that was found in the pond near here?"

The boy nodded. "Yeah. Her mom don't live here no more."

Candice gave him a patient smile. "Can you possibly give me her phone number or address so that I can talk to her about what happened to your cousin?" The boy appeared to waver. "We just want to ask her about a person of interest in another little girl's disappearance," Candice pressed. "You'd really be helping by telling us where to find your aunt."

After another moment's hesitation, the boy shrugged. "Wait here," he told us befrore partially shutting the door and dashing off into the interior of the house. He came back some minutes later holding a black address book. After flipping through several pages, he read the phone number and the address out loud to Candice, who scribbled it down while I held the umbrella over her head.

We then thanked Patrice's cousin and rushed back through the downpour to the car. As we strapped in, my stomach gurgled. "Uh-oh," Candice said with a smirk.

"Sorry. I only had time for toast and coffee this morning."

Candice eyed the clock on the dash. "It is after twelve," she said. Then she peered out at the rain. "Come on. Let's get some lunch and call ahead to Patrice's mother to tell her we want to talk."

"That is a great idea!" I said. (I was mostly talking about the lunch part.)

We ate at a place called Papa's Café, which served a lot of burgers, shakes, and fries—my kind of sustenance.

Candice called Patrice's mother, whose name was Loraine. It was a good thing we called ahead, because the woman needed lots of coaxing before she agreed to talk with us. And I could only imagine that her reluctance was due to the pain of losing a child and not wanting to revisit that awful day.

Luckily, by the time we'd finished our meal, the rain had given way to a steady drizzle, which was definitely preferable to what we'd ridden through earlier.

While Candice drove, I read her the instructions Loraine had given, which weren't that great, and before long we were definitely lost. "What's that sign say?" Candice asked as we approached another street sign.

"Zephyr Road," I said.

"What street are we looking for?"

"South Stewart Street."

"Are you sure we weren't supposed to go west on I-Twenty?"

"You wrote down east."

Candice grimaced. "I'm turning back," she announced.

"Why don't you use your iPhone?"

"Remember how it got us lost before?"

"Good point. There's always pulling over and asking for directions."

Candice sighed. "Okay," she agreed. "I think there was a gas station back the way we came."

Candice turned around and headed east. At the next intersection she turned right. "Where are you going?" I asked.

"This is the way we came."

"Uh, no, it's not." I was pretty sure it wasn't.

"Yes, it was," Candice insisted.

Because she sounded so certain, I began to doubt myself. Truth be told, the area we were in was pretty sparse, so much of it looked the same to me. "Okay," I conceded. "If you say so."

Abruptly we came to a blinking red light and, just beyond that, a section of the road that was covered with water and a sign that read LOW WATER CROSSING.

"Crap," Candice snapped.

I was now positive that we had not come this way, because I would have remembered the water. "I knew this wasn't right," I muttered to myself.

I expected Candice to turn around, but she inched forward tentatively. "Where are you going?" I asked her.

"See that?" she said, pointing up the road. "That's a gas station. We can ask them for directions."

Immediately I had a bad feeling. "Uh . . . Candice?"

My partner edged closer to the water. "Hold on, Abs, I'm trying to see how deep it is."

"I don't think we should cross it."

Candice sat up and smiled. "It's only an inch or two," she said confidently, and pressed the accelerator. We moved into the shallows with ease, water splashing around the wheel wells. "See?" she told me with a grin. "Easy peezy."

My heart was hammering in my chest, and my radar was sounding the alarm, but there was little I could do.

Not even a moment later the car began to turn at an odd angle. "What's happening?" I gasped, gripping the side of the car.

Candice eased off the accelerator and tried to correct by turning the wheel. No sooner did she do that than the car turned even more sharply and slid along the path of the running water. "Damn it!" she exclaimed.

"Ohmigod?!" I shouted, feeling something hard slam against the underside of the car. Water started leaking through the crack in the bottom of my door. "Candice! We're taking on water!"

"I'm working on it, Abby!" I could see her turning the wheel this way and that, trying to find purchase while she punched the accelerator, but it had no effect; we were sliding right off the road into the river next to us.

My eyes focused on the river for a moment and a terrible feeling really set in. "Ohmigod! *Look out!*"

But there was nothing we could do. Within a few heartbeats the car was caught in the current and Candice and I were in serious trouble.

The Porsche twisted and turned and huge chunks of debris slammed against the sides. All the while the interior continued to take on water. In total panic now I tugged at the door, trying to get it open. "We have to get out of here!" I shouted.

Candice reached over and undid my seat belt, then hers. "Abby!" she commanded. "Try to remain calm!"

In the next instant a giant tree limb slammed into our windshield, spraying us with glass and water. I screamed and flailed my hands around wildly.

Candice grabbed my wrist, pulled me to her, and shook me. "Focus!" she commanded, while water poured into the hole made by the tree trunk.

"We're going to die!"

"No, we're not!"

The car tipped then and sent us tumbling over. Candice fell right on top of me and for one terrible moment my head was completely submerged. I began to flail about again and all I could think about was how I didn't want to drown.

Something else slammed hard into the car, and for a brief second, it tipped up again, allowing Candice to move off me enough for my head to get above water. I sputtered and coughed and felt Candice grip the back of my neck tightly with one hand while she pushed her torso against me.

I had no idea what she was doing until I heard more glass breaking, and realized she was kicking out the glass from her side window. "Stay with me!" she yelled when she finally got the glass free.

I tried to focus on her instructions, which were short and to the point. "Push yourself to the top of the window and get out of the car! Once you're free, hold on until I get out. Whatever you do, don't go into that river without me!"

The moment she finished speaking, I clawed my way forward, through the window, and out onto the side of the car. I held on for dear life, but nearly lost my grip when the car slammed into a large rock and wedged against it. Rushing water surged all around and pressed me up against the side of the car so hard that it was difficult to breathe. *"Candice!"* I screamed, fearing that something had happened to her inside the car.

To my relief she finally appeared, and shimmied out of the window. "Hold on!" she commanded.

But as she said that, movement out the corner of my eye caught my attention. To my horror I watched as a giant tree limb came barreling down the river, aimed straight for us!

I looked up at Candice for a split second. She shook her head no. *"Don't!"* she cried, knowing what I was thinking. She then made a desperate grab for my arm. But I knew there wasn't time for her to help me. That limb would smash me flat in the next second.

And so, with a hard shove I pushed away from the car, and was immediately sucked into the torrent.

Chapter Ten

Okay, so, in hindsight, maybe letting go of the car and taking my chances with a raging river wasn't the best idea, but at the time, it certainly seemed preferable to getting smunched.

Some of what happened next is still a little fuzzy, but pretty much I found myself immediately submerged and tumbling around underwater like a rag doll in a washing machine.

For several panicky seconds, I had no idea which way was up, and I found out quickly that swimming was futile. For the most part I just prayed a lot and tried to hold my breath, hoping that with lungs full of air I might pop back up to the surface before I actually drowned.

Instead, I got clobbered by something heavy that raked against the top of my head and sliced along my scalp. Reflexively I put my hand up and felt the rough uneven texture of bark. I grabbed for it almost without thinking, and that minor move, more than anything, is what saved my life.

I managed to get a firm hold on my first try and pull my head above water. The moment my mouth cleared the surface, I sucked in a huge lungful of air, and continued pumping my chest like a bellows to feed my starving lungs.

Once I was properly fueled with oxygen, I could take stock of my situation—which was grim at best. I discovered that the same massive tree that had come charging at me while I was clutching the side of the car was the one that had chased me downstream, conked me on the head, and was now taking me on a log ride. Together we were barreling down the river with tons of other debris, and in the distance I saw the unmistakable sight of white water. There were rapids ahead. "Oh, *fork* me!" I gasped, and in the back of my mind, for no good reason I mentally patted myself on the back for not swearing, even though my life was about to end and it no longer really mattered.

I eyed the banks on either side of the river. Both were impossible to reach with this kind of a current. I then tried steering the massive piece of wood that was keeping me afloat, but it was too big and the water too fast to get it to cooperate. I tried to think of something, anything, that I could do to avoid the rapids, but absolutely nothing came to mind. I was S.O.L., people. Sheep outta luck.

And then, out of nowhere something long and dark flew out across the river so fast that I almost didn't catch it. In the next instant I heard a *thwang*, followed by a *snap*, and I was suddenly staring at a red rag, dangling from a rope suspended over the river seventy to eighty yards ahead. *"Grab the rope!"* someone on the right bank shouted.

I looked desperately along the right bank for the owner of the command, but couldn't see anyone. *"Focus on the rope!"* he shouted again, and I quickly obeyed, turning my head to focus on that rag dangling just above the water.

My heart felt like it would burst out of my chest; it was beating so hard. The rope was getting closer and closer, and if I didn't manage to grab it, there was little doubt about my chances in those rapids.

"Please, please, please, please, *please* let me make it!" I whimpered as the distance closed between me and the rope.

"Put your arm up!" the voice commanded.

With a trembling hand I did as he said.

"Try and loop your arm over the top, then let go of the tree and grip the rope with your other hand!"

The rope was low enough that I felt I could do it. I was headed straight for that red flag. Drawing closer, and closer, I had all my attention focused on it when something smacked hard against my shin and I cried out. As I did so, I lost my grip on the limb, sank under the water, and lost sight of the rope. Using every ounce of energy I had left, I kicked my legs and reached overhead. My palm connected with something and reflexively I closed my fingers around it.

I could have wept with relief when I realized I'd somehow managed to grab the rope! Holding on for dear life with one hand, I managed to clutch it with my other too, but quickly discovered that the current was working against me. It was so strong that it wouldn't allow me to get closer to the rope so that I could pick my head up out of the water.

I tried twisting and turning, but that almost cost me the hold on the rope. With significant effort I pulled myself up like doing a chin-up and managed to get my mouth clear enough to take a gulp of air before I had to relax my arms again and sank under the swift water. I realized that my situation was incredibly dire. I knew I probably had enough energy for one or two more chin-ups before my arms would give out. I barely had enough reserve strength to hold on to the rope. Still, I counted to three, and pulled. I managed to get my chin above water long enough for a couple of pants while I considered my options.

I thought about trying to shimmy sideways along the rope to make it to the bank, but that would take time, and I knew I couldn't hold my breath long enough to make it.

What I really needed was air, and that's what drove me to relax my arms, sink under the water, and use my body to twist onto my back. With my arms crossed behind my head, I was able to prop my head just above the waterline. I closed my eyes and just focused on filling my lungs with air.

I was at that point where I was ready to consider

what I could do next to get out of this mess when I felt a tremendous tug on the line. Arching my back and looking over my left shoulder, I found the source; there was a huge tree branch snagging the line. And, just behind that, something that looked like a refrigerator coming fast and furious down the river.

Luckily, it was far enough off to my left not to hit me directly. Unluckily, I figured that once it hit the rope, it could very well snap the line and all that effort I'd exerted just to hold on would be wasted.

About then I reached that moment that happens in a life-or-death situation where you're just so tired, and your situation is just so bad, that you mentally give up and let go. There was no way I was going to make it; too many variables were against me. It was useless.

In those next few seconds my life did not flash before my eyes. I didn't think about Dutch, or my family, my friends, or even my dogs.

I wasn't sad, or afraid, or worried about what would happen next. I suppose I just felt numb. Almost peaceful. Really, I think I was simply resigned.

I took one last big gulp of air.

Counted to three.

Closed my eyes.

And let go of the rope.

I sank under the water for only a second before something fixed around my waist and slammed me into something hard. I felt a crushing blow to my ribs, but I was so tired and so defeated that I did little more than jerk reflexively.

And I wasn't really able to figure out what was happening to me, although I was aware of moving against the current. Slowly, methodically, I was traveling upstream.

And then that instinctual reaction we have to breathe kicked in, and I got my head above water again and gasped for air. "Hold on to me!" someone shouted.

I was too exhausted to speak, and even though my eyes were open, I couldn't get them to focus. And I was certainly too exhausted to hold on to anything. My arms and legs were like rubber and I was now fully aware that the water was cold and I was freezing. Odd how I hadn't noticed that before.

"You have to try! Come on, ma'am! Put your arms around my neck and hold on!"

Was he kidding?

"I can't move us to the shore if you don't help me!"

Nope. Not kidding.

I closed my eyes again and wished to be anywhere else in the world except here. Where could a girl get a pair of ruby slippers when she needed them?

That arm acting like a vise grip around my waist shook me, and my eyes opened. Lazily I stared up and managed to focus my gaze. Antoine LaSalle's fierce expression did a lot to revive me. "I am not letting go of you!" he shouted so loud I winced. "You are *not* drowning today—do you hear me?"

I managed a tiny nod.

"So put your arms around my neck so we can get out of this river!"

Tears welled in my eyes. How the heck was I going to

manage that? I could barely stay conscious. Still, I decided to try.

Slowly and with a great deal of difficulty, I managed to cup my hands behind Antoine's neck. He then shifted his weight so that my legs looped around his waist and I was pinned to him by the force of the river.

"Don't let go!" he shouted in my ear.

I winced again and thought he didn't have to yell at me. I was doing my best after all.

I placed my head against his chest. He was so nice and warm compared with the water. I watched it race past us, and felt it against my back. I thought it was a good thing that Antoine was so tall. He could touch the bottom here. I could feel him taking slow, methodical steps through the water. I could also see the strain on his neck muscles as he gripped a rope attached to something onshore and slowly, step by step he pulled us forward.

And then, my back cleared the water. A few moments later, my hips were above the waterline too, and just another couple of steps and Antoine had us out of the raging river.

He sank to his knees, breathing hard, and laid me gently on the ground. I closed my eyes, grateful for having met this man that I'd obviously misjudged, and waited for feeling to return to my limbs. Around us I heard crashing sounds and I opened my eyes to see a bunch of firemen charging through the woods to get to us.

Antoine unfastened the harness that was tied around his waist, and tossed it to the side. Rescue workers swarmed around us and I was eased onto a backboard, then bundled by a blanket and told not to move.

A penlight was flashed into my eyes, and the paramedic hovering over me made a comment about a head wound. I reached up and felt the top of my head, realizing it was throbbing. Sure enough, when I pulled my hand away, it was smeared with red.

"Easy there," said the paramedic, laying my hand by my side. "Just try to lie still."

"Abby!" shouted a familiar voice.

"Candice?" I said, my voice no louder than a whisper.

"Ohmigod!" she replied from just off to my right. "Abby!"

Out the corner of my eye I could see her, soaked to the skin and bundled in her own blanket, as she tried to push through two rescue workers to get to me. "Ma'am!" one of them yelled at her as she shoved her way forward. "Let our men work on her for now. You can see her in a moment."

"Is she all right?" Candice asked, her voice pitchy and panicked.

I managed to lift my hand and wave at her. "I'm okay," I croaked.

Candice's knees gave out from under her and she would have sunk to the ground if the rescue workers hadn't been holding her. They helped her back over to high ground, and my backboard was picked up by four rescue workers who then carried me up a slope to a waiting ambulance. Before I could even protest, I was loaded into the back, and after Candice was helped up to sit next to me, we were whisked off to the hospital.

Later that afternoon the atmosphere got *really* chilly. A cold front in the form of our significant others blew into south Dallas and greeted the both of us with some mighty frigid air.

Candice and I had both agreed that, upon reaching the hospital, we would do our best to cover our tracks and not tell Dutch and Brice what had actually happened, and we were well on our way to inventing plausible scenarios for how we'd managed to get so banged up when we saw a CNN broadcast on one of the hospital TVs, featuring an overhead shot of Candice perched precariously on top of her yellow Porsche while the river raged around her. In the next scene, the helicopter news crew captured my rather dramatic rescue as Antoine waded the last few feet to shore with me clinging to his chest.

And just two hours later the cold front blew in.

"What the hell were you two *thinking*?" Brice demanded, pacing the floor in front of my gurney.

"The water didn't look that deep," I said, trying to defend Candice from the earful I figured she was about to get.

"Don't you know not to drive through running water?" Brice snapped. I noticed he was not directly addressing Candice. Instead he kept his comments focused on the floor while he paced angrily back and forth.

"I've driven through way deeper water than that," I

replied. "It rains in Michigan all the time, and I've never had a problem crossing water back home."

"There's a difference between moving water and still water," Brice growled, looking up to lock eyes with me. "It only takes a few inches of running water to carry a car off a road."

"Oh," I said. I glanced at Candice, who looked terribly guilt-ridden while she sat in a nearby chair, wearing a pair of scrubs and a thick blanket. "I should have known better," she admitted. Glancing up at me with pitifully sad eyes, she said, "I am so, *so* sorry, Abby."

I tried to shrug, but I was too stiff and sore to pull it off. "It's okay," I told her. "We both made it."

Dutch had not said a word. Instead he wore his cop face, but his lips were pressed together so tightly that I knew he was super pissed.

"What the hell are you two doing this far north anyway?" Brice asked. Clearly he wasn't through giving us a tongue-lashing.

"Investigating a case," Candice told him.

Brice stopped his pacing abruptly and his head finally snapped in Candice's direction. "What case?"

"A little girl went missing and I was hired to look into it. Abby's been helping me out with some of the legwork."

At that moment Antoine LaSalle popped his head into my room. "Oh, sorry," he said, seeing it full of people. "The nurse said I could come see you."

I almost laughed at Dutch and Brice's reaction when they took in the six-foot-five man of steel in the doorway. "Lieutenant!" I said, happy to change the subject.

Belatedly I noticed the thick bandages on his hands, wrists, and arms. "God! What happened?"

LaSalle waved off my concern. "Rope burns," he said. "Nothing major."

But as he took a step, I could see that he favored his left leg, and like me, he had scratches all along his cheeks, upper arms, and forehead.

Dutch stepped toward him and offered his hand. "Special Agent Dutch Rivers," he said formally.

"Lieutenant Antoine LaSalle," my savior replied, holding up his bandaged hand sheepishly. Dutch lowered his immediately.

"Sorry," he said.

"Don't sweat it, sir," Antoine told him.

"I take it you were one of the rescuers?" Dutch asked.

"I helped Ms. Cooper out of the river."

"Helped me out of the river," I repeated with a smile. "It's like he's talking about giving me a hand out of the pool. The lieutenant here saved my life, although I'm still not sure how you managed to get that rope across the river in time."

Antoine seemed amused. "Crossbow," he said, holding his arms the way he would if he were shooting one. "I got a rope attached to the end of the arrow and shot it into a tree on the far side of the river. I then had to hope you could hold on long enough for me to get to you, using my climbing harness and another line."

"You're a regular G.I. Joe," I said, thoroughly impressed.

"How did you even find us?" Candice asked.

Antoine cleared his throat and almost didn't answer, but as we all waited for him to say something, he finally admitted, "I followed you after you left my house."

Dutch moved away from LaSalle to stand next to me. The move was subtle, but I knew it was meant to let La-Salle know that I had protection.

"Followed them?" Brice said, his eyes narrowing. "Why were you following them, exactly?"

The lieutenant seemed to take the question in stride. "Ms. Cooper and Ms. Fusco came to my house to ask about my little sister, and I wasn't sure if they were legit or not."

"I don't understand," Candice pressed. "Why wouldn't we be legit?"

"The state of Texas has no record of your PI license, ma'am."

Candice's cheeks flushed bright red and Brice gave her a look like, "Told you so."

There was an awkward silence before I said, "Well, I'm certainly not going to hold it against you, Lieutenant. Thank you very, very much for checking up on us. And thank you double for risking your own life to save mine."

Antoine nodded knowingly. "Maybe you'll give me a call and let me know how your investigation is progressing?"

My eyes swiveled to Candice. We both knew that he'd more than earned that with his heroics. "Sure," she said, but her eyes and tone suggested otherwise. "We'll make sure to loop you in the moment we have new intel."

LaSalle studied Candice for a brief moment; he saw right through her words. But he didn't press it. Instead he bowed his head formally, wished me a speedy recovery, and departed.

After he left, Brice turned on Candice. "I can't believe you're walking around conducting investigations without a PI license!"

It was obvious that Candice had officially had enough of being yelled at because her eyebrows lowered dangerously and she replied, "Really? Given the extensive search you've personally conducted into my background, *you* can't believe it?"

"I'm serious, Candice," Brice said.

"I never said you weren't."

"All it takes is one complaint to the state licensing board and your request for PI status is denied."

"Do I look stupid to you?" Candice snapped. "Seriously, Brice! Sometimes you act like you're the only one who's aware of the consequences. Some of us are also educated enough to fully understand the risks involved and are still prepared to assume them."

Brice folded his arms across his chest and glared hard at her. "Yes. We've all seen firsthand today what you're willing to risk, and the consequences that follow."

Candice's eyes grew huge and her mouth fell open.

I sucked in a breath and held a hand to my mouth.

Even Dutch cleared his throat uncomfortably. "Sir,"

he said softly, but Brice held his stance and continued to glare hard at Candice, who glared hard right back. Dutch left my side and walked over to Harrison. Laying a hand on his arm, he said, "Sir, come on. Let's get some air."

But before they could leave, Candice lost it and yelled, "I want you out of my condo, *tonight*!"

Brice appeared taken aback, but quickly recovered. "No problem!"

"Good!"

"Great!"

"Stop it!" I shouted as the nurse came running into the room.

"*What* is going on in here?" she demanded.

Candice pointed to Brice, who pointed back at her, and together they both insisted that the other one started it. In any other situation, the scene would have been comical, but here in the hospital after what I'd been through that afternoon, it was really upsetting.

I started to cry as Dutch worked to calm both Harrison and Candice down, and the nurse told them all to leave until the doctor could bring me the results of the CT scan.

Candice got up and shuffled out of the room and Harrison followed. Dutch was about to go as well when he looked back at me and saw that the floodgates had opened. He and the nurse exchanged a look, and she nodded at him that it was okay to stay with me before she also left the room.

Dutch came over and surprised me by climbing right

into bed and wrapping his arms tight around me, which only made the crying worse.

"Shhh," he whispered, kissing my temple. "It's okay, dollface. You're okay. You're safe and I won't let anything bad happen to you ever again."

After a bit I was able to collect myself. "Sorry," I said, feeling a little embarrassed that I'd dissolved into tears. "I don't know what's wrong with me."

"You've got a screw loose."

I pulled my head back to look up at him. "What?"

Dutch touched the side of my head. "In here," he explained. "Loose screw." I just blinked at him, trying to understand how he could say something like that to me. "I've heard it rattling around, you know," he added. "Every time you get yourself into some big mess, I hear it clinking around inside your skull." He then cupped the side of my head and tilted it slightly to the right, then to the left. "Hear that?" he asked. "Clink, clink, clink. Loose screw." And then he broke into a grin.

I couldn't help it; I smiled too. And then I started to laugh, and once I'd started, I really couldn't stop.

Dutch was laughing too, and that's how the doctor found us when he brought my scan into the room. "Glad to see you're feeling better," he said to me.

I wiped my eyes, still giggling a little. "They sent in a comedian," I said, nudging Dutch.

The doctor looked at him as if he wanted to share the joke, but Dutch just pointed to his chest and said, "Mechanic. I was sent here about a rattle."

The doctor was still looking at us expectantly, but we

didn't fill him in. Instead we just continued to chuckle and nudge each other. Finally the poor man in the lab coat got to the point of his visit. "Your CT scan is clear," he said. "There's no evidence of concussion or internal hemorrhaging."

"Phew!" I said.

"I'd still like to keep you here for observation, but I know when we talked earlier, you were dead set against it."

"I was."

"Is there someone who can stay with you tonight and watch for any symptoms of trauma?"

I nudged Dutch again. "My mechanic friend here might be willing."

"I'll take care of her, Doc."

"All right, then, Ms. Cooper, I'll release you. Remember that the staples in your scalp will need to remain in place for the next fourteen days. Don't wash your hair or swim in a pool until they've been removed, and wear a shower cap when you bathe."

I scowled. "Great. Two full weeks of bad hair."

"Better than getting an infection and having your whole head swell up," the doctor replied.

"True."

The doctor reached inside his pocket and pulled out a prescription pad. He scribbled out two separate scripts for me and handed those to Dutch. "Your antibiotics and pain meds," he said. Then he wished me well, said a nurse would be in shortly to help me get into some scrubs (my own clothes were still wet), and that I'd be free to go.

Dutch left me when the nurse came in, and I was very grateful for her help into the scrubs because my body decided it'd been tossed around enough for one day and pretty much everything hurt. "You'll want to take it very easy for the next couple of days," the nurse told me as I eased into the wheelchair. I thought that it was mighty good of her to point out the obvious.

When she wheeled me out to the front, I was relieved to find Candice and Brice looking slightly less hostile. They were even sitting next to each other in the waiting room, and Dutch was talking softly to them. I figured he was brokering a peace agreement.

Brice went to get the car when I showed up, and Candice and Dutch both helped me into the front seat, where I'd have the most legroom. Brice drove first to a pharmacy, where Dutch dropped off my script; then we hit a drive-through for some grub, which was a relief because I was famished. We ate while they filled my prescriptions, and I barely noticed the lack of conversation.

I fell asleep almost as soon as we hit the road again and woke up to find Brice lifting me out of the car. "Where's Dutch?" I asked, startled that Harrison was the one toting me out of the car.

"I'm right here, doll," Dutch said. "Agent Harrison offered to take you inside because of my back."

"I'll try not to drop you," Brice joked.

"Can't be worse than anything else I've been through today," I replied drily.

Dutch hurried to unlock the door and Brice paused

at the entrance and said, "Shall I carry you over the threshold?"

I laughed but stopped abruptly when I caught sight of the look on both Dutch's and Candice's faces.

Uh-oh.

"Actually, sir, I think I can make it from here," I told him, and tried to wriggle out of his arms.

Harrison made a derisive sound and carried me in through the door anyway, where he gently laid me on the couch, which still had the pillows and blankets from Dutch's turn there.

Harrison then smiled, leaned over, and gave me a peck on the cheek before turning back to Dutch, who did not look happy. Like ... at ... all.

Still, Brice didn't appear to notice because he gave Dutch a pat on the shoulder and said, "I'll swing by and pick you up in the morning."

"Thank you, sir," Dutch said stiffly.

Brice moved to the doorway, where Candice also stood rigidly, but her expression was cool and contained. Still, Brice must have been far more attuned to her, because he paused and asked, "What now?"

Candice took a breath, shifted her eyes to me, and said, "Good night, Abby. I'll call you in the morning to see how you are."

"Thanks. Have a good night."

After they left, Dutch fluffed up my pillows and covered me with a blanket before taking a seat at the other end of the couch. "Now that they've gone," he said, "spill it."

"Spill what?"

Dutch cocked an eyebrow at me. "What?" I said, still trying to figure out what he meant.

"Lieutenant LaSalle?" Dutch said, his question hanging in the air.

Uh-oh. He was on to us. "Great guy," I said with enthusiasm.

Dutch sighed. "You're impossible," he growled.

"I don't know what you want me to say." I was sticking to my guns for all it was worth, really hoping he hadn't already connected the dots.

Dutch tapped his finger on the arm of the couch, still looking skeptically at me. "Really?"

"Really."

"Funny how his last name fits the missing-persons file of a little girl from the boxes you audited ten days ago."

Aw, crap. He'd figured it all out.

"It was Candice's idea!" I said in a rush. I'd deal with the guilt of throwing her under the bus later.

"Oh, I'll bet it was," he said. "And I'll bet you jumped right on that bandwagon."

"You know how hard she is to stop once she's got her mind made up."

Dutch sighed heavily and rubbed his eyes. "What am I gonna do with you?" he whispered.

"Make me some tea and cookies?" I suggested helpfully.

Dutch actually laughed, but he remained on the couch and leaned his head back to stare at the ceiling. "I hate it when you and Candice go off investigating."

"You hate it when I go off with anyone to investigate.

I mean, you almost didn't let me go with Oscar the other day."

Dutch swiveled his head to stare hard at me. "Yes," he said. "And look what happened."

"Okay, so that was a bad example."

"No, Abs, you see, that's just it. That wasn't a *bad* example. That was a *typical* example of what happens when you work a case. It's like you have a giant target on your back, and bad stuff just finds you."

"But at least now I know how to shoot a gun," I suggested.

Again, Dutch laughed, but it sounded hollow. "I'm never going to win this argument, am I?"

"If by winning you mean chaining me to the couch or a desk and ordering me not to help out Candice or you guys in the field now and again, then yes. You're never going to win."

"I could turn you in to Harrison, you know. He'd completely lose it if he knew you two were working one of his cases."

"Yes," I agreed. "You could do that. But I don't think you'd like the consequences." For emphasis I eyed the couch meaningfully.

"You'd kick me out of the bedroom?"

"In a heartbeat, cowboy."

"Harsh."

"Just the way I roll."

"How's your head?"

I smiled. "It makes this rattling noise every time I move it. I think there might be a screw loose."

Chapter Eleven

I was in no shape to do any further investigating for the next several days. If I'd thought my body was sore the day I'd nearly drowned, it was nothing compared with how I felt the next day. I could barely move. Dutch offered to stay home and watch over me, but Candice showed up with a breakfast burrito and coffee, then insisted on hanging out with me so that he could go to work.

Brice picked Dutch up about ten minutes later, which was a relief because my sweetheart was starting to hover, and not in a good way.

"Thank God," I said after the door closed behind him.

Candice chuckled. "He's just worried about you."

I slanted my lids a little. "Brice seemed pretty worried about you too, ya know."

"Oh?" Candice said, her voice mocking me. "What gave it away? The yelling, the pacing, or the issuing of blame?"

I shook my head. "You just don't get it, do you, Cassidy?"

"What don't I get, Sundance?"

"Have you noticed that Brice never loses his cool with anyone—and I do mean *anyone*—but you?"

"I hardly think that means he cares."

I laughed. "Oh, I think that means he cares way more than he wants to."

Candice considered me for a moment. "So you believe he's acting like a jerk *because* he likes me?"

"No," I said. "He's acting like a jerk because he *adores* you. He was pissed off yesterday because you managed to get yourself into a situation that almost killed you."

Candice winced, and I realized she still felt terribly guilty. "That was one of my dumber moves," she conceded.

"Honey," I said, leaning forward with a grunt to grab her hand. "How could you have known? Where we come from, you see a big ol' puddle, you drive right into it and just hope your exhaust pipe doesn't clog."

"I am really, *really* sorry, Abby."

"Don't be," I said. "It was an accident and they happen to even the most cautious and careful of people. We both survived and we're both fine, so 'nough said."

Candice grinned. "You're pretty much the best person I know."

I rolled my eyes and felt my cheeks heat. "Oh, whatever," I said with a laugh. "The point of this conversation was not to make you feel guilty. It was to let you know that Brice has some pretty intense feelings for you, and you can either continue to push him away or you can sit him down and take a chance and tell him how *you* feel."

"Why do I have to go first?"

"Someone's got to."

"He's moving out later today, you know."

"Wait, what?" I was stunned. When I saw them together in the waiting room, I thought that Dutch had managed to help temper their feud. "Why didn't you try to make up with him and tell him to stay?"

"I let him stay the night last night," Candice said weakly.

"Oh, and I'll bet you handed him a pillow and pointed him toward the couch, right?"

Candice flushed. "You don't understand," she said. "Abby, this is the first serious relationship I've had with anyone since my ex-husband, and we both know what a train wreck that was."

"What about that married guy you dated?" I asked. "I thought that was pretty serious too."

Candice waved her hand as if she were shooing away a fly. "Oh, please. Like being the other woman is ever a serious relationship."

"Okay, so why is this so incredibly scary for you?"

Candice fiddled with the zipper on her leather jacket. "Because I like Brice the most," she finally said.

"And?"

"And if I screw it up—as I'm likely to—I don't know how I'll come back from it."

If I'd been able to move, I would have gotten up and gone over to my friend and given her a great big hug. "Sweetie," I said gently. "The only way to screw it up is to forget how much you care about him. As long as you take pains to remember how much you love him every day you're with him, there's no way this can't work out."

Candice looked up and met my eyes. It was odd, but in my mind I felt like she'd just had one of those "Aha" moments.

"Okay," she said. "I get it."

"Good. Now call him. Tell him not to move out."

Candice looked panicked. "What? *Now?*"

"Right now," I said firmly. "This second."

My friend eyed her watch. "But I don't think he's even made it to work yet."

"What does that have to do with anything?"

"Dutch'll overhear."

"Excuses, excuses," I sang. "Call him."

It took a few more minutes of insisting, but Candice did eventually break down and call Brice. She wandered off to another room to talk to him, and when she came back, she looked both relieved and happier. "How'd it go?"

"Good."

I sighed and mocked, "Whoa, there, girl! Don't unload all the details at once!"

Candice sat back down on the couch, smiling. "I told him that I'd thought about it, and I really wanted a chance to cool down and talk to him about our relationship and that I didn't want to rush him into making any sudden drastic decisions."

My brow furrowed. "Where in that did you happen to mention the part about him not moving out?"

Candice grinned. "Right after that. He promised to cancel the moving van and stick it out at my place for another week or two."

While not the gigantic declaration of love I was hoping for, at least with these two, it was a start. "Good for you," I told her. A short silence followed that and I asked, "So what now?"

Candice got up and walked toward the door. "Now that you're fed and watered, I'm off to the Apple Store to replace the Mac."

I made a face. "It was in the car with us yesterday, wasn't it?"

Candice nodded. "Yep."

"Did you lose everything?"

"No, thank God. I back up my laptop every night, and I was smart enough to scan the girls' files into my computer the day I made copies—so it should be easy to just transfer the data and print them out again. I should only be gone a couple of hours and I can bring you back some lunch after I'm done with the data transfer."

"You and your technobabble," I said. "You know what I hear when you say stuff like that?"

Candice grinned. "What?"

"Blah, blah, blah, laptop, blah, blah, blah, copies, blah, blah, blah, lunch in two hours."

Candice sighed dramatically. "I'll pull you into the twenty-first century yet, Sundance," she said, then turned to the door. She seemed to have second thoughts, though, and pivoted back around to me. "Say, while I'm at the Apple Store, did you want me to replace your phone for you?"

I perked up at that. By some miracle, my purse had been recovered by the firefighters when they dragged Candice's car out of the river, but the phone was toast. "Oh, man! I've wanted an excuse to buy an iPhone forever! I can write you a check," I said, wondering where I'd put my checkbook when I'd unpacked the other day.

Candice slung her purse over her shoulder. "Forget about it," she said. "This one's on me."

My eyes widened. "You sure?"

Candice stepped through the doorway. "Yep. It's the least I can do after almost killing you yesterday. Are you going to be okay for the next couple of hours?"

"I should be fine."

"Great. I'll be back with some lunch around noon."

Dutch came home at six to relieve Candice. She'd spent most of the afternoon putting together the soggy notes from the river with what she'd managed to recover from her backup hard drive. She also called Patrice's mother and apologized for not showing up for the interview, saying only that we'd had car trouble. The two talked on the phone and scheduled another meeting for the following Monday.

After Candice left, Dutch retrieved something from the car. It was gift wrapped. "Awww!" I exclaimed when he handed it to me. "You got me something?"

"I did," he said. I thought it was adorable how his chest puffed out a little like he knew he was all that and a bag of cheese puffs.

I ripped open the package and stared at a brand-new BlackBerry. "Uh . . . ," I said, completely surprised.

"To replace the phone you lost in the river," he said. "I know you didn't really like your old one, and I thought this might be a good fit for you."

"Uh . . ."

"It has e-mail and a camera and great service. And don't worry, it doesn't have a GPS signal embedded in it. I'll be completely unaware of your every move." That had been a sore spot for us in the past.

I laughed nervously, just as my brand-new iPhone chimed with an incoming text.

"What's that?" Dutch asked, glancing to the side table where the iPhone was still making noise.

"Nothing!" I said quickly while holding up the Black-Berry and trying to distract him. "This is the greatest gift in the whole world, Dutch! Thank you!"

Dutch nodded but ignored my efforts to distract him. Instead he reached over and picked up the iPhone. "Incoming text from Candice," he said, eyeing the screen. "She says she's so glad that you and she now have the same phone."

When he looked back at me, I gave him the biggest smile I could muster. "I can return the iPhone!"

Dutch sighed and handed me Candice's gift. "Have you already set up your playlists?"

I felt a pang of guilt. I'd spent most of the afternoon buying songs on iTunes. "Maybe?"

He took the BlackBerry out of my hands. "How about I swap this out for a sound dock so you can play your tunes in here?"

I fluttered my lids at him. "I think I love you."

Dutch chuckled and got up. "I'll make us some dinner. And then there's something I want you to look at."

After dinner he handed me a file. "What's this?" I asked, opening it and immediately wishing I hadn't. "Gah!" I said, eyeing the grizzly crime-scene photo of the body of a man—sans head—covered in bruises and burns and cuts. Clearly he'd been through some kind of hell before his head was lopped off.

"Sorry. Forgot the first photo is a rough one."

I closed the file. "Thanks, at least, for letting me eat dinner before showing me that."

"You're welcome," he said with a smile. "Did you get anything?"

"Did I get anything? Like, you seriously think I'm going to take one look at that god-awful picture and tell you who done it?"

Dutch smiled patiently. "It's a lot like those other two cases. Remember the other two men who were found decapitated? You said you didn't think they were drug related but that there was a definite connection between them?"

I blinked. "Oh, yeah," I said, opening the file back up but avoiding the photos and flipping to the written details. "Similar MO here."

"His body was found about a month after Felix Lopez, in April of two thousand nine. The only thing we can find that connects the three cases is that they all lived within the same two-mile radius."

While Dutch was talking, I was taking in the facts on the page I was skimming. Avril Brown was an eighteen-year-old male of mixed race. He'd been living in Houston with his single mother until he got into serious trouble at the early age of fourteen when he'd participated in the gang rape of a thirteen-year-old girl. He'd been tried as an adult, but because he'd made a deal with the DA to identify the other assailants, he'd spent only two years in jail before his release.

The notes in the file documented interviews with friends, family, and acquaintances, who all swore that once Brown was released from prison and taken in by his paternal grandfather in Dallas, he'd turned a major corner and been really trying to get his act together. At the time of his death, he was on his way to completing his GED, was working forty hours a week at his grandfather's mini-mart, and often helped some of his elderly neighbors with odd jobs around the hood.

"I talked to the grandfather this morning," Dutch was

telling me. "He swears on his grandson's grave that Avril wasn't involved in any gangs or narcotics dealing."

"But this has the signature of a Mexican Mafia hit," I said. The clincher was the decapitation. "Have they found the head?"

"No."

"He was tortured," I said. "That's different from the other two cases."

"Yep."

"He either knew something or it was personal," I added, feeling my way along the energy. "Someone tortured him to get information or wanted him to really suffer before he died."

"What could he know?" Dutch asked me.

"I have no idea," I said. "But I don't think this was drug related. There's something else here. It's like, someone wanted information, but they also really wanted Brown to feel the pain. I don't know who he pissed off, Dutch, but it was someone with a grudge."

"One of the guys he accused in the gang rape?"

I nodded, but I wasn't sure my radar agreed. "Maybe," I said. "It might be worth taking a look at who Avril turned over to get a lighter sentence. If one of them got out and tracked Avril down, then he could have been involved in the murder."

"But what about the other two guys?" Dutch pressed. "How do they relate to that theory?"

I rolled my head from side to side trying to relieve the stiffness. "I don't know," I admitted. "Maybe the three guys knew each other—I mean, they were living in the same two-mile radius. Maybe they were friends, and if Avril was the last one killed, then maybe the first two were killed to get information about where Avril was."

Dutch's brow furrowed. "It wasn't like he was hard to find, Abs. A basic records search brought him up right away."

I sighed and shrugged my shoulders. "Okay, so I know it doesn't add up, but I have to be true to what my gut is saying, and it says there's a connection."

Dutch took the file back. "You're sure?"

I closed my eyes and focused all my intuitive power on the three dead men. "I'm sure."

Dutch leaned in and gave me a kiss on the cheek. "Okay, Edgar. I'll take some guys off the other stuff you've given us and put them on this."

"Good," I said, but deep down I was really afraid it wasn't going to make a bit of difference and that the one missing piece in how these three deaths were connected was the most urgent to identify.

Dutch and I spent much of the weekend taking it easy and recovering from our various flesh wounds. And I would have been happy to continue being a lounge lizard if it weren't for the fact that I couldn't shampoo my hair. What was worse was that I'd also been advised by the discharge nurse not to brush it, as if I wasn't careful, I could end up pulling out one of the staples.

I missed the shower something fierce—baths just weren't cutting it—and I didn't know how I was going to make it a whole two weeks before I could scrub-a-dub-dub under the showerhead.

Monday morning Dutch headed in early, probably to talk to Harrison about the Avril, Felix, and Jason connection, and a bit later Candice showed up with a hot cup of coffee and an enthusiastic, "Ready?"

For the record, I was not ready. "My hair looks like crap."

"It looks fine," she lied. "Just pull it back with a scrunchie and let's roll."

"I can't go out looking like this!" I protested.

Candice wheeled me around and trotted me into the bathroom. Being very careful, she managed to comb out some of the worst patches, and pull my locks into a ponytail with a triumphant, "Ta-da!"

I made a face in the mirror. "Maybe I should wear a bag. You know, like the Unknown Comic?"

"Or you can stop worrying about it and come on already. We've got to get to Patrice's mom's by noon."

I sighed dramatically and shrugged into my jacket. "Fine."

Candice drove at very moderate speeds all the way to Dallas, which impressed me, because I will admit I was a little nervous when we went outside and I saw that the yellow Porsche had been replaced by a red one.

"This the new car?" I'd asked.

Candice shook her head. "Just a rental. The other one was fully insured, thank God, but I don't know that I'm going to stick with Porsche. I need a few more days behind the wheel to be sure this is the make and model for me."

At least in the loaner the navigational system was

working and we found Loraine Walker's house without issue.

We parked in the drive and headed up the cement walk, which was badly cracked and in need of repair. The same could be said of the house. It looked like it had seen far better days. The once white paint had faded to a dirty gray, peeling in several patches, while the worn shutters hung limply at odd angles.

The flower beds and lawn were strewn with weeds and debris, making the place appear cluttered. The wooden steps leading to the front door creaked loudly, protesting our weight, and somewhere around back a dog barked. Candice knocked and we waited several seconds before the door was pulled open.

A woman in her mid to late forties stood opposite us. She appeared haggard and defeated. Her large brown eyes widened slightly when she saw us, but other than that, there was little expression. "You the investigators?" she asked.

"We are, ma'am," Candice confirmed, extending her hand. "I'm Candice Fusco, and this is my associate Abigail Cooper."

Loraine pumped Candice's hand only once before she let go and waved us in. "Might as well get this over with," she said.

She didn't have any hint of an accent; in fact, there wasn't much in her voice at all. Her tone was flat and somewhat hoarse, the product of too many cigarettes or too much hard living.

The house smelled terrible, like must, sweat, and

smoke all overpowering my nostrils together. I noticed right away the lit cigarette on the far side of the room next to an easy chair. Loraine sat down and immediately picked it up, striking that smoker's pose with one arm across her middle and the other arm propped up on it by the elbow. "What you wanna know?"

She said the words "What you" like "Whatchoo," and given the hoarseness of her voice to my ears, it sounded like a sneeze.

Candice took a seat on a nearby chair, and I decided to stand and let my radar feel the space out.

"As I said on the phone, we're investigating the ab-duction of two other little girls about the same age as Patrice when she went missing," my partner began.

"Patrice drowned," Loraine said, and there was a note of sorrow in her voice as she spoke her daughter's name.

Candice clasped her hands together. I could sense she was working to be patient with this woman. "Yes, ma'am," Candice said. "I've read about your daughter's death in the newspaper and I'm so sorry for your loss. But I'm not sure that what happened to Patrice was an accident."

For the first time since we'd entered the shabby home, there were signs of life in Loraine's eyes. "You don't?"

Candice shook her head. "That's why I wanted to talk with you, Mrs. Walker. After looking into these other two abductions, we think that perhaps your daughter might fit the profile of these other two cases."

"You think someone took her and murdered her?"

"We think it's a possibility."

Loraine took a long pull off her cigarette. Her fingers shook slightly as she inhaled. "I been telling that to the police for years," she said. "But they don't want to listen. They said that Patrice walked all the way to that pond and fell in. They said she was the cause of her own death, but I knew different. I *knew* that child wouldn't'a done that. Patrice couldn't swim and she was scared of water. She didn't even like to take a bath. She wouldn't go there on her own, nuh-uh."

"What can you tell us about the day that Patrice disappeared?"

Loraine jammed her bud into the ashtray on the table and immediately reached for a replacement. Once she had it lit, she said, "Was a Tuesday. I remember 'cause I had to work the afternoon shift at the hospital."

"You worked at a hospital?"

"I'm a nurse," she said, and seemed to catch herself. "*Was* a nurse. I had my license pulled last year 'cause they said I stole some OxyContin."

Neither Candice nor I commented on that admission. I knew that Loraine had stolen the drugs—I could see the guilt in her energy—and I'm pretty sure Candice picked up on it too. "What time did your shift start?" Candice asked, steering us back to the topic at hand.

"Three. Patrice usually got home around three fifteen, and she'd call me and leave me a voice mail when she got in to let me know she was safe. But that day I didn't get no voice mail, and we was really busy too, so I didn't have a chance to call her until my break at seven."

"Did you speak with her?"

Loraine shook her head. "She didn't answer the phone. So then I got worried and called my neighbor to go over and check on her, but Patrice wasn't home and my neighbor said it didn't look like she'd come home from school."

"Did you call the police?"

Loraine bit her lip and lowered her eyes. "No."

Candice and I exchanged a look. "No?" she asked.

Loraine took a deep ragged breath. "Patrice was only ten years old. She was mature for her age, but I was scared the police would ask me why she was home by herself and call CPS on me. I had just gotten my nursing license and we was living in my mama's house—she was in hospice by then—and Mama said that me and Patrice could stay there rent free until I could save up enough to get us our own place. Weren't no one to look after Patrice but me, and I had to work to put food on the table."

"So when did you alert the police that she was missing?"

"The next day, after I spent all night looking for her myself."

I could tell that Loraine had been harshly judged for that decision. It showed in her eyes as she stared defiantly at Candice, as if she was waiting for her to say something cruel like Loraine should have known better.

"That must have been a very difficult call to make," Candice said kindly. "I'll bet you've second-guessed yourself about waiting to place that call a thousand times since then."

Loraine looked surprised. "More like a million times," she said. "I knew I could lose Patrice either way."

"I'm so sorry."

Patrice smoked her cigarette for a minute before saying anything else. "The police didn't find her until six weeks later, and I knew the minute that patrol car stopped in front of my house she was dead. They told me they found her in a pond a mile away. I told them that if that's where they found my baby, then they needed to find out who killed her 'cause Patrice wouldn't go there by herself. She just wouldn't."

"What'd they say?"

"They gave me some bullshit about letting the medical examiner determine the cause of death first. If the ME could say it was a homicide, then they'd investigate."

"And the medical examiner couldn't rule out that Patrice had accidentally drowned, so they dropped the case?"

Loraine made a derisive sound. "I'm a nurse, miss. I know what happens to a body that's been left in a pond for weeks on end. With no other evidence, wasn't no way they were gonna say that Patrice didn't drown on her own."

Candice glanced at her notes, then asked, "In the days leading up to Patrice's disappearance, did you notice anyone out of place in the neighborhood?"

Again Loraine made a derisive sound. "There's a lotta folks in that hood gotta get by any way they can, miss. So there's a lotta other folks comin' and goin' that's outta place, if you know what I mean."

Candice smiled. "Right," she said. "What I mean is, did you ever notice any vans or contractors or workmen that might have looked out of place in that neighborhood?"

"Probably," she said bluntly. "Like I said, we used to get all kinds on that street."

"Did you ever notice anyone taking a special interest in your daughter?"

Loraine sighed. "No. Patrice was a good girl, but she was shy and I had put the fear of God into her early on. She didn't have many friends and she stayed inside a lot 'cause Pecan Valley ain't no place to play."

Candice looked over at me, silently asking if I had anything to add, but there was nothing here to go on. Loraine didn't know anything about who might have abducted and murdered her daughter—of that I was certain—and try as I might, there wasn't a lot of her daughter's residual energy around for me to bounce my radar off. I shrugged my shoulders and shook my head slightly to let her know there wasn't anything I wanted to ask.

Candice stood then and offered Loraine her hand. "Thank you so much for meeting with us," she said. "I promise you that we will do everything in our power to find out what really happened to your daughter."

"No offense, but I heard that before."

Something pinged in my head then and I asked, "Who told you that?"

"The last private investigator who came here promising me some answers."

Candice turned her head slowly to look at me before addressing Loraine again. "*Last* private investigator? Who and when?"

"I don't know," Loraine said dismissively. "Some tall strappin' man came by here about six months after Patrice's funeral and said he thought she was murdered and he was gonna look into it for me."

"Did he leave you his card?"

"Yes."

"Do you still have it?"

"No."

"Do you remember his name?"

"No."

Candice had asked those questions in rapid-fire succession, and I could see her posture stiffen as she again worked to rein herself in and be patient. "Can you describe this man for me?"

"Why?"

"Because as far as we know, Mrs. Walker, we're the only private investigators to look into your daughter's case in the past two years. If someone already did some legwork, then they might have come across something that could be vital to not only solving your own daughter's mystery but our other two cases as well."

Loraine reached for her cigarettes again. "Was a brother," she said. "And a big handsome one at that. He didn't say much except to ask me some of the same questions you-all did."

"How tall exactly?" I asked, hitting on that descriptive detail.

Loraine shrugged. "Maybe six four, or six five. And probably close to two hundred fifty pounds. But not a ounce of fat on him. He looked like a bodybuilder."

"Was his name Antoine LaSalle?"

Loraine's lids blinked heavily and she pressed the two fingers not holding her cigarette to her temple. "Maybe," she said. "That does sound familiar, but I can't say for certain."

Candice and I exchanged another look. "Thank you again, Mrs. Walker," my partner said. "Here is my card. If you can remember anything more that might help us, please don't hesitate to call me day or night."

Loraine accepted the card and laid it next to her pack of cigarettes. I had no doubt that the moment we were out the door, she'd toss it in the trash. She just didn't appear to have any more hope in her.

We left Loraine to her chain-smoking, and as soon as we got in the car, Candice set the fan on high. "Blach," she said. "I smell like an ashtray."

"At least you can take a shower," I groused while we pulled out of the driveway.

My friend looked over sympathetically. "Don't they make some sort of dry shampoo or something?"

"That stuff's for cats and dogs."

"We could find a pet-supply store," she said with a smirk.

I glowered at her. "Ha, ha," I said flatly. "*High-larious.*"

"How about a hat store?"

I brightened. "What kind of hat?"

"We're in Texas, darlin', home of the ten-gallon."

I pulled down the visor and eyed myself in the mirror. "Do you think I could pull off a cowboy hat?"

"I do."

"Then I'm game."

"Terrific. There's just one stop I want to make first. Then we'll find you somethin' purty."

The stop turned out to be Antoine LaSalle's. I had a feeling that Candice would want to speak to him again after what we'd learned at Loraine's. Still, when we pulled up to his house, it didn't appear that he was home, and after ringing the doorbell and knocking a few times, we gave up and headed to the highway. "What are you going to say to LaSalle when you see him?" I asked.

"I'm going to ask him if he did a little investigating on his own after Keisha went missing."

I knew in my gut that he'd been the "PI" that had talked to Loraine. I was pretty sure that he'd posed as a private investigator in an attempt to find out what might have happened to his baby sister. "You know it was him, right?"

"Yep."

"But you'll remember to be nice to him when you ask, because he saved my life and all, right?"

Candice sighed dramatically. "Oh, if I must."

"He won't tell you anything anyway."

"I said I'd be nice."

"It's not that. It's that he read you like a book at the hospital when you said you'd loop him in, but we all knew you wouldn't."

"It was that obvious, huh?"

"Pretty much," I told her honestly. "And LaSalle's just the kind of guy that won't give you something for nothing. If we want to find out what he knows, we might have to be honest with him."

Candice was silent for a bit before she said, "I don't know that I trust him, Abs."

I could see her point—Antoine was simply scary and formidable—but I kept thinking about how he'd risked his own life just to save mine. "I know," I told her, "but maybe we don't tell him everything we've discovered. Maybe we just string him along with the unimportant details until we get what we need from him."

Candice looked at me sideways. "You're forgetting that we know next to nothing, so there's hardly any information to protect."

"All the more reason to bring him into the loop, then. I mean, what harm could it do?"

Candice inhaled deeply and focused on the road. "Maybe you're right," she said softly, and I almost didn't hear her. "But I still don't trust him."

"Well, think about it at least," I encouraged. I was all for working together as long as it advanced the cause,

and I figured we had more to gain by cooperating with
Antoine to get the information we needed, because I
was fairly certain he had some detail important to our
case that he was withholding. I didn't know for certain
why he would keep information from us, but thought it
might be his army training that caused him to be cautious about what he revealed.

"Okay, Abby, " Candice promised, "I'll work with
him." She then pointed ahead. "There's the outlet
mall."

I squinted. "Do you think they'll have cowboy hats
there?"

"Sundance, they've got *everything* at the outlet
mall."

Candice was right. The huge span of name-brand
stores lining the south side of I-35 *did* have everything.
We discovered a Western store almost immediately and
found some awesome hats. I even got one for Dutch, although I doubted he'd be caught dead in it. After that,
we grabbed lunch and discussed our next steps.

"Other than talking to the lieutenant again, I'm not
sure what other leads we have," Candice said, glancing
over her notes from the case.

"How about the church?"

"What church?"

"The one that Mrs. Dixon goes to."

Candice looked at me like I was speaking a foreign
language. "Huh?"

"Remember?" I asked, even though she clearly didn't.

"She told us that she got the name of the painter off the bulletin board at her church. I know it's a long shot, but maybe the painter was a member of the congregation and someone can help identify him."

Candice beamed at me. "God, I'm glad you're my sidekick!"

Chapter Twelve

Candice dropped me off at home around three and I was surprised to find Dutch already there, tossing a ball in the backyard to Eggy and Tuttle. "You playin' hooky?" I asked, bringing out two beers from the fridge before settling into a lawn chair.

Dutch came over to get one of the beers and eyed me with a smile. "Nice hat."

"Covers the staples."

"You look good in it."

"Yeah?"

He took a swing of the frosty beer, then leaned down to give me a cold nibble on the neck. "Yeah," he said, his voice low and throaty.

I giggled because his lips tickled, then remembered

my original question. "So, what're you doing home, again?"

"I'm waiting for the test results," Dutch said. "Brice said I could work from here if I wanted to."

I did a mental head slap. "That's right! I forgot that the doctor was going to call you today. Have you already heard from him?"

"Nope."

"Did you call his office?"

"Nope."

I looked at my watch. "It's after three."

"Yep."

"Feeling pretty monosyllabic today, aren't you?"

"Yep."

With a sigh I got up and headed toward the door.

"Where're you going?" Dutch asked.

"I got you a hat too. You shouldn't be out here in the sun without one."

"I'm wearing sunscreen."

"You still need a hat." When I got inside, I pulled Dutch's present out of the bag. I'd had to guess at the size, and I hoped I got it right. Then I moved over to the phone in the kitchen, where we kept all the important numbers and messages. Digging through the pile, I located the doctor's office number and picked up the phone to carry it outside.

I finished dialing the doctor's number just before I reached Dutch's side again. When it started ringing, he frowned. "What'd you do?"

"Just ask them for the results and put us both out of *your* misery."

With a smirk, Dutch took the phone and I listened to his half of the conversation. At one point there was a lot of silence and he whispered to me, "She's putting me through to the doc right now."

After an exchange of pleasantries, the doctor seemed to get right to the point, and I read the relief in Dutch's eyes even before the smile spread to his lips. "That's great," he said. "Thanks, Doc. I really appreciate it."

He chatted for a few more minutes and then hung up the phone and threw his new hat on without hesitation. "I'm in the clear," he said, pulling me into his arms and hugging the stuffing out of me.

"I told you!"

"Yeah, yeah," he said, and squeezed me tight one more time.

When he let go and I looked up, I realized how sexy he looked in that new hat. "Lord, cowboy," I said with a drawl and a headshake.

"What, purty lady?"

"You sure are a good-lookin' son of a gun, ain't cha?"

Dutch grinned wickedly. "Care to ride my little pony?" he asked, bouncing his eyebrows.

About ten minutes later, Dutch and I had ourselves a little rodeo.

Yee-haw, ladies. Yee-haw.

*   *   *

Candice picked me up bright and early the next morning. "Where's the new hat?" she asked as I got in.

"It got a little smunched."

"Smunched?"

"Um . . . ," I said. "How can I put this delicately?"

Candice held up her hand. "No need," she said quickly. "I'm pretty sure I can guess."

I sighed contentedly. "I love that man."

"Lucky you," she muttered.

"Hey," I said, only now noticing she seemed a bit grumpy. "What's up with you?"

"Nothing."

"Okay."

"Brice slept on the couch again last night."

"Did you guys have another fight?"

"No. We're still having the same one."

"You mean you haven't talked to him about how you feel yet?"

"No."

"Why not?"

Candice squared her shoulders. "Because I shouldn't have to go first. He should be the one to say that he wants to stay with me and work it out."

"But he does want to stay with you and work it out."

"Has *he* said that?" Candice practically shouted.

My eyes widened. "Gettin' a little loud, honey."

"Sorry."

I gave her arm a squeeze. "You need to take that leap, my friend. You need to tell him that you are crazy about him, that all of this is just bluster from the both of you so that if someone bails, you can blame the other guy. It's ridiculous, and you need to get over it because you're killing any future for your relationship."

That seemed to get to Candice. "You really think it's hurting our chances?"

"Yes," I said bluntly. "You're destroying this really good thing. Maybe the only chance you'll have for a very long time to be with someone you could really love, and if either of you lets that happen, then I will be *so* ticked off!"

I'd tried to sound stern, but Candice started laughing. "Oh, Sundance," she sang. "What would I do without you?"

I made a face at her. "You'd be an old spinster woman with twelve cats."

We made it back up to Fatina's grandmother's house and Mrs. Dixon greeted us at the door with less suspicion this time. "I've been racking my brain trying to remember the name of that painter man," she said after we were seated again in her living room. "I swear it's right on the edge of my memory, but every time I try to pull it forward, it slips away."

"Sometimes not thinking about it is the way to get it to surface," I suggested.

She nodded. "Maybe you're right."

Candice waited for Mrs. Dixon to look at her before she asked, "We were wondering if maybe there was another way to figure out who this man was," she said. "You mentioned that you found this painter's number at church. Do you think he might have been a member of the congregation?"

Mrs. Dixon's eyebrows rose in surprise. "You know, I never thought of that," she said. "Maybe."

"Have you seen him since? Maybe at one of the services?" I asked.

Mrs. Dixon's eyes shifted to me and there was such sad resignation there. "No, ma'am. I don't go to church no more. Got no reason to. Any God that would take so much from me ain't worth prayin' to."

My radar was already on when we entered the room, and now I fully understood the profound sense of loss and sadness that permeated the space all around her. Not only had the poor woman lost every person that ever mattered to her, but she'd lost her faith as well, and it was a pain even more acute than all the others in her life.

"Oh, Mrs. Dixon," I said sadly. "I'm so, so sorry!"

"Why you got to be sorry?" she asked me sharply, taking offense.

"Because it's causing you so much pain," I said, ignoring her tone. "I think you miss God just as much as you miss your family."

Mrs. Dixon's lower lip trembled and she looked down at her hands. "Some people can have their children taken from them and their faith gets deeper. But I been through too much. And I don't have the energy to go looking for my faith again."

I took a deep breath and called out to my crew for help. I had a series of images come to mind and I smiled. "Mrs. Dixon?" I asked.

"Yes?" she replied, not looking up from the hands folded in her lap.

"Where's your piano?"

Her head snapped up and she let out a tiny gasp. "My what?"

"Your piano."

I watched her carefully, and sure enough, she looked over her shoulder to a section of her living room near the window that, to my eye, suddenly seemed open and empty. "How'd you know I had a piano?"

I didn't answer her. Instead I just continued to look at her like I knew her secret.

Finally she said, "It's in storage."

"How long has it been since you played it?"

She pursed her lips, clearly displeased that I was asking her about it. "Long enough."

I made a point of looking around the room, up and down at the walls. "I think that what this house really needs, ma'am, is to hear your music again. I think that what these walls miss the most is the sound of your piano and your voice."

Again Mrs. Dixon's lower lip trembled and I knew I'd found that tiny crack in her fortress of self-imposed misery. "How'd you hear about that?"

I tapped my temple. "I'm a person who knows such things, Mrs. Dixon. I see things before they happen, and I can catch glimpses of the past without any prior knowledge. When I look at you, all I see is the rich and good life you had before you stopped living. And it was filled to bursting with music and song and faith. So maybe you don't need to have the energy to go looking for God again, ma'am. Maybe all you need is just to play a song on that piano every so often, and God will find you."

We left Mrs. Dixon's a short time later with the name and address of her old church. As we got in the car, Candice let out a heavy sigh. "I swear I could barely keep from grabbing that woman and hugging her until she promised to get her piano back."

I winked at her. "Trust me, she's going to have them deliver it out of storage soon."

"You swear?"

I laughed. Candice had a soft spot for grandmothers. "Cross my heart."

We got to the church about five minutes later. It was a fairly nondescript structure: gray masonry walls, one large stained-glass window on the side, double doors at the front.

After parking, we walked in quietly, mindful of any afternoon services, but the place was all but vacant save for a woman dusting the pews. "Can I help you?" she asked when she saw us.

Candice strode forward and introduced herself before jumping right to the purpose of our visit. After she'd explained that she was there on behalf of Mrs. Dixon and was looking into her granddaughter's disappearance, the woman directed us to the office building next door. "You'll want to see the church secretary, Genevieve.

She's been here for twenty years and knows everyone who's ever come or gone from this place."

We found Genevieve in a tiny office suite on the second floor of the building we'd been directed to. I guessed she was about sixty, but she looked much younger with a smooth caramel-colored complexion and beautiful amber eyes.

Candice introduced us and told her why we'd come. "Oh, how is Francine?" she asked when she heard we'd just come from Mrs. Dixon's.

"I think she could use some company," I said bluntly. "I believe that poor woman is as sad and lonely as they come."

Genevieve clenched her fist and placed it over her heart, like it pained her greatly to hear that. "You know, when Fatina went missing, Francine came here every day to pray. But when it became clear that her grandchild wasn't coming back, she just lost all faith. It was like she felt personally betrayed by God. She stopped comin' to church, so the reverend and me went to her every Sunday. But soon she stopped answering her door and she refused to take our calls. After a while, I guess we gave up on her like she gave up on us."

"I think she could use another visit," I said. "And I think she could use her piano back."

Genevieve's mouth fell open. "Where's her piano?"

"She said it was in storage."

"Oh, that poor woman!" she exclaimed. "She loved

her music more than breathing. She used to play and sing for our choir. Lord, Lord, that woman has a voice!"

"Maybe some members of your congregation can help her get the piano out of storage?"

Genevieve grabbed a pad from her desk and scribbled on it. "I'm makin' myself a note," she said. "We'll get to it right away."

After making sure that Mrs. Dixon was taken care of, we focused on the painter. Candice explained that a week before Fatina had gone missing, Mrs. Dixon had had her house painted by someone who posted his information on the church's bulletin board. "Do you currently have anyone in your congregation who might make a living as a painter?" Candice asked.

Genevieve tapped her lip thoughtfully. "We have quite a few men who might fit that description. I'll have to go through our records to find out, but if Francine got that name off of our bulletin board, then the man would have had to go through me. No one's allowed to post anything up there without my permission, and I make sure that anyone wantin' to sell anything or advertise is either a member of the congregation or related to someone who is."

Candice and I brightened. That was exactly what we'd been hoping for. "He would have posted his ad sometime near the spring of two thousand eight. So you can exclude anyone fitting that description who wasn't a member before then."

"Leave it to me," she assured us. "It might take me a few days, but I'll get you a list together."

We left the church buoyed by the fact that we might finally have a solid lead, and Candice drove us over to Antoine's. This time we got lucky; he was outside in his driveway washing his Jeep.

"Had a feeling I'd see you two again," he said cordially as we walked up the drive.

"Wonder why," Candice muttered under her breath.

"Thanks again for saving my life," I said loudly. I felt a little guilty over the fact that we had to ask Antoine about talking to Loraine Walker.

Antoine scrubbed his car with a sponge. "Part of the job," he said, and for the first time I saw the hint of a wry grin on his face.

"Part of the job?"

"Protect and serve," he recited.

Candice and I exchanged a look. "Ah," she said. "Well, we really do appreciate it, Lieutenant."

"But you're not here to talk about that."

"No."

Antoine tossed his sponge into a nearby bucket and turned to face us. Placing his hands on his hips, he said, "Did you find Keisha's killer?"

"Not yet," Candice said.

"Got any leads?"

I had to marvel at how quickly Antoine took control of things like conversations and drowning women.

"No," Candice told him bluntly. I was a little disappointed that she didn't at least share the possible lead we'd just gotten from Genevieve.

"Then what's this about?" Antoine asked.

Candice kept her voice level, calm, almost friendly. "Did you perhaps investigate your sister's disappearance on your own?"

"Of course I did," he said. "She was my baby sister, ma'am."

I was surprised at his honesty. For once he was being completely forthcoming.

But I could tell that he still wasn't winning points with Candice. "I see," she said. "In the course of your own investigation, did you perhaps interview a woman named Loraine Walker?"

"Yes."

"So you lied to us when we first talked to you. You knew about her daughter, Patrice, before we mentioned her."

"Yes."

"Why didn't you tell us?" I asked, shocked to discover that Antoine had told me a bold-faced lie and I hadn't picked up on it.

Antoine regarded me coolly. "When you two showed up on my doorstep, I had no idea what your motives were. I mean, why would you want to dig into a cold case that even the FBI hadn't been interested in?"

He had a point, but I countered with, "Does it really matter what our motives were as long as we were looking into it?"

Antoine gave me a crooked smile. "I've been in a war zone for the past year, ma'am. We learn not to trust strangers pretty quick."

"Are you willing to be straight with us from now on?" Candice asked him pointedly.

"I will if you will," he replied, and it was clear he didn't believe we had nothing new to share with him.

Still, Candice withheld. "The moment we get something solid, Lieutenant, I promise to bring you into the loop."

Antoine's eyes studied her for a long moment before he pushed away from his Jeep and went to pick up the sponge again. "Sure you will," I heard him mutter.

Candice waited a moment to ask her next question. I knew his ability to read her was throwing her off a bit. "Lieutenant, did you discover anything that might be important to our investigation?"

But my savior was out of patience with us. "I'm done answering questions, Ms. Fusco. When you want to open up to me, I'll open up to you."

Candice pressed her lips together, clearly frustrated. "Thank you again for your time, Lieutenant. We'll stop bothering you now and let you get back to washing your car."

Once we were safely out of earshot, I pressed Candice to consider being straight with Antoine. "What do we have to lose?" I asked her as we got in the car.

She didn't answer me right away, and I thought it was mostly a pride thing for her. Other than me, she hated working a case with someone peering over her shoulder. It's what prompted her to leave the big firm she used to work for and hang her own shingle. "I don't know," she finally said. "But I'd prefer to have him butt out and work this case with just you and me."

"Okay, but at some point we'll have to fill him in."

Candice smiled. "Right," she agreed. "The moment we haul Keisha's killer in, I'll personally place that call."

The next few days held little in the way of progress. There wasn't much we could do until we heard from Genevieve, so after a few days of waiting for the phone to ring, Candice placed several calls to the St. Louis PD and county morgue to try to track down Fontana Carter, and when that seemed to go nowhere, she did another search of public records to see if there were any more possible victims from our killer that maybe we'd overlooked.

"Whoa," she said as she sat on the love seat opposite me in her condo.

"What?"

Candice swiveled her laptop around so that I could see the screen. The face peering out at me was another adorable little girl with a slight overbite and almond-shaped eyes. A cold prickle tingled my skin. To my mind's eye her image was flat and two-dimensional. "Who is she?"

"Essence Jackson," Candice said. "A missing-persons record was filed with the Dallas police on October tenth, of last year."

"Did it go to the FBI?"

Candice moved her laptop back to face her. "I doubt it. She'd turned fourteen two months before she went missing."

I cocked my head. "Why does that matter?"

"Children who disappear under the age of thirteen are considered critical missings, and protocol dictates that the FBI is looped in. But if they're fourteen or older, they aren't considered critical and are handled only by the local PD. I missed this one somehow in my first search."

I got up and went over to sit next to Candice. "She's a little older than the other girls," I said.

Candice nodded. "Yeah, but look at her, Abby. She looks younger, doesn't she?"

"She does," I agreed. With those big doe eyes, Essence didn't look a day over twelve.

Candice then read some of the details out loud. "Essence Jackson, age fourteen; missing since the evening of October sixth."

"Why did her parents wait so long to report her missing?"

Candice's eyes darted across the screen. "She lived with foster parents, and according to this, she'd run away from their home on several previous occasions, but had always come back within a few days. It sounds like it was a difficult relationship."

"Well, if you're wondering, Essence is no longer with us," I said sadly.

Candice's shoulders slumped. "Same guy?"

I closed my eyes and focused on her energy. "I think so."

Candice shut her laptop and got up to fetch her purse. Retrieving her notepad, she walked back to me and sat down again. "We need to map this out," she said, and began jotting down names and dates. "So far, we know that Patrice was murdered in March of oh-eight and Keisha was murdered in May."

"Then Fatina was murdered in January of two thousand nine."

"And now Essence in October of last year."

"He's still killing," I said. I'd hoped that since Fatina had died over a year ago, maybe the serial killer had been imprisoned on another crime or even killed himself. Essence's death was evidence that, as of the previous October at least, he was still out there.

Candice sighed and rubbed her eyes tiredly. "We've got to find this guy, Abby."

"Did you call Genevieve?"

"This morning. A small electrical fire burned through a section of the church's basement over the weekend. They put the fire out quickly, but Genevieve told me she's had her hands full for the past couple of days. She did promise me she'd get to our list soon though."

"Maybe you could call her again and beg her to make it a top priority?"

Candice nodded. "I think I'd better." Candice then checked her watch and made a face.

"What?"

"I have to go."

"Got a date?" I asked hopefully.

"Brice and I are having dinner tonight. I'm making his favorite dish and I'm planning to declare my undying love and devotion to him, or something slightly less ridiculous."

My eyebrows rose. "Can it be that Candice Fusco is finally stepping up to that plate?"

"Someone's got to," she said, tucking her laptop into its case and gathering the rest of her things.

I thought I'd give her a little encouragement, so I said, "Speak from your heart and you'll be fine. Just tell him how you really feel, and the rest will take care of itself."

"You'd better be right about this," she warned playfully. "If he tells me at the end of tonight that he just wants to be friends, I'm gonna come lookin' for you."

I laughed. "I'm perfectly willing to have you take that chance. Now get out of here and go make that dinner!"

As soon as I'd closed the door behind Candice, Dutch called. "You got a minute?"

"Sure, cowboy. What's up?"

"Can you come down to the office?"

I eyed the clock. It was quarter to three. "Um . . . sure. Want to tell me why?"

"I'll tell you when you get here."

On that cryptic note I was left to pull my awful-looking hair into a scrunchie, slather on far too much makeup to distract from the bad hair, pout fiercely at my reflection, and dash out the door.

When I arrived at the office, I found that little had changed since I'd been there last—except that there was a big old "9" on the whiteboard under number of cases solved. I smiled in satisfaction that not only had we met the goal set forth by D.C. and by Brice, but we'd pretty much blown those numbers right out of the water in less than a month.

Dutch waved at me from Harrison's office and my smile vanished. With a little dread I saw that the blinds were closed. "Uh-oh," I muttered, walking forward with a pounding heart. I'd never been fired from a job before, and I expected that's what this was probably about. Either IA had determined that Rodriguez and I were at fault, or Brice had discovered that Candice and I were investigating an FBI cold case on our own.

When I entered Brice's office, I was surprised to see Rodriguez already there, looking just as nervous as I felt. "Hey," he said when he saw me. "Heard about that close call you had in Dallas. You okay?"

I sat down in the chair on his left and squeezed his good hand. "I'm fine," I assured him. "Thanks so much for asking."

"How's the scalp?" Brice asked from behind his desk.

"Ready for a shower," I admitted. "Only a few more days before the staples come out."

Dutch closed the office door and took a seat next to me. I could see that a single file had been placed on Brice's desk. With Rodriguez's presence, I assumed it had to be IA's findings.

"We've called you both in to let you know that the Internal Affairs investigation has been completed, and while they did find fault with you, Agent Rodriguez, for taking an untrained civilian employee to a possible crime scene, they have determined that you could not have foreseen that, given the lack of information from the original investigation. Your old partner admitted that when he followed up with the garage owner, he left out of his notes the fact that Clady's son had been the one who'd towed the kids' car and then dropped them off at the motel. Your old partner had also failed to do a background check on Darrell. Therefore, you had no reason to suspect anyone at Clady's—especially given that you didn't know previously Russell had a son.

"Further, given that you, Ms. Cooper, have had no firearms training whatsoever, the fact that you were so effectively able to take out the assailant is a commendable accomplishment. IA is making sure to note this in your file."

I realized I'd been holding my breath and I let it out slowly, but I was still a little unsure what all that meant. "Soooo," I said slowly, "are we off the hook?"

Brice winked at me. "Yes. You two are officially off the hook. And you, Ms. Cooper, are up for a commendation from D.C."

"I am?"

Dutch reached over and gave me a gentle squeeze to my shoulder. "Congratulations, Abby," he said softly.

I shook my head, as if I could rattle some sense into it. "Does this mean we can go back to work too?"

"It does," Brice assured me. "I realize we've called you in on short notice, so if you would prefer to start back with us the day after tomorrow, that's fine by me."

"I'd like to put in a couple of hours today, sir," Rodriguez said. I could only imagine that he'd probably gone a little stir-crazy at home.

"Of course, Agent Rodriguez," Brice said, and turned expectantly to me.

"Can I come back tomorrow?" I asked. I'd been unprepared for this little turn of events, and there were some errands that I had to run.

Harrison smiled. "Certainly. We'll see you tomorrow around eight thirty, Ms. Cooper."

Dutch walked me out and gave me a big ol' hug in the hallway. "I'm proud of you," he whispered into my ear.

"For what?"

Dutch seemed surprised by my question. "For everything."

"Everything?"

Dutch grinned. "Have you seen the whiteboard, Edgar? We're solving cases right and left in there."

I blushed. "You coming home for dinner?"

Dutch wiped his face with his hand. "Wish I could, dollface, but there are a couple of cases I'm working and we're still trying to sort through all the possible connections."

"You mean the one with those three dead guys we were talking about the other day?"

"Yep. Sure could use your input on that tomorrow."

"Absolutely! I promise to help you guys out first thing."

Dutch wrapped his arm around my shoulders and walked me to the door at the front of the office. "Any luck with the missing girls?" he asked before seeing me off.

"We have some intel we're waiting to hear back on. It's a long shot, but if it pays off, it could be gold."

"Just make sure Harrison doesn't hear that it's one of our cases."

"If the lead comes in, how about I tell you what we've found and let you take the case back?"

Dutch's eyebrows rose. "Is Candice going to be okay with that?"

"Probably," I said. "I mean, I'll ask her, but I think if I phrase it right, she'll agree that it's better than telling Brice we've been working one of his cases behind his back this whole time."

Dutch gave me one last hug, promising that he'd try not to be out too late, and I left to run errands.

Later that night around nine I got an odd text from Candice. It read simply that she was off our case until further notice, and that she'd catch me up on the details the next morning.

I sent her back a note asking if she wanted to talk because I had a strong sense that something upsetting had happened to my friend. She waited nearly an hour to reply and it was only two words: "Not now."

To add to the confusion, around ten o'clock just as I was drifting off to sleep, I heard the front door open and thought it must be Dutch, but another voice told me he had company.

I waited for him to come upstairs and he confirmed that he'd brought someone home with him. "Are you okay with Harrison crashing at our place tonight?"

I sat up and stared at him. "You brought Brice home?"

"Yes."

"Why?"

"He and Candice had a major fight and the poor guy was ready to camp out on his couch at the office."

I blinked several times, trying to catch up with this sudden turn of events. "Uh, sure," I said. "Of course it's okay with me. And put him in the spare bedroom at the end of the hall. I just washed the sheets in there, actually, and there are fresh towels in the closet."

"He's good on the couch," Dutch replied, and I gave him a stern look.

"Oh, for cripe's sake, Dutch! He's *not* sleeping on that lumpy couch." When Dutch blinked dumbly back at me, I rolled my eyes and got up to grab my robe.

After heading downstairs, I found my boss sitting like a dejected little kid on the edge of the sofa. "Hey, Abby," he said when he saw me.

"How you doin'?"

"Been better."

I turned to Dutch, who'd followed me down the stairs, and scowled. "What?" he asked defensively.

"Can't you see the poor man needs a beer?" Again I got nothing but a few blinks from him, and impatiently I hurried into the kitchen to retrieve a brewski. After handing it to Brice, I said, "There's a room upstairs that's all made up, sir. Why don't you go on up and you can stay as long as you like?"

He smiled gratefully. "I don't want you to go to any trouble. Really, I can crash on your couch and be out of your hair in the morning."

It was then that I noticed the duffel bag next to him on the floor. I stepped forward, grabbed it, and turned to the stairs. "Don't be silly," I insisted. "You'll be much more comfortable upstairs. And I mean it when I say you can stay here until you figure things out."

I glanced back over my shoulder and saw the way Dutch and Brice were exchanging dumb blinks back and forth. "I'm not taking no for an answer, sir," I said firmly.

Brice gave me a half smile. Standing up, he saluted and said, "Yes, ma'am."

"That's more like it."

Chapter Thirteen

Dutch joined me back in our bedroom after Brice had been given the tour of the spare bedroom and the adjoining bath. "That was nice of you," he said once he'd closed the door.

I shrugged out of my robe and got back under the covers. "Candice would have done the same for you."

"I'll remember that the next time you kick me out of the house."

"Do you know what their fight was about?"

Dutch sighed. "Candice received a formal complaint from the Texas state PI licensing board. They're accusing her of conducting investigations before her license has been issued."

"*What?*" I gasped. "*Who* complained?"

"According to Candice, it must have been Brice."

"*Why* would she think that?"

Dutch put a finger to his lips. "Abs," he warned, "can you keep it down? I don't want Harrison to know we're discussing this."

I cocked an eyebrow at him. "Oh, like it's not obvious that we'd be talking about him. Seriously, why does Candice think it was Brice who complained?"

"Because of what he said when you were in the hospital after you two nearly drowned."

I thought back to that afternoon, and I did remember him warning her that it would only take one complaint to the state licensing board for her application to get bounced. "Did Brice *actually* send in the complaint?"

Dutch climbed in bed next to me. Pulling me close to spoon with him, he kissed the back of my neck. "He swears it didn't come from him, but Candice doesn't believe it, and in the course of their shouting match, I guess it came out that she's been investigating one of our cold cases and then he blew up."

I gulped. "Am I in trouble?"

Dutch laughed. "No. Harrison thinks Candice talked you into letting her investigate the girls."

I sighed. "Which is actually the truth."

"He also wants you to brief him on any new leads you've uncovered in the morning."

"Uh-oh."

"And I think he wants you to go to bat for him with Candice again."

I squirmed around to look at Dutch. "He wants me to *what*?"

"He wants you to convince Candice that he had nothing to do with the letter from the licensing board."

"How'd I get stuck in the middle of this?"

Dutch chuckled. "By putting yourself there, sweethot."

"Crap on a cracker," I grumbled, turning back around. "Have I mentioned lately that I hate it when you're right?"

"No," he said, nuzzling my neck playfully. "And frankly I think you're overdue."

The next morning can best be described in one word: awkward.

I still couldn't bring myself to call Brice by his first name when we were in a casual setting, so seeing him the next morning coming out of the bathroom in his boxer shorts made for one flush-cheeked moment. I had no idea how I was going to get through a debrief with him without thinking about my boss in his boxers.

Harrison left before either one of us, and I rode in with Dutch, somewhat excited to get back to work again, but wishing I looked better. "I cannot wait until Friday," I said.

"Staple-removal day?" he asked.

"Yes, and a nice hot shower. I may stay in there all day."

"You've still gotta work, you know. Now that you're off the hook with IA, you'll need to put in those eight hours."

I spent the rest of the ride thinking about what Dutch

had said, and I started to realize that, grateful as I was for the steady paycheck, working in a cubicle five days a week wasn't very satisfying.

What I had enjoyed was palling around with Candice— like old times. We had the freedom to call our own shots and not worry about punching a clock every morning. Somewhere deep inside I knew that if I worked at the CCS for too long, I'd eventually burn out.

After getting settled at my desk again, I was invited into Harrison's office with Dutch to debrief him on the missing girls from Dallas. I gave Harrison the details, working to make it seem like it was more my idea than Candice's, and finished by letting him know that we'd discovered a possible fourth victim and hit a dead end unless Genevieve came up with a name for us to investigate.

The whole time I was speaking, Harrison didn't comment or interrupt. He listened, took a few notes, thanked me for the debrief, then excused me from his office.

I was so stunned at the fact that he didn't say one thing about my flagrant breaking of the rules that I sat there for a minute, looking at him blankly. "Something you wanted to add, Ms. Cooper?" he asked when I didn't get up and leave.

"Uh . . . ," I said. "Well, actually, I'm kinda surprised you're not mad."

He and Dutch exchanged a humorous look. "I would have preferred you'd asked if you and Ms. Fusco could tackle this on your own," he admitted. "But knowing her as I do, I've learned that attempting to stop Candice is like trying to stand in front of a steamroller; if you don't get out of the way, you're likely to get flattened."

I laughed. "Yeah, she's pretty determined when she wants to be." I then thought of something. "Sir, would you mind if I asked you if you really had nothing to do with that complaint to the licensing board?"

"I had nothing to do with it, Abby," he said firmly. "Nothing."

I nodded. "Okay. I believe you. And I'll make sure to mention that to Candice."

Harrison fidgeted with the alignment of his nameplate. "Thank you," he said. "And now if you'll excuse us, I have some reports and cases to go over with Agent Rivers."

I stood up to go. "Yes, sir."

Dutch got up too and opened the door for me. As I passed him, he said, "Remember, I need your input on those three cases we talked about."

"Absolutely. Come find me when you're done here."

"Ms. Cooper?" Brice called, stopping me in the doorway.

"Yes?"

"Would you be up for another of your classes today for the agents?"

I smiled ruefully at him. "You mean, because the last one was so packed with interested pupils?"

Brice twirled a pen between his fingers and motioned toward the whiteboard where the tally for our month was proudly displayed. "Oh, I think you'll have a few agents more than willing to sit in this time. Can you prepare something for us by ten?"

I still had all the notes and ideas from the first class in my desk drawer. "Of course."

"Excellent. See you then."

I spent much of the rest of the morning going over and refining my notes for the class. Brice sent an e-mail letting the squad know that I'd be in the conference room at ten and hinting that he strongly encouraged them to attend. So I wasn't surprised when at five to ten they all began moseying toward the conference room.

On his way in, Rodriguez made sure to whisper a note of encouragement in my ear. "I'm glad you're doing this," he told me.

I took a sip of water and tried not to look nervous. But then I considered that trying not to look nervous probably made me look nervous, so I busied myself by handing out my supportive material to the group as they entered.

Dutch and Brice were the last ones in, and even Katie had come in to see what I had to say.

"Good morning," I said to the agents. My voice cracked a little and I felt my cheeks heat up. Public speaking isn't really my forte. "Today I'm going to go over the very basics of developing your own intuition. I'm not going to spend any time on the theory behind PSI or the promising scientific studies showing definitive proof of its existence being done in Europe right now, but if you're interested in any of that, please don't hesitate to see me later and I'll point you to some Internet links and such."

I looked around the room at the blank stares of the attendees and thought I should get to the good parts and quick. "What I'm going to attempt to do in the course of these classes is to have you listen a little more carefully to your own gut instincts. I would imagine that if you've made it to the level of investigative agent, you're already well schooled in relying on your own intuition when it comes to solving a case. I just want to hone those inherent skills and take you one level further."

I paused here and looked around again to see if they were following. The most any of the men did was blink or nibble on a snack they'd brought in with them. "Okay!" I said, clapping my hands. "Let's get busy. What most people don't realize is that, at its heart, your intuition isn't just a sixth sense; it's a personal language and it's made up of symbols and images that string together to form ideas that plant themselves either at the far corners of your thoughts, or in the forefront of your mind. So what you as individuals need to do to utilize your already keen ability to tap into your intuition is begin to build your own language so that these insights can guide you more successfully through these cold cases."

I paused to see if the group was still with me here, and I was encouraged to see that the blinking and nibbling had turned to something like interest. Encouraged, I continued. "To build that language, we're going to be using the same techniques your mother utilized when you were a child and she taught you the basics of English. We're going to associate some simple and common images with their word counterparts to form the building blocks of your new language.

"To make sure this ends up being a useful tool to you, we'll begin with some basic crime-fighting words and images, and as time goes on, we'll be able to build on that initial vocabulary to include some of the more subtle associations. I don't know that you'll all be predicting the future by the end of these lectures, but you should be able to glean some solid information out of the past by using your new skills."

I then began to hand out sets of flash cards that I'd had Katie print up for me. On the front of each card was a word associated with crime. There were cards for the basics like "suspect," "weapon," and "victim," along with more complicated words like "homicide," "fraud," "bank robbery," "terrorism," "illegal gambling," "cyber crime," "kidnapping," "organized crime," etc.

After all the cards had been handed out, I said, "The thing to remember is that most of this exercise will be done with your eyes closed. On the front of each card is a word associated with crimes the FBI investigates. The other side is blank. What I want you to do is to close your eyes, think about that word, and see what image comes to mind. Once you have that image, write the description down on the blank side of the card.

"Those of you who have good imaginations will find this exercise easy, but those of you who are perhaps more analytical might have some difficulty. If you do encounter some issues creating an image for the word on the card, open your eyes and draw a picture. It doesn't have to be detailed, and it's okay if it's completely abstract, but you will need an image to associate with that word, so don't give up until you have it."

All the agents in the room seemed eager to get on with the exercise and I was anxious to see what they would come up with, so I eyed the clock and said, "I'll give you until ten forty-five, and your time starts now."

The agents went to work and I felt a wave of relief that they were all following my directions. I could tell the men with the most natural intuitive abilities; they kept their eyes closed for almost the entire period, opening them only to jot down a few notes per card.

Others stuck to doodling images on the backs of the cards. Only one person seemed to really struggle, and that was Harrison. The poor guy spent a lot of time tapping the side of his temple with his pen and staring blankly at the wall.

And I believe I finally understood why it'd been so hard to convince him in the beginning that I was really psychic; he had precious little natural intuition of his own, so of course he couldn't understand it in someone else.

Finally, at ten forty-five I told the agents to put their pencils and cards down. I felt it might be important to get some feedback from them to gauge their progress. I decided to start with a friendly face first. "Agent Rodriguez," I said, "can I ask what image you wrote down for the word 'homicide'?"

Rodriguez eyed his paper. "I drew a chalk outline."

I beamed at him. "Excellent!" I said, relieved that he'd

captured the exercise so well. "That's a fantastic image to use. Now, what did you write down for 'suspect'?"

He smiled sheepishly. "I drew a wanted poster," he said.

I wanted to hug him. "Perfect!" I exclaimed. "You're really good at this, Agent Rodriguez. Are you sure you haven't had any other training?"

Rodriguez blushed. "I swear this is my first time."

"Well, you're a natural," I said, then turned to another agent. "And what about you, Agent Cox? What did you get for 'kidnapping'?"

Poor Agent Cox looked like a deer caught in headlights. "It's weird," he said to me, obviously embarrassed about what he'd written.

"Weird is actually good," I encouraged. "The stranger the image, the more it will stand out when you're focusing on a case and your intuition suggests it."

"Well, I immediately thought of Patty Hearst. You know, she was kidnapped before she was brainwashed into robbing that bank."

I could feel my shoulders really relax. These guys were naturals. "Agent Cox, I think that's a perfect image to use. But let me ask you, what image came up for 'robbery'?"

"Chris Douglas."

"Who?"

"He was the first guy I ever busted for robbery back when I was with the Philly PD. I haven't thought of that kid in years, but when I saw the word 'robbery,' that's what came to my mind."

"If it makes sense to you, then that's all that matters," I told him.

After picking on a few more agents, I decided to show them how they could begin to use their new language practically. I dug into my folder of notes searching for an old case that I'd helped Candice solve a few years ago. Pulling out copies of a photograph along with several blank sheets of paper, I handed these to the first agent and told him to take one of each, then pass them around to the group. "That is the photo of a building where a crime took place. What I'd like you to do is simply consider the photo, then close your eyes and write down whatever images spring to mind using your new vocabulary. But also note, gentlemen, that if a new image comes into your head, don't hesitate to write that down as well."

I waited for several minutes while the agents did as I asked. When the last pen went down, I gave the next set of instructions. "Now I want you to take those images and jot down the story of the crime. What do you think happened in that building?"

The agents went back to their paper and began to write out their thoughts. It took no longer than three minutes for them all to complete it. I decided to start with Agent Rodriguez again. "Tell me what you think happened."

"It was a robbery," he said, lifting up his flash card where there was a cartoon image of a man wearing a mask with a bag of money in his hand. "I get two suspects," he added, holding up another card with the image of a wanted poster. "One male and one female." I couldn't help it. My jaw dropped and I just stared at him. "What?" he asked nervously when he saw my reaction.

I laughed. "You're going to put me out of business, buddy," I said, before looking around the room. Every person there was leaning forward, looking intently at his own notes and at me. "Who else got robbery for the crime involved?"

Almost every hand in the room went up. The only one that didn't raise a hand was poor Brice. "I wrote down homicide," he said.

"Don't sweat it," I told him. I then beamed at the other agents. "The crime committed was an elaborate embezzlement scheme involving two criminals. One male, one female. Who else had the detail of a female accomplice?"

Five hands stayed in the air and all of the agents seemed really stunned.

I wanted to clap my hands. These guys were fantastic. "Did anyone get a detail that seemed out of place?"

Dutch waved his hand and I called on him. "I kept seeing a boat."

Excitedly, I dug into the file and pulled out the photo of a large ski boat. "The Kalamazoo PD found most of the embezzled funds in the bow of this boat belonging to the suspect," I said. The look on Dutch's face suggested I could have knocked him over with a feather.

"Whoa," he said.

Brice leaned over to eyeball Dutch's notes. He shook

his head enviously. "I think after all this time, she's rubbed off on you, Rivers."

Dutch looked at me and winked. "I think you're right, sir."

I glanced at the clock and decided to quit while we were ahead. "Let's stop here, gentlemen. Thank you so much for coming. Next week we'll expand on your vocabulary and learn some additional techniques."

As everyone exited, I was thrilled to see most of the agents comparing notes with one another, and the buzzy excitement of the exercise carried out into the squad room.

Dutch squeezed my hand as he passed. "Great job, Abs," he whispered, and I felt giddy with happiness that I'd finally managed to break the ice with these guys.

The rest of that morning and early afternoon I was very busy, and my desk saw a lot of traffic. Some of the investigators came over to get my intuitive input on the progress they'd made so far on their cases; others stopped by to ask me questions about intuitive theory and for a few of those Web sites I'd talked about in the meeting.

By the end of the day I noticed a real shift in the energy of CCS. It was as if we all had a secret and we'd bonded over it.

A little before six, Dutch swung by my desk. "You ready to go?"

I leaned back in my chair and stretched. "I didn't get much of a chance to focus on your case," I said, referring to the three men who'd been murdered.

"Don't sweat it. This was your first day back. Let's have a meeting with the agents I've assigned to help work it in the morning."

I got up and reached for my purse. "Perfect." I was about to suggest dinner out when I noticed Brice still in his office working on his computer. "Is he coming back to our house tonight?"

Dutch slapped his forehead. "Damn," he said. "I forgot to make him a spare key. Can you give him yours?"

I took my keys out of my purse. "I'll be right back," I said, and moved toward Brice's office. Poking my head in, I said, "Sir? I thought I'd give you my keys so that you can let yourself in when you come home."

Brice eyed the squad room. No one was left but me and Dutch, and I could see his shoulders relax. "Thanks, Abby," he said, reaching for the keys. I turned to go, but he stopped me. "Can I ask you a favor?"

I turned back. "Of course, sir."

Brice reached into his desk drawer, pulled out a thin folder and extracted a legal-sized paper from it. "If you're going to see Candice in the next few days, would you give her this?"

"Um, sure," I said, wondering what the paper was, but not wanting to appear like I was prying by reading it in front of him.

Brice seemed to know that I was curious, because he explained, "It's a contract."

"A contract?" That surprised me and I glanced down at the paper.

"It's a consulting contract to retain Ms. Fusco's services. In the paperwork we acknowledge that she is not currently licensed within the state of Texas, but the FBI finds her services invaluable and understands that the paperwork with the licensing board is merely a formality. Oh, and when she signs it, she won't need to date it. I've done that for her."

I felt a smile spread slowly to my lips, especially when I took note that the date Brice had posted was for March 30, a full week before she and I began investigating the case of the missing girls. "She can show this to the state licensing board," I said.

Brice focused back on his computer. "I believe it would present her with an excellent defense if she could show that she was acting on our behalf and that no intent to deceive existed. And please tell her that if she agrees to the terms and finds them acceptable, she can return the signed document to Katherine and have her ID photo taken at that time."

"ID photo?"

"For her civilian-profiler badge," Brice said. "Just like yours."

I glanced down at the badge hanging from the lanyard around my neck. "Sir," I said, smiling broadly now, "can I just state for the record that I think you're a really great guy, and that this is pretty awesome of you?"

Brice actually laughed. "Thank you, Abby. And you guys shouldn't wait up. I've got a few hours left here."

Dutch and I had dinner at a wonderful Indian restaurant called the Clay Pot. After that, I asked him if he wouldn't mind dropping me at Candice's. "How're you going to get home?"

"She can drive me," I said. "Or I can take a cab."

Dutch rolled his eyes. "If you're going to have a heart-to-heart with Candice, there's probably going to be wine involved. Call me when you're through with your pow-wow and I'll come pick you up."

"You might be the best man I know," I said.

"Might be?"

"I'll change it to 'are most definitely' when you come get me." I then pulled him close for a little smooch.

Candice was in a pretty foul mood when I arrived on her doorstep. "He's a son of a bitch," she snapped by way of hello.

"Hi, honey!" I sang, pushing past her into the condo and waving the doggie bag full of leftovers Dutch and I had taken from the restaurant. "Hungry?"

"I'm serious, Abby," Candice said stubbornly. Still, she marched over to the kitchen and started pulling plates out of the cupboard. "How am I supposed to make a living now that I can't get a license?"

"I don't think Harrison was the one who complained," I said, setting down the bag and unloading the contents. "Get a plate for me, would you? I could go for more of this rice."

"Of *course* he's the one who complained!" Candice insisted. "You heard what he said at the hospital! He couldn't wait to get me in trouble!"

I took a deep calming breath and pulled out the contract from my purse. "Honey," I said softly. "He didn't do it. And this proves it."

Candice's brow furrowed as she took the paper and began to read it. "What's this?"

"Brice drew it up," I explained. "It's a consulting contract between you and the bureau."

"How does this help me?" she asked, holding the paper like she was ready to discard it into the trash.

"For starters, Brice notes in the third paragraph of the contract that the FBI knows you don't yet have your license from the state licensing board, but is aware that the paperwork has been filed. Until such time as you become licensed, you will be acting as a civilian profiler with the FBI. Oh, and I almost forgot the best part—look at the date." For emphasis I tapped the date at the bottom of the page. "Brice made sure to tell you that he'd already filled that in for you."

Candice scrutinized the bottom of the contract and I saw her mouth fall open a little. "No way," she whispered.

I dished out a healthy portion of food onto her plate. "Way."

She looked back at me in disbelief. "I can present this to the board. It'll totally exonerate me."

I pointed a finger and said, "Bingo. And it'll also allow you to keep investigating the missing girls in the meantime. Worst-case scenario, Candice, even if the board denied your license, you could still act as a consultant for the FBI. Brice made sure there was no end date on the contract—and he's willing to turn his good faith into money. He's matched your hourly rate."

I'd had time at dinner to go over all the details of the contract, and I had to hand it to Brice: He'd worked hard to make sure that Candice wasn't adversely affected in any way should the worst happen, and her PI license was denied. She'd have a job with the FBI as long as she liked.

It was a risky move too; I mean, not only was he willing to fudge the date, but she and Brice *were* seeing each other. I wondered how the higher-ups would feel if a complaint came through that both the special agent and assistant special agent in charge at the Austin bureau had their girlfriends working for them.

"He didn't send the complaint in," Candice determined as she finished reading the contract. "And the potential to cause him trouble personally if I sign this is significant."

Candice had assumed the same thing I did. "Still, our dear Mr. By-the-Book Harrison went ahead and drafted it anyway."

"Wow," Candice said, looking meaningfully at me.

"Wow," I agreed.

Candice pushed her food around with her fork. "I think I owe him an apology."

"Yeppers."

She glanced at the clock. "I should do it in person," she mused. "But I don't even know where he is."

"He's either still at work or he's at our place."

Candice's eyebrows rose in surprise. "Your place? You guys took him in?"

"You would have done the same for Dutch," I reasoned.

Candice smiled. "You never would have kicked Dutch out."

"You're probably right there. But remember back when we were first dating? We didn't always get along so well either."

Candice laughed. "Oh, I remember," she said. "I never thought you two were going to work through it. Back then, I gave you guys a month, tops."

"And yet, three years later, here we are."

Candice looked thoughtfully at me. "Here you are," she repeated softly. "Okay, I'll call him and see if he wants to talk tomorrow."

"You can drop off your contract when you see him," I suggested. "He wanted me to tell you to give it to our office manager, Katie, and make sure you get your photo taken for your civilian badge."

"Oh, I'm not signing this," Candice said.

I did a double take. "Say what, now?"

Candice folded the paper and set it to the side. "I can't. If Brice ever got called on the carpet because of it, I'd never forgive myself."

I blinked furiously, trying to catch up to her logic. "But, Candice, if you don't sign that, then the board could deny your license."

"They may," she said. "But I can't let Brice risk his career for a mess I created."

She picked the paper up again and moved to tear it in two when I reached out and grabbed her arm to stop her. "Will you just wait until you talk to him first?" I begged. I wasn't getting a negative feeling from the contract. I knew logically that it was risky for them, but I also didn't feel that by signing it she would get either herself or Brice in trouble. I told her as much, but she still looked unconvinced. "Just give it some thought. Talk it over with Brice and make sure you're both okay with it."

Candice agreed to at least wait a day and I called Dutch, who picked me up, and we headed home.

Chapter Fourteen

Dutch and I got into the office bright and early. I wanted to review the cases of those men as soon as possible because I felt a tremendous sense of urgency that I couldn't quite explain. I could just feel a sense of foreboding in the ether, and I knew I didn't have much time left to put the clues together before they would all just slip away.

We sat down together when the other three agents arrived. Assigned to the case were Agents Todd, Ruben, and Cox.

Dutch brought me up to speed on their progress so far. "We've interviewed an additional twenty-two family members and friends, and no one knows why these guys wound up dead, much less decapitated."

"No connection to drugs or the Mexican Mafia?" I asked.

Agent Cox shook his head. "The first time I looked at these crime-scene photos, I could have told you these were made to look like cartel hits but they weren't."

"How can you tell?" I pressed.

I'd heard that Cox was a gang and organized-crime specialist from Houston, but I wanted to hear why he didn't think these murders were cartel related. "Well, for one thing, La Familia doesn't just behead anyone. When they take off a head, it's to send a powerful message to anyone thinking about crossing them. These three guys had no connection to organized crime. At most, they were street punks that La Familia wouldn't have bothered with. And the coroner ruled in all three cases that Lopez, Cushing, and Brown likely died before they were decapitated. Not La Familia's style. Those sickos tend to go for maximum gore, if you know what I mean."

My stomach clenched and I had to swallow hard. "No need to elaborate," I told him.

Dutch took over the conversation then. "As Agent Cox said, we really think we can rule out the Mexican Mafia for this, but whoever did kill these guys wanted to make it look like a Mexican Mafia hit."

"But why?" I wondered out loud. "I mean, why go to all that trouble?"

Agent Todd said, "Maybe the best way to cover up three murders is to make them look gang related. La Familia's been in the news a lot in recent years. Maybe our killer got the idea to cover his tracks by watching the evening news."

I sat back in my chair and thought about that. "You

think we've got a serial killer here, targeting young men?"

"That was one of the theories we were batting around," Dutch said. "To our knowledge, he hasn't killed anyone in almost a year, which means he could have moved out of the area, got thrown in jail, or someone killed him."

"Or he might just be lying low, waiting for another opportunity," said Todd.

"What's your radar saying?" asked Dutch.

I eyed the driver's license photos of the three men that Dutch had placed on the conference table. "Yeah. That could be it. I mean, my intuition strongly suggests they were all murdered by the same guy."

"What we're having a hard time with, Abby, is identifying what characteristics connect them to each other."

"What do you mean, 'what characteristics'?" I asked.

Dutch pointed to the photos and said, "Jason was white, Felix was Latino, and Avril was mixed race. They don't look alike, they're not the same age, and other than the fact that they lived in the same two-mile radius, they have nothing in common. We've done extensive checks into their backgrounds; Jason and Felix attended the same high school but at different times and floated in different social circles. Avril moved into the area after he got out of juvie and never attended high school. None of their family will admit to any of them being either gay, or in a gang, and as far as we can tell, their paths never crossed except maybe by pure coincidence."

"I hate to ask this next question, but did the coroner note any signs of rape or molestation?"

Agent Cox said, "I checked, and the answer is no."

I sighed. My radar said very clearly that there was a clue right in front of us that we were missing. I wanted to say it was even obvious, but no one had connected the dots yet. I stared again at all three photos and closed my eyes. In my mind I saw Santa Claus reviewing a list of names, and as I focused harder, I saw that the scroll in his hand had the heading "NAUGHTY," and down a few spaces were the names Jason, Felix, and Avril and one additional name I couldn't make out. "They were on a list," I whispered.

"List?" Dutch asked.

I opened my eyes, and stared at Dutch. "Yes."

"Like a hit list?" Agent Ruben asked.

I shook my head. "No," I said, feeling that out intuitively. "I think their names were maybe mentioned publicly, like in the newspaper or something. And whatever they were noted for, it was for being bad."

All four men just stared at me blankly. They obviously had no idea what I was talking about.

"I know that sounds odd," I admitted, "and I'm sorry I can't help you more than that, but I do want to mention that there could be a fourth victim."

"You mean, he's killed someone else?" Dutch asked.

I took a deep breath and tried to inch along the thready energy I was picking up. "No," I said slowly. "But he will if we don't stop him."

"What's the name?"

I shook my head. "I don't know. But I do know that unless we figure out how this guy is targeting his vics, we won't be able to narrow the field and he'll strike again."

The meeting broke up shortly thereafter, none of us looking like we felt it'd been very productive. "Sorry," I whispered to Dutch as we left the conference room.

He gave me a funny look. "Why are you sorry?"

"I wasn't very helpful in there," I admitted. "I only gave you guys the most obscure tip ever to follow up on."

"How do you know you weren't helpful?" he asked plainly. "Seriously, Edgar, you know how this psychic stuff works better than I do. Maybe the fact that you told us to focus only on one direction was because that's the only direction that will yield us one more clue."

I smiled up at him. "You're a pretty understanding guy—you know that?"

Dutch grinned back. "You realize I'm going to quote you on that the next time you and I get into an argument, right?"

I laughed. "What? You and me argue? We *never* do that!"

"Never do what?" Brice asked, walking in on the last part of the conversation.

"Jump to conclusions," I said quickly. I didn't repeat the inside joke to him, knowing it might hit a little too close to home.

Brice nodded, but he seemed distracted. "I'm headed out to meet with Candice for a few. Dutch, you're in charge until I get back."

"You got it, sir."

"Good luck," I added as he turned to leave.

He stopped and looked over his shoulder at me. "Will I need it?"

"Probably," I told him honestly, and his face fell. "Try starting off by telling her how nice she looks. She's a sucker for flattery."

Brice's lips pressed together, but he nodded and hurried off. Dutch shook his head. "I think we need to stop sticking our noses in their business from now on."

I waved my hand dismissively. "Too late, cowboy. We've entered the vortex and there's no getting out until they resolve it or split up."

"I'm not sure which to hope for," Dutch said.

"How about wishing for a sandwich?" I asked, pointing to the clock, which read noon. "Drama always makes me hungry," I added when Dutch gave me a humorous look.

Brice returned about two hours later and I noticed that he carried the folded contract with him. Close to five I found the courage to head to his office and ask him how it'd gone. "She signed it," he said.

My eyebrows shot up. "She did?"

Brice leaned tiredly back in his chair. "It took a great deal of coaxing, but I finally convinced her that I could weather any fallout that might come out of it better than she could."

"Awesome!" I wanted to ask him how the talk had gone between them, but I considered what Dutch had said about butting out, and decided it might be time to do just that. "Very well, sir. Will we see you for dinner tonight?"

Brice nodded. "Yes, but let me pick it up this time. I'll be over around seven. Just text me what you two are in the mood for and I'll grab it on the way."

Dutch and I left the office around six, and I'll admit, I was so tired and had such a headache I could hardly think straight. "You okay?" Dutch asked as we drove.

I realized I was squinting from the throbbing behind my temples. "Fine. Just another headache."

"You get your staples out tomorrow," he reminded me.

I brightened a little at that. "I know. And thank God! I cannot wait to shampoo my hair."

Dutch was about to reply when my phone bleeped. I dug it out of my purse and said, "It's Candice."

"So answer it."

I punched the screen and greeted my good friend. "I signed the contract," she said right away.

"Good for you!" I didn't want to let on that I already knew.

"Brice insisted."

"I figured he would."

"I'm still worried this could come back to bite him in the butt."

"I'm not," I told her firmly. "Really, Candice, the energy isn't there for trouble. It actually feels like now that you've signed the contract, a lot of stuff is going to fall into place for you."

"You promise?"

"I do."

There was a bit of a pause then, and I had to bite my lip to keep from asking her if she had told Brice her true feelings. Waiting paid off because she said, "We didn't talk about anything other than the contract."

"I figured."

"But I *am* going to talk to him soon."

I sighed. "You know, Candice, for someone who used to jump out of airplanes all the time, I'm amazed at how scared you are to take this one tiny leap."

"It's not a tiny leap," she insisted. "This is way bigger than that."

"See, and it's because you're thinking it's some huge thing that you're putting it off. It's just a conversation, honey. And through that will be an exchange of information. Either he feels the same as you do, or he doesn't. My money is that he does, because Brice Harrison does not strike me as the type of man to take risks with his career lightly. But he's doing that for you."

It was Candice's turn to sigh heavily and this was followed by an even lengthier pause. "So I heard from Genevieve," she said, changing the subject.

"Yeah?"

"She's almost through with the list. She's going to fax it to me in an hour or so."

"So you're back on the case?"

"I'm contractually bound to investigate," she said, and I detected the humor in her voice. "I need to bring this one home for Brice."

"Good for you," I said as we pulled into our sub. "Keep me in the loop, okay?"

"Will do," she assured. "And speaking of keeping people in the loop, I've decided to bring Antoine in on this."

"Really?" That was a surprise.

"Yes. I have a distinct feeling he was the one who turned me in to the board."

"Uh . . . then why would you want to loop him in?"

Candice sighed. "Because I think you were right to recommend we do that in the first place. The guy did save your life, and if I were him, and someone was purposely stonewalling me, I'd probably mess with them a little too."

I smirked. "Really?" I mocked. "That doesn't sound *anything* like you."

Candice ignored the sarcasm. "Yeah, well, maybe once he sees that we trust him with our information, he can trust us with his. And who knows? If we show him the names we get from Genevieve, maybe one will register with him."

"Oh, honey! That's a great idea!" But even as I said it something nagged at me but my headache prevented me from digging too deeply into what felt off and as Dutch pulled into our driveway I was actually anxious to get off the phone with Candice and go find some Excedrin. "Listen, hon, we're home and I've got a killer headache. Can you and I chat later?"

"Oh, sweetie! I'm so sorry. Of course, of course. Go take care of yourself."

*   *   *

The doorbell rang at seven thirty. I got up from the table where we'd all just sat for dinner to answer it, thinking it was probably Dave—because no one knew when we were having a nice hot meal better than that man. I was surprised then when I opened the door to see Candice looking sheepish on my doorstep. "Hey," she said.

"Oh, hey! What's up?"

Candice held up several sheets of paper. "Genevieve's list of congregation members who have occupations as handymen or contractors."

I motioned for Candice to come in, and she stepped through the door, already shrugging out of her coat when she happened to catch sight of Dutch and Brice, sitting at the table and looking quite surprised by her appearance. "Ooops," she said, her voice almost panicky. "I didn't mean to interrupt. I can come back later."

I flattened my back against the door, barring her hasty exit. "Don't be ridiculous! Please, come join us for some Chinese."

With her back to the table, Candice gave me a steely glare. "I don't want to impose," she said loudly.

I narrowed my eyes right back at her. "It's no imposition at all! There's plenty. And you look hungry. We'd love it if you'd stay, right, Dutch?"

From the other side of the room I saw the deer-in-the-headlights look on Dutch's face, but one warning glare from me and he quickly recovered. "Sure," he said. "There's plenty of food for one more."

"And Brice wants you to stay too, right, sir?"

I expected that since Brice had been caught off guard,

he'd mutter something stupid, like, "Uhhhhh. . . ." But he completely surprised me when he actually got up from the table and came over to us. "I've got your favorite, kung pao chicken," he said calmly, taking Candice's sweater from her and motioning to the table.

"Uhhh . . . ," Candice said, and I stifled a giggle.

We had a wonderful time at dinner and it reminded me of old times. At first, Candice and Brice were a little stiff and formal with each other, but soon their obvious attraction took the edge off, and by the end of dinner they were laughing and sneaking goo-goo eyed glances at each other.

I cleared the dinner dishes, suggested they take advantage of the lovely evening and go for a nice walk. "It's such a cute neighborhood," I coaxed as I grabbed plates and glassware. "Really, you two look like you could both use some fresh evening air."

Candice smiled slyly at me and I pretended not to notice. Brice got to his feet and offered Candice his arm. She blushed and could hardly refuse. Once they'd gone, Dutch came in to help me with the dishes. "You're pretty proud of yourself, aren't you?" he asked.

I realized belatedly that I was wearing a rather smug grin. "Had to be done," I told him. "I mean, I'm so sick of hearing all their excuses for not talking to each other. They're worse than a soap opera."

"They'll figure it out."

"How can you be so sure?"

Dutch tossed the kitchen towel he was using to dry the dishes over his shoulder and lifted my chin with two fingers. "Because we did," he said, and kissed me gently on the lips.

"I'm thinking we shouldn't wait up for them," I said, turning off the water and snuggling into his arms.

"I'm thinking you're right," he agreed.

The next day was fairly routine; Candice had left a copy of the church list on the dining room table along with a note thanking us for dinner and asking me to take a look at the names over the weekend to see if anyone jumped out at me. Skimming through the pages, I guessed there were close to fifty names on the list. "Yikes," I muttered. The church obviously catered to a large blue-collar base, but fifty names were a lot for my radar to deal with, and I mentally made a note to ask her to narrow it for me if she could.

Brice was still with us that morning, but he assured us over coffee that he would be out of our hair by Saturday. "I'm thinking of checking into a hotel," he said.

I opened my mouth to protest, but Dutch subtly squeezed my arm and said, "Whatever is most comfortable for you, sir."

Brice nodded. "Thank you for your hospitality," he added. "But I really think it's time for me to find my own accommodations and let you two have your house back."

On the way to work, I got a call from the doctor's office to confirm my appointment for the staple removal. I'd scheduled it over lunch, and it was close enough to Candice's that I could pop over there and take a quick shower.

When we got to the office, we checked in with Todd, Cox and Rueben about the murdered young men, and I was surprised when Cox said he thought he might have something. "I found a connection," he said.

"What?" I asked.

"Facebook."

I blinked. That was so *not* what I thought he was going to say. "Say what, now?"

"All three guys had accounts on Facebook," he said.

"Uh," I said, wondering how he could possibly think that was a lead. "Isn't the whole world on Facebook?"

"I'm not," Cox said stubbornly.

I bit my tongue and asked, "Did they friend each other, then, or something?"

"No, but Avril and Felix were both fans of Jay-Z."

"How do you know?"

"It's on their profile page," Cox told me, pointing to his computer screen like he'd just cracked the case wide open.

"Ah," I said, and eyed Dutch skeptically. "Keep digging," he told the agents before motioning me to follow him to his office.

"What's up?" I asked when he pointed me to a chair.

"You're squinting again."

I took a seat and rubbed my temples. "I can't seem to get rid of this headache," I confessed.

"Are you coming down with something?"

I shook my head. "No, this usually happens when I overwork the radar."

"Can I get you some Tylenol or something?"

"I've been popping Excedrin since yesterday and it hasn't even made a dent."

"Did you want to go back home?"

I took a deep breath and forced myself to smile. "I'll be fine. Really. I just need to push through it."

Dutch looked unsure, so I got up and forced an even bigger smile. "Work on Agent Cox, would you? That Facebook thing isn't even close to a lead."

"Is there anything else you can suggest that might help us narrow where to look for this list that these guys are on?"

I rubbed my temples again but stopped the moment I saw Dutch's face. "All I can tell you is what I saw in my mind's eye, Dutch."

"What was that exactly?" he asked.

"It may sound weird, but the image I had was Santa reviewing his naughty list, and Felix, Jason, and Avril were on it."

Dutch considered me for a long moment. "You're right. That does sound weird."

I threw my hands up. "It's all I've got."

"Okay, Abs. I'll keep working it with Cox, Rueben, and Todd. Now go get some coffee and take it a little easy today, will you?"

He didn't have to tell me twice, especially since the moment I began auditing files, my head was throbbing like a souped-up bass.

At eleven thirty I reminded Katie that I was taking a long lunch and hurried to my doctor's appointment. The process to remove the ten staples in my scalp was remarkably quick, and I could barely contain my excitement afterward when I showed up at Candice's door with shower supplies in hand. I rapped loudly on her door, but no one came to answer it. "Crap," I said, and knocked again. "Come on, Cassidy! Sundance needs a shower."

A few more seconds passed and the door was opened abruptly. I took a huge step back when I came face-to-face with a rumpled-looking Brice Harrison wearing Candice's silk robe and several smeared lipstick stains on his face. "Abby!" he said, clearly flustered when he saw me standing there all slack-jawed.

"Uh . . . ," I said, feeling my cheeks heat.

"Errr . . . ," he said, his own face turning red.

And then no one said anything more. I simply turned on my heel and hurried away, wishing that once I got outside, a freak solar flare would burn away my retinas and I'd never have to see *anything* like that again.

I dashed back to the office, stopping to pick up a sub on the way, and when I got there, I grabbed several Bankers Boxes and told Katie I'd be working on them in the conference room. I didn't know how long I'd be able to avoid seeing Brice after that encounter, but I was hoping it would be at least for the rest of the day.

I got my wish, as I was left to work undisturbed for the afternoon, and it wasn't until four thirty that the door opened and Dutch poked his head in. "Hey," he said when he saw me.

I sat back in the chair and squinted at him. "Hey, yourself."

"How'd it go at the doctor?"

"I'm no longer the bride of Frankenstein," I said, dipping my head so he could see my scalp.

"Didn't have time for that shower at Candice's after all, huh?" he said, coming into the room.

I felt my cheeks heat again. "Nope." And I left it at that.

"You look beat."

"I am beat. And this headache is now like a raging bull."

"Too much intuiting?"

"Definitely."

"Harrison said we could knock off early."

"He won't get any argument from me," I said, shoving the folders back into their boxes.

As we walked out, I asked, "Any luck tracking that connection to Avril, Felix, and Jason?"

"Not yet. But I keep thinking back to your vision. There's something obvious that we're missing."

"Tell me about it," I agreed.

We arrived at Dutch's car then and I handed him his keys. "Mind driving?"

Dutch unlocked the doors, and while I was getting in, my phone beeped. After digging it out of my purse, I noticed that there were three missed calls and three voice mails, all from Candice. "Uh-oh," I said.

"What?"

"Candice called."

"Why is that an uh-oh?"

I tore my eyes away from the phone display and

quickly decided against telling Dutch about the encounter with Brice earlier that afternoon. "I didn't have a chance to look at the list of contractors and handymen from the church," I said quickly.

"She'll understand. Call her up and tell her you'll get to it later this weekend." I didn't say anything and Dutch must have interpreted that to mean I was still feeling guilty over it. "Really, dollface, you should think about taking it easy for a day or two. You look a little pale."

"I think I'm getting a migraine," I admitted, realizing the constant throbbing headache I'd had all day was starting to intensify.

"Now, that's an uh-oh," Dutch said.

And he wasn't kidding. Over the course of the next day and a half, all I did was lie in bed with a cold compress on my forehead as the most god-awful headache took hold and refused to abate.

It was so bad I had to lie in bed with all the blinds closed and the lights off. I couldn't even tolerate the light from the television.

Dutch came in to check on me about every hour. He tried to get me to eat something too, but I was just too miserable.

Finally, by Sunday morning I began to feel better and eventually made it out of bed long enough to tolerate a nice long shower.

When I headed downstairs, I found Candice in my living room holding her car keys and looking terribly worried. She and Dutch were whispering and they stopped abruptly when I appeared. "Abs!" Dutch said, getting to his feet to come over to me as I moved slowly down the stairs. "What are you doing out of bed?"

"I'm a little better," I said. "And I think I'm hungry."

Dutch grinned. "Well, then, I know you're better. The time I worry is when you're not eating."

He then went off to make me a sandwich and I sat down with Candice on the couch. "I'm so sorry you're not feeling well," she said to me.

"It's okay," I assured her. "This happens when I overdo it with the radar."

"How many cases are you focusing on at the bureau?"

I sighed tiredly. "Not sure. Maybe . . . fifty a day."

Candice looked at me like I'd just said something crazy. "*Why* would you think you could handle that kind of volume?"

I attempted a smile. "That's part of the job description." And even as I heard the words come out of my mouth, I knew that pace would be the death of me.

Candice was shaking her head back and forth. "Abby," she said gently. "You're not built to do that. You can't even read more than six clients a day!"

My eyes welled with tears. I knew she was right, but to admit it meant admitting I'd failed. "What can I do?" I asked.

"You can quit," came a deep baritone voice behind me.

I jumped a little. I hadn't realized Dutch had come back into the room. He set my sandwich on the coffee table and sat down on the couch next to me. "I can't quit," I told him, and more tears leaked out of my eyes.

Dutch and Candice exchanged a knowing look, and my sweetheart tucked a strand of my hair behind my ear. "Of course you can," he said. "And we can rehire you as a consultant. You could work for us part-time. Just a few hours a week, whatever you think you can handle."

"I've already talked to Brice," Candice said. "He's good with it if you are, although he really wants you to continue teaching the classes for the agents. He says that's the most important element you bring to the table."

"Even more than the audits?" I asked.

Dutch snaked an arm over my shoulder and pulled me backward into him. Kissing the top of my now squeaky clean hair, he said, "We can do our own audits. Once you teach us how to differentiate the viable files from the dead ones, we should be off and running."

I glanced up at him. "You're sure?"

He grinned. "Miss Cooper, as your supervisor, allow me to inform you that you've been officially let go from full-time status with the CCS. We'd like to offer you a consulting position instead. And we're willing to pay you at your former hourly rate."

My eyebrows arched. "You realize that even working part-time I'd be making more money than before when I was on salary."

"Yes," Dutch said. "But you'd be responsible for your own benefits like health insurance, etc."

"I've paid for that before."

"You and I can get a group rate," Candice assured me. "Especially when you come to work for me!"

I laughed. "I don't think I've ever changed jobs so fast in all my life."

"Civilian profiler one minute, private investigator the next," she sang.

"We always did make a good team," I told her.

Candice grinned. "And just think about how well we'll do when Milo joins us."

Dutch leaned forward. "Milo's agreed to move to Texas?"

"He says he'll be down in the fall, right before the new school year. He doesn't want to take his son away from his friends too early. He wants to give him the summer to say good-bye."

"That *is* good news!" I sang, and just like that, I felt much better.

A little later I walked Candice out to her car. "So, after I heard that you were having a migraine from overusing your radar, I called Mrs. Dixon about Genevieve's list. I'm headed back to the church tomorrow morning to meet with her and Genevieve. Hopefully Mrs. Dixon will recognize a name or two, and if not, I thought maybe Genevieve could help narrow the scope."

"Can I come?"

Candice smiled. "Of course! But only if you think you'll feel up to it."

"I'll be okay," I assured her.

Candice nodded. Then, out of the blue, she said, "I'm really sorry about Friday. Brice told me it was you at the door."

I cleared my throat uncomfortably. "Please don't mention it," I said. "Like, ever again."

Candice laughed. "Agreed."

"You two are back together again?" I couldn't help it; I had to know.

Candice blushed. "Um . . . yeah," she said, and then she took something out of her pocket and put it on her left ring finger before waggling her hand at me. "You could say that we're permanently back together now."

I swear I did the Wile E. Coyote *baaaarruuuugah!* eyes. "You're *engaged*?!" I shouted, and then I believe I launched myself right into her and hugged her until she protested that she couldn't breathe.

I made Candice tell me all the details—well, not *all* the details—I was pretty sure I had a feel for what happened immediately after she'd accepted the ring, but the part leading up to it was what I was most interested in.

"I wish I could take credit for telling Brice that I was crazy about him and didn't want him to move out, but the truth is that he came over Friday for lunch, and while I was fixing us some salad, he got down on bended knee and offered me the black box with this beautiful ring inside. He told me that he'd never been so in love and he couldn't imagine life without me, and if I wanted to say no again, I could, but he wasn't going to stop asking until I eventually said yes."

I sighed contentedly as I held her hand in front of my

face and tilted it back and forth to catch the fading afternoon light. "I'm so glad you finally said yes," I told her. "I mean, it's about freaking time! For a minute there, I thought we'd all be old and gray by the time you two got around to saying 'I do.'"

Candice smiled. "I'm not the only one putting off commitment, you know."

I looked up from oggling her ring. "Huh?"

"I'm talking about you and Dutch, Abs. What's up with this whole we're-just-living-in-sin stuff anyway?"

I blinked at her indignantly. "Hey, we have a *great* relationship."

"Oh, I'm not saying you don't. What I *am* saying is that you guys don't practice what you preach."

"Will you please speak English?"

"One of you needs to pop the question already," Candice said, moving over to her car and opening the door.

I stood there completely dumbfounded in my own driveway. I had no words to muster a retort, and Candice waved daintily from behind the wheel and left.

It took me about five whole minutes to collect myself and walk back into the house. The truth was that I really *did* love my relationship with Dutch. We'd never talked marriage or next steps. Living together came so easily to us that it seemed a shame to go messing with that. Still, when I saw him sitting on the couch watching a ball game, I asked, "You're happy, right?"

Dutch held up his beer in one hand and the remote in the other. "Ecstatic."

"No," I said. "Seriously, Dutch. We're good, right?"

He reluctantly pulled his eyes away from the TV. "Yeah, doll. We're good."

I nodded. Dutch went back to watching the game. "I mean, you don't want anything more than this, right?"

Dutch's posture stiffened. He then muted the TV and focused on me. "More?" he asked carefully.

His reaction confirmed my suspicion. Talking about marriage and stuff like that—even in the most general of terms—was enough to cause tension between us. "Forget it," I said, and pushed a smile onto my face to show him that I was only kidding. "Stupid Candice put a crazy thought into my head."

Dutch's stiff posture became downright rigid. "What kind of crazy thought?"

"She and Brice are officially engaged."

The muscles of Dutch's jaw bunched. "Well, we knew that was coming," he said after a pregnant pause.

I nodded. "Yeah, but now that she's got a ring on her finger, Candice thinks one of us should pop the question." I then laughed to show him how ludicrous I found that idea.

He laughed too.

We sounded like a couple of tortured hyenas.

"I'll let you get back to the game," I said.

"Thanks."

"Oh, and Candice and I are headed up to Dallas tomorrow."

"You are?"

I nodded. "We're going to try and have Mrs. Dixon and the church secretary help us narrow the list down. If we can isolate a few individuals, we'll be able to turn the names back over to you guys to follow up on."

"That'd be great," he said, his posture finally relaxing a little. "But just to be clear, none of the names on the list flagged your radar?"

I shook my head and turned to the stairs. "I honestly haven't looked at it yet. It's a long list and I really wanted to give my noggin a break."

"How many names are there?"

"About fifty."

"Good thinking. You two be careful, okay?"

"Aren't we always?"

Dutch laughed, and unmuted the TV. "No."

"Good point. Okay, we'll be careful this time. I pinkie swear."

Chapter Fifteen

I woke at some point in the middle of the night with the most foreboding feeling. I couldn't pinpoint the source of it, which made it all the worse. Sleep proved impossible and eventually about four a.m. I got up and tiptoed downstairs.

I made myself some coffee and just sat huddled in an afghan waiting for the sun to rise.

Dutch found me at five. "Abs?" he said, from the middle of the staircase.

"I'm down here."

He came to sit next to me on the couch. "Couldn't sleep?"

"No."

"Is the headache back?"

I shook my head. "Something bad is going down."

Dutch rubbed his face tiredly. "Something bad is going down," he repeated. "Care to elaborate?"

"I'm not sure I can," I said honestly. "I just have the worst feeling that I've failed in some way. Like, there is something I'm missing, and because I didn't connect the dots, someone's going to pay . . . big time."

Dutch reached for my nearly empty coffee cup, inspected the contents, and got up with it to shuffle into the kitchen. He was back two minutes later with a fresh mug for both of us. "Drink," he ordered. I took a sip. "I'm going to cook up some breakfast. Once I know you've eaten, we can talk about it."

Dutch got busy in the kitchen and I joined him by taking a seat at the kitchen table. We didn't speak while he cooked us up a couple of omelets, plus one for Eggy and Tuttle to split. He wouldn't let me talk until I'd taken a few bites. The truth was that the foreboding was so intense that I didn't have much of an appetite. "So talk to me," Dutch said when I settled for pushing my eggs around the plate.

I sighed. "I think someone's going to die."

Dutch eyed me over his mug of coffee. "Do you know who?"

I closed my eyes and tried to sort out the pieces. There was so much jumbled information swirling around in my head that it was really hard to figure it out. "I think our serial killer may have found his next victim," I said sadly. "I feel such a strong connection to Jason, Felix, and Avril, like everything points to them."

"Is it going to happen today?"

I closed my eyes and waited for my radar to figure it all out. "I'm not sure," I confessed. "I'd like to say no, but only because I feel the energy could go either way. Regardless, events are set into motion today, and the consequences seem grave. That's the only thing I'm sure of."

"What do we do?"

I opened my eyes again as the familiar throb began to pound behind my eyes. "Put all your men on the case, Dutch. There has to be some sort of connection that ties those three together, and if you can figure that out, then maybe you can stop this guy from claiming another victim."

"Done. Do you want to come into the office with me?"

I thought about that for a minute, weighing it against the promise I'd made to Candice and an uncanny sense of urgency I felt to go with her. "No, I feel like I really need to head to Dallas. But keep me in the loop on anything you guys find that might be a lead, okay?"

"Got it." Dutch kissed me on the cheek then and said, "If I'm going to get a jump on this, I gotta shower and get to the office."

"No sweat. I'll do the dishes," I told him.

Candice came by around seven to pick me up. "Ready to roll?"

I got in and buckled up. "I am."

"We're going to stop at Antoine's first," she told me.

I remembered then that she'd mentioned wanting to show the church list to the lieutenant to see if any names jumped out at him, but as we pulled out of the drive I had a strange vision come into my head. I saw the image of a tiger dressed in fatigues and sitting on a stony perch eyeing every movement while its tail flickered back and forth.

"You okay?" Candice asked.

I realized I'd been staring straight ahead while I tried to figure out the imagery. "Fine," I told her, still puzzling over it. I felt that Antoine was the tiger, and I remembered thinking of him in that same way when we'd first met him, but that was before he'd saved my life. Still, there was this nagging feeling in the pit of my stomach. "Maybe we shouldn't show him the list," I said after a bit.

"Who?"

"Antoine."

Candice chuckled. "Are you kidding me?" When she saw the serious look on my face, and realized I wasn't, she asked, "Why the change of heart, Sundance?"

I wanted to tell her that my radar didn't think it was a good idea, but the more I thought about it, the more I knew I could be jumping to conclusions here. Yes, Antoine was stealthy and dangerous like a tiger—but weren't most war veterans? The guy had just come back from a war zone, so who knew what dangers he'd had to face down? And the man hadn't even hesitated to save my life, after all. "Forget it," I said. "You're right. Showing him the list is the right thing to do. I think this headache is still playing havoc with my radar."

"You sure?"

I wasn't, but I didn't know why I wasn't, so I insisted we head to Lasalle's anyway.

Two and a half hours later we pulled up to the lieutenant's house. He was sitting on his front porch, dressed in
fatigues and looking like he'd been waiting for us and the
imagery of the tiger flashed through my mind again. "I
have to get to work soon," he said by way of greeting.

"Sorry for the holdup," Candice told him, and pre-
sented him with the list from Genevieve. "We think there
is a slight chance that one of the names on here might be
a person of interest in your sister's disappearance."

LaSalle remained seated while he studied the names
one by one. Slowly, he shook his head. "No one jumps
out at me," he said, and I breathed a sigh of relief when
I sensed he was telling the truth. "But that might be just
my first reaction. Can I make a copy of this and think on
it for a day or two?"

My radar weighed in again, and it strongly suggested
that Antoine could definitely help point us to the man
who abducted his sister, so without any further hesitation I said, "Of course."

LaSalle got up and turned to his door. "I'll just scan
this into my computer and be back in a second."

"Take your time," Candice told him sweetly, and I
couldn't help noticing that she wore her new civilian
badge on a lanyard around her neck, just in case La-
Salle wanted to send another letter to the state licensing
board.

The lieutenant came back out in just under three
minutes. "Thank you," he said, and for the first time he
smiled genuinely at both of us. "I really appreciate you
two bringing me in on this."

"Certainly," I said, easily, even though I still had an unsettled feeling in the pit of my stomach.

After leaving LaSalle's, we headed over to the church. Genevieve greeted us warmly and I noticed with satisfaction that when Mrs. Dixon arrived, the two hugged each other fiercely and a few tears were shed before everyone took their seat. We showed the list first to Mrs. Dixon, who took her time and studied it name by name. I kept my fingers crossed that someone there would ring a bell.

As she was looking it over, my phone bleeped. Caller ID said it was Dutch. I excused myself to the hallway and answered. "What's up?"

"I've figured out your list," Dutch said.

I looked back through the open doorway at the huddle of women poring over a long set of names. "How'd you get a copy?"

"What?"

"Of our list?"

"No," Dutch said. "Not your church list, your naughty list."

I rubbed my forehead, which had begun to throb again. "Why do I feel lost?"

"Abs," he said patiently. "Remember your Santa Claus vision?"

And I immediately understood what he was getting at. "Oh! *That* list. Okay, so what'd you figure out?"

"Felix, Avril, and Jason were all registered sex offenders."

I gasped and a jolt of electricity shot right through me just as my radar started firing off alarm bells in my head.

"Dutch," I said quickly, my heart pounding, "I'm going to e-mail you that list of names from the church. I need you to run it through the sex offender database, and I need it done ASAP."

"I thought you wanted me to focus on the dead guys."

"Just do this for me, will you?" I snapped.

There was a pause, then, "Okay, Abby. Send me the list and I'll pull Todd off the other investigation to run it through."

"Thank you," I said gratefully. "And one more thing: I need the last known addresses for the three dead men."

"Addresses?" he asked.

"I have a theory."

"Want to fill me in?"

My hands were shaking slightly as I reached into my purse and pulled out a pen and a piece of scrap paper. "No time. Just give me those addresses and work on that list. Call me back the moment you get anything."

After taking down the addresses, I had Candice e-mail Dutch the list from her laptop. Genevieve and Mrs. Dixon were still huddled together, looking through the names, one by one. "Anything?" I asked them.

The pair looked up. "Not yet," said Mrs. Dixon, and I could tell she felt bad about not recognizing any of the names.

"It's okay," I assured her. "We'll figure it out." I then turned to Candice, who was watching me closely. She knew something was up. "Can you pull up Google Maps?"

Candice opened up the file and I had her type in the addresses for all three dead men. Small red pins dotted the homes in a nice tidy triangle. "Now can you plug in the addresses for Keisha, Patrice, Fatina, and Essence?"

Four more red dots appeared within the red triangle. "Whoa," Candice whispered. "Abs, what's going on?"

I was about to answer her when my phone bleeped. It was Dutch. I put him on speaker so Candice could hear. "One name on your list hit the registry," he said. "Ronald D. Mundy. He goes by his middle name, Don."

Out the corner of my eye I saw Mrs. Dixon's head snap up. "That's him!" she gasped. "That's the man who painted my house!"

"Don Mundy?" Genevieve repeated. "I know him. His mother is one of our most active members."

"Where do they live?" I asked her quickly.

Genevieve thought for a moment. "Well, his mother still lives on Pecan Valley Drive—that's about five miles from here—but Donny, he's real close. Just behind us in the apartments next door in fact." Genevieve pointed to the large window of her office and my eyes traveled to a set of apartments just beyond the parking lot.

"Abs!" Dutch said through the speaker. "What's going on?"

But I didn't answer him right away; instead I asked a question. "That sex offender registry, Dutch, is that something anyone can access?"

"Yes. It's available online. You can just plug in your own address and it will give you a map of any registered sex offender within a two- to three-mile radius of where you live."

"Oh, God!" I whispered, and closed my eyes as I thought back to that moment when I'd agreed to let Antoine take the list inside to scan into his computer.

"What?" Candice said. I opened my lids to see her staring at me with concern.

"LaSalle," I whispered. "He's the only one it could have been."

"What are you talking about?" she and Dutch asked together.

"He's been clearing his neighborhood of sex offenders. He must have pulled up the registry after his sister went missing, and killed anyone in his neighborhood who might have been a suspect. That's why no new men have been murdered in the last year!" I said, sliding one more piece into place. "LaSalle's been in Afghanistan. And that's also why he wanted us to keep him in the loop, so that he could get to any additional suspects before we did."

"We gave him the list!" Candice gasped, her face going a little pale.

And the weight of the terrible mistake I'd just made hit me like a punch in the gut. "Dutch!" I nearly shouted. "Send any available agents to the army base in Killeen. You've got to bring LaSalle in for questioning *immediately*."

"On it," he said. "And I'll also send some agents to pick up Mundy for questioning. You two sit tight, you hear?"

"Got it," I said, and clicked off.

For a long few moments no one spoke; we just looked worriedly around at one another. Candice got up then and went over to the window. I fidgeted in my chair, holding my phone and wishing it would ring soon.

The tense silence was broken when Candice suddenly exclaimed, "Son of a bitch!"

I jumped as she whirled around, drew her gun, and went running out the door.

I sat there for all of two heartbeats before I bolted after her.

Keeping up with Candice was tough. That woman can run. Still, I managed to follow her down the two flights of stairs, out through a back door, across the parking lot, and over to Mundy's apartments.

I had no idea what she'd seen to cause such a reaction until we reached the parking lot of the complex, and passed by LaSalle's green Jeep. Candice paused by his car and swore. "Shit! I forgot to get Mundy's address!"

With shaking fingers, I pulled out my iPhone and tapped on the Internet icon. A few seconds later I had the sex offender registry up, and found him. "He's in three-B!"

Candice dashed to the stairs leading up to the third floor and I pounded after her. When we got to 3-B, we could clearly hear sounds of a struggle from inside. Candice used her arm to halt me and press me flat against the side of the building. "Stay here!" she hissed. Holding her gun up, she stepped back from the door two paces, then used her heel to kick it in. In the next instant she was through the entry and shouting orders for LaSalle to drop his weapon.

A muffled voice inside screamed in agony, and La-Salle shouted, "This is none of your business!"

"Drop it, LaSalle!" Candice yelled again.

I closed my eyes and the most horrible image floated into my mind. In a flash I saw LaSalle, flat on his back with a bullet through his brain, and lying nearby was Candice, a large knife sticking out of her chest.

I inhaled sharply, gathered my courage, and stepped through the door. "LaSalle!" I shouted, moving quickly to Candice's side.

The lieutenant was standing menacingly behind a chair, where a bloodied, bruised, and battered Don Mundy was duct taped. His eyes were huge, and it was obvious he'd been tortured, as various tools lay strewn about the chair, all of them tipped with red.

"Get out of here, Abby!" Candice commanded, her voice more furious than I'd ever heard her.

I ignored her and took one bold step forward, putting myself squarely between LaSalle and Candice. "Listen to me!" I shouted at him, my eyes on the huge army knife he held in his hand. "It's over, Lieutenant! Your sister is not coming back! And killing Mundy will not change that!"

"I'm not looking to change it," LaSalle told me. "I'm looking for revenge."

I held up my hand in a stopping motion. "But don't you want to know where she is?" I tried. "If you kill Mundy, you'll never really know what happened to her!

Don't you owe it to Keisha to bring her body home and give her a proper burial?"

LaSalle's eyes flickered for an instant between me and Mundy. I used the opportunity to take another step forward.

"Abby!" Candice shouted, and I felt her hand grab my arm but I pulled with all my might and tugged myself free. LaSalle crouched slightly with that big knife in his hand, and for a moment I thought he was going to make a move to stab one of us, so I turned as Candice made another grab for my arm and shoved her hard, out of range of the knife. She fell and Antoine took that opportunity to step menacingly toward me.

"Please, Lieutenant!" I begged, holding my hands up in surrender, while hearing Candice scramble to her feet behind me. I knew she wouldn't hesitate to shoot him if she thought I was in danger so I didn't mince words with him. "Please just stop and think this through for a second!" LaSalle hesitated and I used the moment to say, "Help us give some closure to the families of these girls! If you kill Mundy before he tells us what he did, and where the girls are, their families may always wonder what happened to them!"

Outside we all heard sirens approaching, and I could tell that if LaSalle was going to make a move, he was going to do it in the very next second, so using every ounce of courage I had, I took one more step toward him and placed my shaking hand on the butt of the knife. Behind me I heard Candice suck in a breath. "You can do this!" I urged him, ignoring my partner and fighting down my own fear to maintain eye contact with him. "You can step back from here, Antoine, and bring justice to your sister and the other three girls."

LaSalle's eyes bored into mine, and all I saw was indecision. "Antoine," I whispered as tears formed in my eyes as the emotion of the moment took over. "You saved my life! *Please*, let me return the favor."

Outside the sirens stopped abruptly and loud footsteps approached. I gripped the butt of the knife as tightly as I could, praying I could stop Antoine from bringing it down into my chest, or Mundy, or tossing it at Candice. And with a suddenness I didn't expect, LaSalle abruptly let go of it altogether just as the police burst into the room and began yelling at everyone to get down on their knees.

I stepped back from Antoine, lowered the knife to the floor, and did exactly as I was told.

It took Dutch the rest of the week to wrap up all three cases. Mundy cooperated fully to escape the death penalty, and led the CCS to the bodies of Keisha, Essence, and Fatina whom he'd buried next to an abandoned gas station somewhere out in the boonies.

LaSalle pleaded guilty to first-degree murder, but given the circumstances of his sister's death, and his sterling military service, he was given a fairly light sentence of life with the possibility of parole in thirty years.

Candice was also able to bring final closure to Mrs. Dixon, matching the photo of Fontana to that of a woman's body brought to the St. Louis morgue in 2006.

Fontana had died of an overdose, just like her mother suspected.

A few days after Fatina's funeral, I was called into the office for a meeting with Dutch and Harrison. I figured they wanted to talk about when my next class would be scheduled or a new cold case.

I figured wrong.

When I walked into the conference room, I was quite surprised to discover the newly promoted regional director of the FBI, Bill Gaston, sitting there waiting for me.

To his left sat a man I didn't recognize, in a black suit, white shirt, and crisp black tie, who gave me the creeps, along with a military officer of high rank, given the number of stars pinned to his cap.

Introductions were made, and I found out that the man in black was actually CIA, and the military dude was a lieutenant colonel. Dutch and Brice joined me in the meeting, but no one else was allowed in. Gaston spoke first. "Thank you for joining us, Abigail," he said.

"My pleasure, sir."

"You're probably wondering why we've called you in here."

"It had crossed my mind."

Gaston smiled at me. I genuinely liked him but was often intimidated by the power and intelligence that just radiated out of him. He was by far one of the sharpest and smartest men I'd ever known—and probably one of the most lethal. "I'm very impressed with the numbers coming out of CCS," he said to me. "I understand much of the credit should go to you."

I felt my cheeks heat. "It's a group effort, sir."

Gaston merely smiled and gave me a nod. "Let me ask you something, Abigail," he said in a casual tone.

"Of course, sir."

"Do you love your country?"

My brow furrowed. "Of course, sir."

"Would you be willing to risk your own life to protect it?"

I blinked. What the hello-dolly was Gaston getting at? "Yes," I said slowly. "I would, sir."

Gaston's eyes flicked to Dutch, who did not look happy . . . like, at all. "It's her decision," Gaston said in a way that suggested they'd already had a pretty intense discussion about me.

Dutch's lips pressed together, and I could tell he was holding his tongue with effort.

"Sir," I said. "May I please ask what this is about?"

Gaston folded his hands on the tabletop and looked at me square in the eye. "We would like to propose a mission, Abigail."

I couldn't help it. I smiled. "A mission? You mean like you need me to be a spy or something?"

But Gaston wasn't joking. "That's exactly what I mean."

I gulped. "Ah," I said. "Where?"

"I'm afraid I cannot tell you that until you agree to help us."

"Okay," I said, thoroughly confused. "Who am I spying on, then?"

Gaston said nothing. Instead he just continued to stare at me, and it became obvious that he would not say anything more until I agreed to the mission, whatever and wherever it might be.

But I was the cautious type, so I cheated. I turned on the radar and keyed in on the energy in the room. "Canada," I said to him, and felt pretty smug when both the lieutenant colonel and the CIA guy blinked in surprise. I focused on the military man. "Something was stolen off a base," I said. "Something critical to our national security."

The colonel's face flushed crimson. "Gaston!" he snapped. "Order her to stop!"

I would have laughed in his face if Gaston's eyes hadn't warned me to back off. "Abigail," he said softly. "Don't tread too deeply here, just yet."

I shut off the radar and sighed. "Yes, sir."

"Thank you."

"Can you give me any details to help me decide if I should accept this mission?"

Gaston considered that for a moment, and again I saw him glance at Dutch. "It is quite dangerous," he said softly. "I must warn you that the other two agents sent to retrieve our resource have both been murdered in the most grisly fashion."

Gulp.

"We feel strongly that what we need is a secret weapon. Someone able to glean information about where our merchandise has been hidden without making themselves suspect. We also need to identify the major players who might be bidding on the merchandise, as apprehending them would help keep our country secure."

"So, what?" I pressed. "You're just going to stick me on a plane and say, 'Go for it'?"

Gaston smiled again. "No," he assured me. "We'll send you in with a very small team. One other agent to help protect you, and a handler to guide you."

That made me feel a little better at least. "Can that other agent be Dutch?"

Every head in the room save Dutch's and Gaston's shook no. Gaston, however, was the one to make the final decision. "Of course," he said, and immediately I saw the surprise and relief wash over my sweetheart's face.

"Okay," I said. "If Dutch is willing, then so am I."

All eyes swiveled to Dutch. I could tell the decision was tearing him in two, and he took a very long time to answer, but finally he said, "Yes, sir. We'll do it."

Gaston looked immensely happy. "Excellent!" he said, and got up from his chair. Everyone else followed suit. "Agent Harrison, I will need Ms. Cooper and Agent Rivers in Washington early next week to be briefed and meet their handler."

"Yes, sir," Harrison said.

Gaston then shook our hands, and left with his companions. When it was just the three of us again, Harrison asked, "Are you two certain about this?"

"No," said Dutch, and he reached out to hold my hand. "But I think Gaston would have talked Abby into it eventually. At least this way, I can try and keep her safe."

Harrison sighed. "I don't like it," he said softly.

And more than anything, that made me worry that I'd just made a terrible mistake.

The next morning was Saturday and Dutch woke me from a sound sleep before it was even light out. "Hey," he said, rubbing my arm to bring me out of my slumber.

"Whaz a matter?" I asked groggily.

"Come for a drive with me."

I lifted my head off the pillow and squinted in the gloom of the room. "What time is it?"

"You don't want to know," he said.

I noticed then that he was showered, shaved, and smelling amazing. "How long have you been up?"

"A little while," he said, moving to the closet to toss some jeans and a sweatshirt at me. "Come on," he coaxed. "There's something I want to show you."

"Can't it wait?" I asked.

"No, honey," he said gently. "I think it's waited long enough."

I looked at him curiously, but he said nothing more. Instead he left me to get dressed, and I had to go looking for him once I had some clothes on. He was sitting out in his car in the driveway. "He done lost his dang mind," I muttered, peering through the blinds.

I grabbed my purse and headed out to join him and he pulled out the moment I closed the car door. "Can we at least get some coffee on the way to wherever it is you're taking me?" I asked. Have I mentioned that I'm not much of a morning person?

"There's coffee where we're headed," he said. "And it's not far at all."

Dutch drove and said nothing more. I tried to get my brain to focus and rubbed the sleep out of my eyes. I had no idea where we were going, and anytime I asked Dutch, he simply said, "You'll see."

I couldn't do much else but stare out the window. It was still a little murky out, but the sky was quickly moving from dusky gray to a peachy purple. The sun was just starting to rise.

Dutch drove first south, then west, and I could just make out that we were heading to higher elevations as we wound our way along a curvy road. Finally we came down a street without much in the way of housing, but off to the right were some really incredible views. The road we were on rose above a valley and I could see miles into the distance. "Whoa," I said, pointing out the window. "Look at that."

Dutch nodded but kept his eyes on the pavement. He stopped at the very end of the road, as it dead-ended into a peninsula that had breathtaking views on all sides. Pounded into the ground was a series of stakes with little red flags.

Dutch parked and started to get out of the car. "I thought you said there'd be coffee?"

Without replying, Dutch moved to the back of the car and opened the trunk. I headed back there with him and watched curiously as he unloaded a large blanket and a picnic basket. "I came prepared," he said, swinging an arm around my shoulders and moving me over to the center of all the stakes.

I watched then as he unfurled the blanket and coaxed me to sit next to him while he got a thermos out and two coffee mugs. I sat down next to him grinning from ear to ear. "You're like the most romantic man on earth, you know?"

"Guilty as charged," he said, and handed me the mug.

I took a sip and sighed contentedly and looked around. "So what is this place?"

"This?" he replied. I nodded and he said, "It's our new home."

My jaw dropped. "It's *what*?"

Dutch smiled and tilted my chin with his fingers. "See right here?" he said, pointing to a series of stakes that surrounded us. "Once Dave and his brother-in-law finish building the two-story Tudor I had their architect design, this will be our little breakfast nook. It faces east so we can watch the sun come up."

I gasped, looking in the distance as the rays just beyond our view shimmered a rich orange against the outer hills. "Ohmigod!" I whispered.

"And that," Dutch said, pointing in the opposite direction. "That is where our living room will be. We'll have lots of windows with blue shutters, and we'll be able to watch the sunset when we share some ice cream."

Tears welled in my eyes, and I had to blink them away to see where he pointed next. "Right there is where the garage goes, and there'll be enough room above it for his and her offices."

I could hardly breathe and a small sob escaped me. "Oh, Dutch," I squeaked.

But my lovely man wasn't finished with the surprises. No, he had one left, as I discovered when I realized his arm had looped around my middle and in his hand was a velvet black box. "And this is the ring that I had planned to give to you the day we arrived here in Austin, but Brice beat me to the surprise by proposing to Candice first. I decided to wait until that fanfare died down a little to make sure it was special for you, but now that we're headed to D.C. next week, I don't think I can wait a minute longer." He paused for just a moment to reach over and gently open the box to reveal an enormous emerald ring. "Abigail Cooper," he asked formally. "Love of my life, would you make me the happiest man on earth and marry me?"

I tried to say yes, I really did, but my voice had left me the moment I realized he was showing me the vision I'd had of our life together in that two-story Tudor with a kitchen that faced east, and a living room that faced west.

After several feeble attempts at a yes, I finally settled for nodding vigorously and covering him with kisses.

Turn the page for an excerpt
from Victoria Laurie's
next Psychic Eye Mystery

EYE SPY

Coming from Obsidian in July 2011.

For the record: burying a dead body is a *lot* more work than it looks like on TV.

Also for the record, burying a dead body while wearing a clingy evening gown, heels, and in the pouring rain—darn near impossible. Of course, I had help, which could be why we eventually got our dearly departed dude six feet under. (Okay, so maybe it was more like three feet under, but who's really measuring at that point?)

"I think that's good," said my oh-so-gorgeous fiancé as he patted down the mud on top of the long mound of dirt covering our dead guy.

"Thank God," I said, holding my hands palms up to let the rain wash some of the mud off. And that's when I realized my engagement ring had slipped off. "Son of a beast!" I gasped. (Yes, I'm still not swearing, which, at times, proves most inconvenient.)

"What?" asked my sweetie.

Before answering him, I dropped to all fours and began to feel frantically around in the mud. "My ring! I've lost my ring!"

My fiancé threw aside his shovel and came to squat down next to me. "When?"

Tears welled in my eyes, and my heart raced with dread. "I'm not sure," I admitted, still scratching at the mud with my fingernails.

"Abigail," he said gently, "if it's in the grave, we're not going to find it now. We've got to get out of here."

"But—!" I began.

"No buts. Now come on. They'll catch on that we've killed him any minute now, and they'll be looking for us. We have to put some distance between us and them."

I was still crying, however, and I couldn't get over losing the most precious thing I owned. "Please, Rick?" I begged. "Just give me a minute to look. I promise if I don't find it in—"

And that's as far as I got before the woods all around us erupted in gunfire. Rick pulled me to him protectively. I stared into his deep brown eyes as he growled, *"Move!"*

He got no further argument from me; we surged forward, and I followed right next to him as we darted through the underbrush. We ran for probably a quarter mile, and I tripped and slipped almost the entire way in my heels. Thank God I'd passed on the stilettos and gone with a modest two-inch heel. The darn things had no traction, however, and if Rick hadn't been holding my hand, I'm sure I wouldn't have made it that far that quick.

We stopped to catch our breath and listen for signs of a chase behind us. I did my best not to quiver in fear while he scanned the area around us. In the distance I could hear the occasional pop of a gun, but nothing seemed close, and for that, I was grateful. I eyed my sore, muddied, and blistered feet, and wished that my black pumps were ruby red and I could click them together and go back home.

"You ready to move again?" Rick asked me.

"Yes," I said.

No, I thought.

"I can see a structure about twenty yards that way," he told me. "I think it might be a hunting lodge or a log cabin. We can make it there and hide out till nightfall. It'll also give us some shelter from this rain."

"Yippee," I said woodenly.

Rick smiled in sympathy and took my hand. "Come on, babe. It's not far."

Now, you're probably wondering what mess I'd gotten myself into this time—right? Let me take all the suspense right out of it for you. It was a doozy!

It all began three weeks prior to our mad dash through the forest, to a time when I was feeling . . . well . . . patriotic.

Of course, when you have three high-ranking members of the FBI, CIA, and armed forces telling you that your country needs you, it can be a powerfully convincing argument.

You see, six weeks ago, there was a breach to our national security that was of epic proportions. Something was stolen that was so crucial to our country's safety that it left each and every one of us vulnerable.

What was it? you ask. Well, if I told you, I'd have to kill you.

Ha, ha, ha! *Kidding!* I'll divulge all; but let me at least start again at the beginning, which, for me, was on a beautiful late April day in downtown Austin, when I was called to a meeting at the FBI office, where I was a civilian profiling consultant. That's really just a fancy way of saying that, as a professional psychic, I assisted the FBI by pulling warm clues out of the ether on cases that had long since gone cold.

At this particular meeting were my sweetheart—assistant special agent in charge Dutch Rivers—his boss, Brice Harrison; *his* boss, Bill Gaston; and a lieutenant colonel with the air force, along with some steely-looking dude from the CIA.

During the course of that meeting, it became evident that something of *great* importance had been stolen off a military base and was then summarily smuggled out of the country. The good news was that the item had been traced to Canada. The bad news was that everyone agreed it would not be there for long.

Now, naturally, our government wanted its property back, and so they'd sent two CIA agents to retrieve it. Those agents' true identities were discovered, however, and I understand that their demise was swift and most unpleasant—something I'd rather not think about, actually.

Anyway, when it became evident that the task of retrieving the article in question was more formidable than first imagined, Bill Gaston thought of me.

I debated the idea of becoming a spy for two whole minutes—something in hindsight I'm still sort of regretting—but I'd agreed, and Dutch and I had flown to Washington, D.C., the following week.

We'd been met at the airport by a lanky young agent with red hair and lots of freckles. He reminded me of Opie from *The Andy Griffith Show*. "Agent Rivers and Ms. Cooper?" he asked, spotting us immediately from the faces in the crowd surrounding the luggage carousel.

Dutch extended his hand. "Agent Spencer?"

Opie shook Dutch's hand warmly. "Yes, sir," he said, offering me a nice smile too. "Our car is this way."

We trailed behind Spencer, toting our luggage to a waiting black sedan. I swear, if the FBI ever wants to blend in right, they need to add a few Priuses or something less conspicuous to their fleet.

Spencer loaded my bag into the back of the trunk, and we were on our way. "Are we going to headquarters?" Dutch inquired.

Spencer shook his head. "No, sir," he told us. "I've been told to bring you to the CIA central office."

I gulped. I grew up at the height of the cold war, so I still think of the CIA as an agency staffed with seriously scary people willing to do *anything* for the cause.

But I held my nerves in check—I mean, I didn't want to appear all fidgety and nervous on my first day of spy school. How uncool would *that* be?

We arrived at the CIA central office, and Opie handed us off to a female agent dressed in a smart black pantsuit and a crisp white shirt; she had no emotion on her face whatsoever.

She took us through security before seeing us to a large conference room, where nearly a dozen men and one woman were already seated.

The lone woman stood when we entered, and I noticed she was at the head of the oval table. "Good morning," she said cordially. "Agent Rivers, Ms. Cooper, please come in and join us."

The agent who'd shown us in backed out of the room and closed the door. I felt Dutch's hand rest on my lower back as he guided me to the only two available seats left at the table. My mouth went dry as I took up my chair, but when I saw Bill Gaston sitting across from us and smiling warmly, I breathed a teensy bit easier.

It struck me then that the table was arranged somewhat by rank. The woman at the head of the table was obviously running the show, and she was flanked by two gentlemen, who I'd guess were in their midfifties; they seemed full of authority. The authority vein trickled down the table from there.

I also couldn't help noticing that everyone appeared quite interested in me, as so many steely eyes were focused my way. I could also see a little disappointment in a few of them as they assessed me from head to toe. Not the first time I'd experienced that reaction and, likely, not the last.

"Welcome to Washington," said the woman at the head of the table into the silence that followed our sitting down. "I'm Christine Tanner, and I'm the CIA director of intelligence here in D.C."

I smiled and nodded to her, and Dutch did the same. And that was it for pleasantries, because Tanner promptly sat down again and clicked a button, which caused the conference room to go dark except for the projection of a slide onto a screen at the other end of the room. "Ms. Cooper, as you have cleared our security background checks, we feel it wise to educate you on the nature of the security breach we encountered three weeks ago."

I focused on the slide, which showed an areal view of a large air force base. "This is a military outpost in southern Utah. On the morning of April sixth, during a routine flight test, one of our military drones went missing." I heard a click, and a new slide showed the image of an unmanned drone aircraft like I'd seen on the news used in air strikes against enemy militant fighters in Iraq and Afghanistan, although this one looked much smaller in scale.

"The pilot claimed that midway through the test flight, the operating system on the drone failed, causing it to stop responding to his commands and eventually crash somewhere out in the desert."

So far I was following. The air force had lost a drone. Got it.

"It is not unheard of for the operating systems on these aircraft to fail, and because these drone are very expensive to replace, as well as the importance of what this particular drone was carrying, an extensive search was immediately conducted to retrieve whatever remained of the drone and its cargo."

I looked at Dutch; he was focused on Tanner in a way that suggested there might be something more to this missing-drone story. "After we combed through the area where the drone was believed to have crashed, no evidence of it could be found, which is why the military began to suspect the pilot's story."

A little way down from me and to the right, the lieutenant colonel who'd come with Gaston to recruit me in Austin shifted in his seat uncomfortably. Into the slight pause that followed Tanner's last statement, he said, "I personally requested that the pilot come in for a polygraph. But when he failed to show up, we went looking for him. We found him on the floor of his shower, shot through the head at point-blank range."

"Suicide?" I asked, already knowing the answer.

"No," he told me.

"Obviously, we no longer suspect there was an operational issue with the drone," Tanner added. "We believe the pilot was coerced or bribed into delivering our drone into enemy hands."

I furrowed my brow. Why was one missing drone causing so much uproar?

Gaston seemed to read my mind, because he spoke next. "It's more than just a missing drone," he told me.

"Agent Tanner, why don't we allow Professor Steck-worth to explain?"

Gaston's eyes had settled at the end of the table on a small man with salt-and-pepper hair and a nose much too big for his small square face. He cleared his throat when all eyes turned to him, and nodded to Tanner, who clicked her remote to project another slide on the screen. It was a photo of a man young enough to be a college student; he was somewhat unremarkable in appearance, except for the fact that enveloping him on all sides was the most beautiful cloud of color I'd ever seen. "Oh, my God!" I gasped, already understanding what I was looking at.

"Do you know what you're seeing?" Professor Steck-worth asked, staring keenly at me.

I nodded. "You've captured the image of his aura." In my mind's eye, when I focused only on the young man in the photo, I too saw a cloud of color, though it wasn't nearly as vivid as what I was seeing on the screen.

Professor Steckworth smiled. "Yes, very good, Ms. Cooper. Your own abilities allow you to see auras, I take it."

"Well . . ." I hesitated, not wanting everyone to assume my eyesight was clogged with images of color, color everywhere. "It's less that I *see* them and more that I sense them in my mind's eye. If I close my own eyes and focus, I can imagine, if you will, what someone's aura looks like."

"Excellent," Steckworth said, and I noticed a few knowing glances exchanged around the table before the professor motioned to Agent Tanner, and she clicked forward again . . . and again . . . and again, and in every slide was the picture of another person wearing a different set of colors that varied in degrees of intensity and vibrancy. I knew why they were showing me the photos. "Each one is unique to the person," I said. "Like a fingerprint."

Professor Steckworth nodded again. "Indeed." He then seemed to want to talk at length and looked to Tanner, who nodded to him. "You see, twenty years ago, I had the most astonishing encounter with a woman who claimed to be psychic. I was working on my PhD at the time, and her abilities so impressed me that I made her the focus of my thesis.

"This woman was also an artist, and for a mere pittance, she would paint your portrait and include your individual aura. Of the hundreds of portraits I viewed of hers, no two were alike, and that began my quest to see if I could prove that auras really existed.

"What I discovered was that each and every human being emits a certain electromagnetic frequency made up of individual wave patterns unique to that person— no two frequencies are alike, not even with identical twins. I then worked with the psychic to match colors to each wavelength and was able to develop a digital photography software to capture the overall effect. I call the system Intuit."

"Amazing," I whispered, completely fascinated by the photos and the professor's story.

The professor took a sip of water and continued. "As

my research and applications turned more promising, the air force became more and more intrigued, and when I needed funding to continue Intuit's development, they provided me all I needed in return for the exclusive use of the system. Even then I could see the far-reaching benefits of my research, and as a former marine, I readily agreed.

"Along the way to developing Intuit, I made several key discoveries using the software, which could prove most useful to our national security. What my research team and I discovered was that when we scanned in a still photograph of test subjects, our software was unable to detect or produce an aura image. However, when we scanned in a *video* image, the software *was* able to capture the aura." The next slide showed a short clip of an infamous terrorist, and it left me stunned. The United States' Public Enemy Number One was surrounded by a bubble of color—mostly gray, black, and red, and then my own intuitive radar began to put the pieces together. "The drone was carrying Intuit," I whispered.

In answer there was a click, and the next slide revealed an areal view of that same air base from before, and on the ground were little blobs of vivid color.

I gasped.

"Jesus!" whispered Dutch.

"The drone was carrying the only prototype of the technology as well as a homing device and a small dummy missile," said Professor Steckworth. "We dubbed the prototype Intuit Tron, and it had reached its final testing phase before being deployed on the morning it disappeared. This is the last image it recorded in fact."

The professor fell silent, and in the room, you could have heard a pin drop, but then Tanner clicked the remote again and a clip of our president's last State of the Union Address began playing. Two seconds in, I saw the man I'd voted for and fully supported surrounded by a huge bubble of brilliant blue, green, and lavender. In that moment I believe my heart skipped several beats, and my stomach felt like it had fallen down to my toes. There was another click, and the slide moved to a clip of the British prime minister, then the French president, and on and on with each allied national leader's aura vividly portrayed.

It took me several seconds to realize I'd stopped breathing.

The lights came on then, and I squinted in the brightness, while my mind raced with the possible horrible implications of having this particular technology in the wrong hands. "Now do you understand why your country so desperately needs someone with your talents, Ms. Cooper?" asked Tanner

"Yes, ma'am," I said gravely. "Whatever you need me to do, I'll do it."

"Good," she said. "Then let's get started. . . ."

FROM

VICTORIA
LAURIE

The Psychic Eye Mysteries

Abby Cooper is a psychic intuitive.
And trying to help the police solve crimes
seems like a good enough idea—but it
could land her in more trouble than even
she could see coming.

OM0014

VICTORIA LAURIE

THE FIRST BOOK IN THE
GHOST HUNTER
MYSTERY SERIES

WHAT'S A GHOUL TO DO?

Don't miss the first adventure in the series starring M.J. Holiday, a sassy psychic medium who makes a living by helping the dead.

ALSO AVAILABLE

Demons Are a Ghoul's Best Friend

Ghouls Just Haunt to Have Fun

Ghouls Gone Wild

Available wherever books are sold or at penguin.com